HEARTS OF FORTUNE

HEIRS OF CAPE CANYON - BOOK 1

E. WINN

HEARTS OF FORTUNE

Copyright © 2024 by E. Winn

All rights reserved.

No part of this book may be reproduced in any form or by any electronic or mechanical means, including information storage and retrieval systems, without written permission from the author, except for the use of brief quotations in a book review.

This novel is a work of fiction. All characters, organisations, and events portrayed in the novel are either productions of the author's imagination or are used fictitiously.

Edited: Amy Maranville from Kraken Communications

Cover Design: Quirah Casey from Temptations Creations

Published by Ardently Romance

For the girls, gays, and theys who find one fictional D is never enough

CHAPTER 1

INCLAIR

"Fuck me, tell me that's not her," my brother Presley leaned in, muttering in my ear.

The three of us stood in a line at the altar beside our father who, like the stupid, lovesick fool he was, had decided to get married.

For the third time.

Wife number one had been my mother, who he'd married when they were eighteen, too young and foolish to realize they actually hated each other. It took them thirty years of tearing each other to shreds, one baby of their own, and my two adopted brothers standing beside me for it to sink in that they were a match made in hell.

Our father bounced back fast, though.

Unfortunately, wife number two was a walking cliché – twenty-five years my father's junior and only with him for his houses, his money, and his malleable personality that meant she could manipulate just about anything she wanted out of him so long as she sucked his dick on demand. She didn't stick around long, but she sure as shit took a hefty sum with her when she left him for the guy who made her coffee at the country club.

Lucky our father had more than enough money to last him seventeen lifetimes, even after establishing enormous trust funds for his three sons. The bitch wife had tried to take half of those too. She'd failed, though, because nobody fucks with me and my brothers. Not as long as I'm breathing.

I didn't think it was likely that this latest wife would be any different than wife number two. I'd met her a few times when she'd started appearing at the house. She played the role of the doting wife and keen stepmother well, but nobody could keep up an act like that forever. Her true colors would no doubt come out the moment she moved in.

Except…this wife didn't come alone.

She came with a daughter; one who was an absolute smokeshow now that we were getting our first look at her. She walked down the aisle towards us in a thin strap silk black dress that screamed sex, even if it did look classy as fuck. It showed off her tanned slender legs, the top half clinging to the perfect handful at her chest. Presley was a tit man, hence why he was drooling over her already. Her long dark hair was loose down her back in waves and her light blue eyes were completely devoid of any kind of emotion. Maybe our darling step–sister wasn't as excited about this union as our new mommy had made out?

She clutched a bunch of peonies in both hands as she took slow steps down the aisle. All eyes were on her. The eyes of total strangers. As far as I knew, she'd never met any of them, myself and my brothers included. Yet her spine was straight, her shoulders back and her head high as she ignored them all.

"How the fuck am I supposed to focus with *that* living down the hall from me?" Dacre muttered from where he stood on the other side of Pres.

My hand tightened on my wrist clutched in front of me, my brothers and I standing tall and stoic as she approached.

Our father grinned at her, desperate to make this marriage work before it had even begun, which meant he would be eager to win this girl over with his version of fatherly affection.

It wouldn't fucking last.

And maybe it wouldn't matter, because our new stepsister gave him nothing. She ignored all of us as she passed in a wave of coconut shampoo and Chanel perfume, to take her place alone on the other side of the altar.

"Fuck me," Dacre said a little too loud.

Our father shot him a hard look. "Don't even think about it. You three are to watch out for her, not try to corrupt her. There's too much riding on this."

We nodded once in acquiesce like good soldiers.

Our father clasped my shoulder. "I'm trusting you, Sinclair. It's your job to welcome her to the family."

My brothers waited until my father had turned back to his ceremony, no longer listening.

"You got that, Sin?" Presley said with a smirk. "We better make sure we welcome her to the family."

CHAPTER 2

DEMPSEY

"If anyone objects to this union, speak now or forever hold your peace."

I objected.

I *seriously* fucking objected.

But if I'd dared to say it during the ceremony, mother would have strangled me in a mass of tulle.

Why she'd been so thrilled to marry a rich asshole who likely only wanted to control her—just like my father had—was beyond me. If it were just her life, it would have been one thing, but she was dragging me to this pretentious world of the wealthy along with her. I struggled to control my expression as my anger bristled.

I didn't want this.

I didn't want any of it.

Not a gated community of mansions filled with cheating husbands and perpetually doped-up trophy wives who raised brats with trust funds so big they didn't know how much a candy bar cost at the store. Why would they? They sent their housekeepers or personal shoppers to places like that. They were all too drunk, high, and horny to care how the other half lived.

My family had been comfortable—albeit miserable—in our old life. But comfortable wasn't a word used to describe my mother's new husband.

Byron Aston was richer than God.

Yet despite the cushy new lifestyle I was about to be thrust into, I didn't want to be here.

Of course, I had no choice. As much as I hated living with my mother, life with her and her new uber-rich, society husband was my only option. Because there was no way in hell I would go back to my father. He'd have to drag me by my hair, screaming my lungs out first. And knowing him, he'd likely do exactly that when he came for me.

For now, I was stuck here with my mother, her new husband, and his three hideous offspring.

Only… *hideous* was a stretch.

It was an undeniable fact that all three of my new step-brothers were hot as sin.

The oldest one stood beside my new stepfather at the cere-mony, watching me with a guarded curiosity as I passed. The middle one, caramel-haired and slightly taller than the other two, had smirked with all the confidence and swagger that only the truly wealthy and untouchable could pull off. While the third looked at me like I was about to become his new favorite toy, a thought that seemed to piss him off if the scowl was any indication. The sight of them as I walked down the aisle had been overwhelming, and I'd had to work hard to stop it showing on my face.

Filthy rich playboys weren't my style. Especially ones I was forced to call family now.

After the ceremony, I stood in the giant glass atrium that had been erected for my mother and new daddy's wedding reception on the sprawling grounds of the compound I was to call home.

It was packed with people I didn't know, the same men whose seedy gazes had trailed over my body as I walked down the aisle, seated next to women who turned their noses up at me. I knew the reputation of women like them. It didn't matter that there were ten, twenty, thirty years between them and me. They saw me as competition. Someone who could potentially steal their sweaty, balding husbands. At least Mom's new one had a full head of hair and a half-decent personality from the few times I'd met him when he'd come to pick up Mom for one of their dates.

I pressed my lips together, comforted by the taste of my favorite peach lip gloss. Right now, it was a small taste of familiarity in this soulless place. Sipping at the chilled glass of champagne in my hand, I propped my other hand under my elbow to keep the glass close to my mouth. Getting drunk and staying that way seemed like my best chance for survival.

I was contemplating my escape—maybe slipping out the back of the atrium to the staffing tent to find a cute waiter I could flirt with and really piss off my mom—when my three brand new stepbrothers cut through the crowded dance floor in my direction.

I stilled.

Well, this should be interesting...

They stopped in front of me, creating a loose semi-circle around me, cutting me off from the party.

"If it isn't our new step-sister," said the one with caramel-colored hair and a smile that promised nothing but trouble, spreading his arms wide and taking a step towards me like he was going to wrap me in a hug. He had Prom King written all over him.

I stopped him with a hand to his chest, which was taut under my touch. "I'm good, thanks."

I'd been dreading this meeting from the moment my mother told me my new step-daddy came with three sons as accessories. Now that it was happening, their collective hotness was unsettling. Overwhelming, even. Not to mention the undeniable power that having money brought.

Surely it couldn't be legal for this much handsome to exist in one family? And surely being attracted to people you were now supposed to call your step-brothers was some kind of crime? Didn't mean I had to act on it though. I'd keep them at arm's length and save myself a world of pain.

"Our super fucking hot new step-sister," the one to my right grumbled, as though the fact I was even vaguely attractive was an intentional move on my part to agitate him.

I could say the same about them.

He was slightly shorter than the other two and looked to be the embodiment of solid muscle. A stupidly hot gym bro.

"Why would my appearance offend you so much?" I cut back, determined to be so prickly they'd leave me the hell alone. "Do you hate women?"

I sipped my champagne as though the entire interaction bored me. In reality, my heart was racing in my chest.

The dark-haired one with fierce green eyes was watching our interactions, hands in his pockets, that same wary curiosity in his eyes that he'd had at the ceremony.

"I love women," the Prom King said, drawing my attention back to him. His gaze dropped down my body and back to my face with a broad grin. "Let's go back up to the house and I'll show you how much."

He moved to take a step towards me again, but Green Eyes stopped him. "Cool it, Pres," his voice was low and commanding to his brother, making my stomach flip.

"Pres?" I asked Prom King, with a frown.

"Presley," he offered. "Mom was big into Elvis. And yes, I move my hips just as well as he could. Happy to give you a demonstration any time, sweet cheeks."

He motioned for me to lead the way in the direction I assumed went back up to the house. The grounds were massive and I'd only been here one night, sleeping in one of the guest rooms with my mom the night before her wedding, which had been a particular kind of torture. We'd been brought down from the house for the ceremony in the world's swankiest golf cart, because it was too far to walk and God forbid we scuff the red bottoms of the three-thousand-dollar Louboutins that were currently biting into my heels. So far, my knowledge of my new home was limited. Just like my knowledge of my new family.

"That's Dacre," Presley said, motioning to pissed off Mr. Muscle.

"A real pleasure." He gave me a hard nod, his bright blue eyes boring into me.

God, I bet girls just fell into bed with him.

"Would you two cut it out? She's our fucking step-sister," Green Eyes said, his gaze never leaving me.

Dacre shrugged and Presley looked thrilled that he'd gotten a rise out of his brother.

"We're not related, it's legal," Presley said with a devious grin.

I turned to Green Eyes. "And you are?"

A ghost of a smile played at his mouth. Other than that, his expression didn't change. "Sinclair, but you can call me Sin."

Sin. The way he said it… like it wasn't just a name, but a promise. One I was sure he could deliver on, given half the chance.

You'll never find out, so stop thinking about it.

"Well, glad we've finally met. Now we can stay out of each other's way. That house is plenty big enough that we'll probably never run into each other."

I was here to focus on school and ensuring my father left me the hell alone. Once I graduated, I'd have options. I wouldn't need either of my parents.

The three boys chuckled and my cheeks flushed with embarrassment. Why the hell were they laughing at me?

"I don't think you understand how this works," Sin said, taking a step to close the space between us. "We're family. Which means you're one of us now."

I scoffed. "One of you?"

The last thing I needed was another man (or men) telling me how to live my life.

The side of Dacre's mouth quirked. "It means where we go, you go. Our father's told us to keep an eye on you, and we take our duty to our family seriously."

Irritation sparked inside me. "I don't need three overgrown babysitters. I can figure this place out for myself."

Pres moved closer, throwing an arm around my shoulders. "Come on, Dempsey. Plenty of girls would love to be in your position. Unfettered access to the Aston brothers? What an opportunity."

He said "Aston brothers" as though they were royalty and I should bow at their feet like a good little subject. I'd rather puke in my purse and carry it around.

I shoved Presley off and he chuckled at my efforts, willingly stumbling back a step.

"Thanks, but I can take care of myself. I don't need help from three trust fund babies whose biggest talents are spending their daddy's money and partying in his houses."

"You bring your own bank account did you, Princess?" Sin's hard voice sliced through me.

I swallowed my frustration, because he had a point: If I had my own bank account padded with cash, I'd be gone already.

I didn't have any money. My father had made sure of that when he'd been hellbent on limiting my options to force my hand. The fact I now had nowhere else to go was the *only* reason I was even here.

There was nowhere I could go where my father wouldn't eventually find me. Being here, under the protection of Byron's wealth and this locked-down community might buy me some time, but I was worth too much to my father for him to let me go. I just had to be ready when he came to collect.

When I didn't reply, Sinclair huffed a laugh at my expense.

"That's what I thought. Pretty girls in glass houses shouldn't throw insults, *Dempsey*."

The mocking way he said my name made me scowl. I downed the rest of my drink and discarded the glass on the table behind me. "I've had enough family bonding for the night. Think I'll go find a satin-covered pillow and a set of one-thousand thread count sheets to lie my pretty little head on."

Without another word, I pushed past them.

"You need any help with that, you just say my name. Preferably between moans," Presley murmured.

I ducked my head as I walked away so they wouldn't see how my cheeks flamed.

CHAPTER 3

Skulking like a desperate wallflower wasn't really the first impression I'd been going for, yet here I was.

My mother had given me what she considered a pep talk last night, while we'd completed a rigorous sixteen-step skincare routine ahead of her bridal debut today. This new life was "a fresh start," she informed me, and she expected me to adapt to this new world order without complaint because the respect of this community was very important to Byron, and so was their support, whatever that meant.

I didn't ask questions, or even respond really, because it didn't matter. I would be required to play the role of the perfect society daughter, because I owed my mother a debt. She'd given up everything for me, which meant now, I wasn't to put a foot wrong. I couldn't jeopardize this for her in any way or I'd book myself a one-way ticket back to the one place I never wanted to be again.

The fact that she held that threat over me, knowing what it would mean, proved just how little she cared about me and how much more she valued her new-found status as Byron Aston's wife.

More than her only daughter.

It didn't seem to occur to her that she'd come out happier and billions of dollars better off with Byron than she'd ever been in a loveless, controlling marriage to my father. She would have stayed with him and died in unconscious misery if it weren't for me.

So, I didn't bother pushing back. What would be the point? I'd be railroaded into the life she wanted for us the same way she'd been yanked and zipped and tucked into her wedding dress until it looked like she'd never indulged in more than a lettuce leaf her entire life.

A waiter appeared, brandishing a tray in front of me, and pulling me from my head. "Seared salmon puff with caviar?"

I stared down at the pastry with little black globs on top. I'd do just about anything for a taco right now.

Glancing back up at the waiter, I shook my head, eyes meeting cool brown ones and a friendly smile.

He was cute. And he could be fun to pass some time with at this hellish event.

Before I could offer up so much as a flirtatious smile, a guy slicker than an oil spill stepped into my line of sight, grinning like a squirrel with a nut stash.

"Act like the hired help you are and disappear," he said, staring down the waiter until the guy backed away and disappeared into the crowd.

I stared at my new friend, a small part of me turned on by his obnoxious attitude, the other part appalled. How screwed up was I that part of me liked the display of dominance?

First I was lusting after my stepbrothers, and now this guy? I needed to see a therapist. My mother could afford the best now that she'd married Byron. Maybe I'd request a trip to space for my next birthday while I was at it.

Hell knows they could afford that, too.

"You know," my new friend said, leaning in close. His body was angled so he blocked my view of the party. "If you flirt with the help, you'll earn yourself a reputation around here."

"Oh, yeah?" I countered, playing along as though his flirting impressed me. This guy was a typical trust fund baby, but he was easy on the eyes and his expensive cologne was getting me high, so I was at least willing to hear him out. "And what kind of reputation is that?"

He smiled in a way only the truly conceited could manage. "That you're not wife material."

I held back a snort. Like I cared. I wasn't looking to become anyone's wife, least of all to a guy who looked like he ironed his jeans and his mom still bought his underwear for him.

But given my only form of entertainment right now was standing alone against a wall, I was willing to play along.

"Not wife material? Then what kind of girl would I be?"

His eyes lit with a fire that fuelled my ego to unimaginable levels. He wanted me. He was probably already half hard just thinking about railing me in the garden. And right now, I was angry enough at my mother that I'd let him.

The idea of acting out against her was appealing. I didn't need to maintain the perfect daughter routine where no one could see me and miss the opportunity for rebellion by boning this Chuck Bass wannabe behind the rose bushes purely because I could.

"You'd be the kind of girl that likes to have a good time. The kind that doesn't give a shit what anyone thinks of her. The kind who's naughty and knows how to take what she wants." He grinned again. "That's mistress material, baby."

I let a smile slip across my face.

Maybe this one was smarter than he looked. He was appealing to my ego. His lines were pure cringe, but I was bored and feeling problematic.

"Well, in that case, how about you get me a drink and we talk about all the ways we could get into trouble?"

He leaned in closer. "Just talk about them?"

I shrugged. "Get me a drink and we'll see."

He walked backwards a few steps, waggling his eyebrows at me like a frat bro about to get laid, then disappeared through the crowd towards the bar. He was nothing like my usual type, but right now I didn't care. I was in a strange place, with people who couldn't give less of a shit about me. I should at least get an orgasm for my efforts to play nice.

"You won't get off by getting with him," came a voice from behind me, a tall body appearing at my side. Presley towered over me, handing me a glass of perfectly chilled champagne.

I took it and downed a large gulp. "Excuse me?"

"Trenton. The loser who was just eye-fucking you."

Trenton? *Yeah, that tracks.*

"You won't get off by hooking up with him."

So far Presley and I had a total of one conversation between us and he thought it was his place to dish out some protective brotherly advice?

"Are you speaking from experience? Did Trenton fail to show you a good time?"

He eyed me sideways, fighting a grin. "I've heard enough from the girls who boned him then came to me for a real fuck that he doesn't know how to work the female anatomy." He shrugged. "Or he's too selfish to give a shit."

I rounded on him. "Wow, you like your women to chat about their prior conquests while you nail them. Interesting insight."

He shook his head, smiling from ear to ear. "The fucking sass on you. Sinclair is going to lose his shit."

Trenton returned to us, two shots of tequila in his hands. He offered my stepbrother a curt nod. "Ah, the football star is here to save the day, like always."

Presley played football?

I eyed him carefully, taking in the toned set of his shoulders, wondering if his legs had the muscles to match. Sports star would certainly explain the confidence.

Trenton handed a shot glass to me with a grin. "Bottoms up, baby."

Presley quirked a brow at me that said *'Really? This guy?'*

I ignored him and knocked back the shot.

"Should we find somewhere a little more private?" Trenton levelled Presley with a look that spelled out what an inconvenience he was.

I nodded, downing the rest of my champagne, and Trenton took both glasses, stepping away for a moment to discard them on a nearby table.

Presley leaned in close, his muscled chest pressed against my bare arm. "Have fun with that three-pump chump."

Then he moved away through the party.

I didn't need any more people dictating how I could live my life. I'd tolerate it from my mother because I had no other choice, but my new step-brothers could take a long jump off a short dock if they thought telling me what to do was going to bond us.

Trenton took my hand and I let him lead me through the atrium, dodging increasingly drunken guests as we went. A man twirled a woman half his age on the edge of the dance-floor and she stumbled into me, my hand slipping from Trenton's. The woman giggled an apology at me before jumping back onto the floor with a guy who looked old enough to be her grandfather.

God, I hate it here already.

As we made our way past the bar, Dacre and Sinclair were propped against it, their hard gazes scorching over my skin.

Dacre shook his head like he was disappointed in me. "Bad idea, Bambi."

I didn't need to understand the nickname to know that I instantly hated it.

"Seems like a great idea from where I'm standing," I cut back.

Sinclair's green eyes were hard. "Don't say we didn't warn you."

Ignoring them, I made my way to the back exit where Trenton was waiting, his hand brushing my lower back as he led me out to the garden.

CHAPTER 4

woke from my sleep in my palatial new bedroom, desperate for a glass of water.

Rifling through the bathroom attached to my new room, I came up empty. The cabinet had every kind of cream, shampoo, product, and towel I could ever hope for, but not a glass in sight.

"I need to speak to management about the way they run this hotel," I muttered to myself, padding across the thick cream carpet that was like walking on marshmallows.

I slipped into the hallway wide enough to host a hockey game, and found it dark and deserted. My three new step-brothers slept on this floor. Byron had let me know they'd be "just down the hall if I needed anything." I'd bitten my tongue to stop myself from telling him I wouldn't be needing anything from his crazy hot spawn, other than to stay far away from them.

As I made my way to the stairs, I was greeted with the sound of bass pounding through the wing of the house. Pausing at the landing, I strained to hear voices, but the steady thumping beat was all that echoed back.

I glanced down at my black silk sleep shorts and matching

tank top. Surely I could make it to the kitchen for a glass of water and sneak back up before anyone saw me.

I paused. Why should I though?

This was my house, too. Byron had gone to great lengths to emphasize that point. I was supposed to make myself at home, which meant no skulking around in the dark because I wasn't wearing a bra or showing a little too much leg.

Screw it.

Bypassing the kitchen, I made my way through the mansion following the growing volume. It was three am, did these guys sleep?

The closer I got, the louder the bass grew, until it was vibrating through the floor and walls. I'd been joking when I'd told my stepbrothers that the house was so big we didn't need to worry about running into each other, but apparently I was wrong.

I paused outside a set of double doors, the music humming through my body now that I was so close. This was the opposite of staying away from them, which meant no good would come from me walking in there. But did I care about being good right now?

Not at all.

Gripping the ornate golden handle that probably cost more than a car, I pushed the door open, only to have my eyeballs instantly assaulted. The music was so loud inside the room, it pounded through my skull, and I pulled a face, both at the noise and the sight in front of me.

Sinclair and Dacre were seated on an enormous U-shaped sectional, Dacre aggressively making out with a girl who looked a lot like one of the photographer's assistants from the wedding. Sinclair sat at the far end of the sofa, his arm around a girl in a navy dress that clung to her perfect body. It was clear from her immaculate makeup and sparkling jewelry that she came from money. They were huddled together, talking only to each other, her hand placed possessively on his thigh.

And yet no one in the room seemed at all fazed by the fact that Presley had a redheaded waitress from the reception bent over the pool table and was railing her from behind, her moans of pleasure mixing with the pounding music.

Presley spotted me, his face splitting in a grin that I was quickly learning was his signature. "Hey! Our new sister has come to join the party."

His hips never faltered as he thrust into the waitress. Her head shot up, and she glared at me.

Don't worry, girl. The billionaire playboy who's clearly into public sex is all yours.

"What are you doing here?" Sinclair demanded, his tone flat and unreadable.

The guy was a damn robot.

We weren't about to hug it out while he reassured me he was the big brother I'd never wanted, but did he have to be such a hardass every time we spoke? Was he happy to see me right now or was he ready to murder me six different ways and make it look like an accident? It was impossible to say. Worse, I found myself wondering if I *wanted* him to be happy to see me.

The thought unnerved me. I didn't want him having that kind of power over me.

"I got lost exploring the house, so I followed the pounding sounds vibrating through the floor."

"You hear that, Pres?" Dacre laughed. "She could hear you pounding Rebecca from the other end of the house."

Presley chuckled, still moving inside the waitress—Rebecca, I guessed. Rebecca's cries of pleasure heightened, and I couldn't help but stare at them. While part of me was disgusted that he was boning her out in the open, it was… kind of hot.

Clearly, Presley knew what he was doing, given the way

Rebecca's face was contorting in ecstasy as she clung to the table. Which was more than I could say for my *fun* with Trenton earlier tonight. Unfortunately, the warnings from my new step-brothers had been accurate. Trenton did not, in fact, know what he was doing.

"You're thinking about it, aren't you?" Presley called, eyes alight with victory.

"Thinking about what?"

"Your time with the three-pump chump and how much better it would have been if you'd gotten with me."

I pulled a face. "Not even close."

Was I that easy to read that my new step-brother who'd only known me for all of a few hours could see right through me? I'd have to work harder to keep my reactions locked down.

Presley's smile widened, his hips thrusting so hard into the waitress that her whole body slammed into the table, making her cry out.

"You're a fucking liar," Presley said, as he maintained a shocking level of control.

"If you think you've seen all you're going to see of Trenton, you're delusional," Dacre said from the couch, the girl beside him now kissing his neck like she was going for an Olympic medal in hickeys.

"What's that supposed to mean?"

Sinclair sat forward, elbows pressed to his knees as he watched me. The girl beside him glanced between us, her expression as equally blank as his.

"It means he's a pussy who turns into a drooling dog over the girls who get him off. So, you've just become his newest obsession."

"If you were any good at it," Dacre added with a laugh.

I stared him down. "I'm more than good at it."

He quirked a brow. "That so?"

I leaned down, gripping the back of the couch. "It's a

shame, *brother*, that you'll never have the privilege of finding out."

Presley's chuckles filled the room as I strolled for the door.

"Try to keep it down during your tacky sex fest," I called over my shoulder. "This whole thing reeks of pretty little rich boys whose Mommy didn't love them enough."

"Hey!" Presley protested with mock outrage.

But I didn't stick around to witness any more. I swiped a water glass from the bar on my way out and slammed the door behind me.

CHAPTER 5

startled awake, covered in a thin layer of sweat, my heart hammering against my chest like a runaway train.

That dream had been intense and so real.

Dacre's lips against my throat.

Presley's mouth between my legs.

Sinclair watching it all with hooded eyes from a chair in the corner.

It was so hot.

And so *very* wrong.

Panting, I scrubbed my hands over my face. There was something seriously warped with me that I was having sex dreams about a foursome with my insanely hot step-brothers. Why the hell was my subconscious mind drooling over them at all?

My mother would murder me if I so much as wore the wrong dress to an event. She'd have me locked in the basement and tell everyone I'd gone to some remote college in the Swiss Alps before she'd allow me to do anything to publicly tarnish the Aston name. And jumping one—let alone all three—of my new step-siblings would create a bigger scandal than this community of cash worshippers had likely ever seen.

Yet that dream had made me wetter than I'd ever been my own.

I strolled into breakfast an hour later, after taking the longest, hottest shower of my life, trying to scrub the memory of my dream from my skin.

What I'd witnessed my stepbrothers partaking in over the weekend was to blame. The crazy hot mental image of Presley railing the waitress was seared into my memories forever, no matter how hard I tried to forget it. A bit of selective amnesia would be great right about now.

So far, my stepbrothers were living up to every expectation I'd had when my mother had dragged me here—they were nothing more than rich, entitled playboys who liked to work hard, play hard, and fuck even harder.

With money came power, but that didn't mean I'd be giving them power over me.

If they thought I was about to fall in line like a good little step-sister because they declared I was an Aston now, they were going to be sorely disappointed. My mother already had enough control over my life; my stepbrothers would have to get in line.

I stopped short at the domestic scene in the dining room in front of me. Byron sat at the head of the table, my mother at his side. In one hand, he held a cup of coffee, and in the other, my mother's hand. He was reading something on a tablet propped in front of him, while my mother scrolled her own tablet, no doubt coordinating her busy schedule of shopping, party planning, and dress fittings. I had no idea how she planned to occupy her time now that the wedding was done and she was officially Mrs. Beatrice Aston.

Presley was seated at the dining table next to Byron, Sinclair on the other side of him, while Dacre was across the table, a seat left empty between him and my mom that was clearly meant for me.

I'd managed to successfully avoid them for the rest of the

weekend by keeping to my room, only venturing out for snacks to break up my marathon of *White Lotus*, *Bridgerton*, and true crime documentaries. When the air in my room had grown particularly stale and the maids came in insisting on cleaning the bathroom and changing my sheets, I'd taken to wandering through the house. I'd discovered the locations of each of the three pools. There were two outdoor and one indoor. The indoor one had to be Olympic-sized, it was so huge, and it featured a sky-high diving board I'd never be stepping foot on with my fear of heights.

Swimming, on the other hand, had been a passion of mine since before I could walk. I'd made the swim team in high school and planned on joining the team at whatever college I ended up at. But my mother had pulled that dream right out from under me the moment she'd decided to force me to live hers instead, which meant going to the fancy college my new stepfather funded.

"Good morning, sweetheart." My mother smiled at me in a perfect imitation of a loving parent. She turned her smile on Byron, the two of them grinning at each other like a picture of wedded bliss.

I wonder how long it will last?

How long would it be before Byron lost interest? Or kept working late? Or stopped coming home at all? How long until Mom's new society friends started whispering about the state of the Aston marriage, or the tension they felt between the newlyweds at whatever events they attended that week? Would they be sleeping in separate beds this time next year? Would they have separate cars taking them to the same place?

Life was never picture perfect. Especially for the rich. They just had the means to hide it better than most. Everyone had skeletons in their closets, but the wealthy had dead bodies buried everywhere.

I took the vacant seat at the table, Dacre's gaze sliding my way when I sat down beside him. The maid—one of many in

Byron's household—placed a plate of poached eggs loaded with hollandaise sauce in front of me.

"Um, excuse me," I twisted in my seat. "I didn't order this."

She looked momentarily perplexed, glancing at my mother.

"I ordered it for you. You need a proper breakfast today," my mother said, barely glancing up from her tablet.

Like hell I was eating that. Hollandaise was foul, an opinion of which my mother was well aware. Perhaps she was distracted by all the new zeroes on the tail-end of her bank balance.

I forced out a smile, turning back to my plate. "I'll just take a bowl of gluten-free granola, if that's okay."

My mother gave me a disapproving frown, which I ignored. She could dictate a lot in my life right now, but my breakfast wasn't going to be one of them.

"Do you have Portadillo granola by any chance?" It was my favorite. I'd eaten it for breakfast everyday back home, something my mother also knew. Maybe she had arranged with Byron's extensive staff to have some on hand for me, I dared to hope.

"I'm so sorry, Miss Dempsey, we don't. I can arrange it for you for another day."

I smiled up at her with a nod, not wanting to let my hurt show. Byron had made such a big show about me being at home here, but it seemed my mother didn't feel the same way.

Conscious of my stepbrothers watching the entire exchange, I handed the plate back to the maid. "Any gluten-free granola you have will be fine, thank you."

She nodded once, accepting the plate of eggs and disappearing through the side door in the direction of the enormous kitchen.

Bryon tilted his head in my direction with a smile.

"Excited for your first day at Cape Canyon College, Dempsey?"

I still didn't have a read on Byron. I'd expected him to be an asshole billionaire who only cared about how much money he could make, how many houses and fast cars he could own, and how many miles he could track in his private plane. But so far, he seemed almost... *nice*. Which was suspicious. Rich people were never nice. It didn't pay to be kind.

"Yeah, I guess so." I toyed with the tablecloth where it hung in my lap. "I don't really know what to expect."

Cape Canyon College sounded like yet another playground for the wealthy. A prestigious, sprawling, ivy-covered campus, that was run more like a prep school than a college. I'd been told in no uncertain terms by my mother that I didn't need to bother with the places I'd worked my ass off to earn at Dartmouth, Cornell, or Columbia, because I'd be going to Cape Canyon College once we started our new life.

Now that my mother had changed her last name to Aston and had a reputation to uphold as the queen of the community, I didn't get to make my own decisions anymore.

"There's an expectation of excellence from any student attending Triple C, but you'll hopefully have a lot of fun there, too," Byron said, eyes filled with encouragement.

How much fun could I realistically have at a college owned and funded by my new stepfather?

Byron has sent all three of his sons there. Presley and Dacre were still enrolled, and Sinclair had graduated two years earlier. Since then, he had started his own tech company, as Byron had told me with a note of pride—pride that made me wonder if Byron might really care about his offspring... or maybe he was just a really good actor.

"No better school in the country than Triple C," Presley said like a walking advertisement. He shovelled a spoonful of scrambled eggs in his mouth to cover his shit-eating grin.

The maid returned, silently placing a bowl of granola with

fresh strawberries and yogurt in front of me. I smiled up at her in thanks.

"Dacre, Presley, you wouldn't mind letting Dempsey ride with you today, would you?" my mother asked, turning her faux smile on each of them.

Dacre's eyes locked on me. "No problem at all."

I shook my head, the idea of being stuck in a car with either one of them making my granola sink in my stomach. The plan had been to stay away from them, not be stuck in a confined space with them on a daily basis.

"No, that's okay. I can make my own way there."

"How?" Sinclair asked, fork halfway to his mouth. "Did you come with a car we don't know about?"

If I did, it would be easy to miss. That garage was the size of a house and had more luxury and foreign cars than I could count on four hands, let alone two.

"Now that you mention it..." Byron said, signalling to someone out in the hall.

His valet stepped into the room, moving to Byron's side and producing a set of keys.

Byron held them up, grinning. "A little gift for you, Dempsey."

I stared at him like he'd grown a second head. He was giving me a damn car and calling it a *little* gift?

When I took too long to accept the keys I was being offered, my mother nudged me, her elbow connecting with my ribs, making me squeak in pain.

"Oh, um... thank you, Byron." I pushed from my seat, reaching for the keys and sitting back down. I turned them over in my hand. "You got me a Bentley?"

Byron's smile widened. "That's right. Can't have you walking these mean streets."

He chuckled, my mom laughing along with him. The only mean thing about these streets were the asshole husbands who thought they could get away with anything and the talons on the women who believed being rich was better than being treated decently.

"I was surprised to see it in the garage, given you already own two," Presley muttered.

Byron either didn't hear him or chose to ignore him. "If you'd prefer not to drive it yourself, I can arrange a driver for you."

I stared down at the keys, then back up at my new stepfather who'd just handed me a two hundred-thousand-dollar car like spending that was pocket change he found in the couch cushions.

"That's okay, I'd love to drive it." I shook my head to clear the disbelief. "Thank you so much for this, Byron."

He nodded, satisfied with my reaction, and went back to reading his tablet.

"You better finish eating and then go upstairs and fix your hair." My mother gave my arm a firm pat. A little too firm. "You don't want to be late for your first day."

"My hair is already done."

"Oh." She scrutinized me like a judge on a reality cooking show assessing a lopsided tiramisu. "Are you sure you want to wear it like *that*?"

My hands clenched at my sides under the table. I jolted in shock when Dacre's warm, reassuring hand closed around my fist.

"You can't hit her," he muttered so only I could hear. A playful smile tugged at the corner of his mouth. I stared back at him in surprise.

"Wasn't going to," I muttered back.

Ignoring the growing feeling in my stomach, I shoved an enormous spoonful of granola in my mouth.

The disapproval on my mother's face almost made her forehead wrinkle. She'd better watch out or Byron would be trading her in for a younger model within the year.

She and I hadn't always been at odds this way. There'd

been a time when we were close. But all that had changed when I was sixteen and she'd turned a blind eye to my father's insanity. We were in the same house, but we might as well have been miles apart. She played Susie Housewife while I went through hell.

Eventually, she'd packed our bags and we'd left, but only after I begged her to save me. And even then, she acted like she was doing me a huge favor.

It took me a while to understand my mother wasn't naturally maternal. She cared more about the men in her life, and now her new money, than she did about her own child. And because of it, we'd never be close again.

"Miss Dempsey," the maid said, returning to my side and holding out a letter. "This came for you this morning."

Sinclair's brow quirked from across the table. "Only been here three days and already getting your mail redirected. How eager."

I took the letter from the maid, offering her a tight smile as I opened it.

"Dempsey can direct her mail here for the rest of her life if she wants," Byron said to Sinclair. "This is her home now."

Sinclair responded, but I didn't hear the words. I was too busy staring down at the paper in my trembling hands. My stomach dropped like an elevator from the top floor.

Inside the envelope, written on a thick, luxurious piece of personalized stationery was a one-line note.

Did you really think I wouldn't be able to find you there, darling?

I screamed on the inside, forcing down the granola threatened to claw up my throat and it was like swallowing a stack of needles. I wanted to vomit it all straight back up on the perfectly decorated table setting.

I knew it would be easy for my father to find me eventually. My mom had married a highly prominent billionaire, their wedding making the social pages of every newspaper in a three-hundred-mile radius. But a part of me had hoped that Byron's wealth and connections would stall my father. I hoped he would've moved on once he realized I was out of his reach.

If I lived a normal life with a loving mother, the smartest thing to do would be to turn to her and Byron for help. But I knew my mother would never allow me to taint her new life with the shameful sins of our old one. No matter how much Byron wanted to preach at me that I was part of this family now, I was only allowed to be part of it under the terms my mother dictated. And my father wanting to use me for his own cruel gain didn't factor into her new reputation.

I was required to keep my mouth shut. Which meant I was totally alone in this.

Shoving the letter back in the envelope, I excused myself from the table and hurried from the dining room. Once in my room, I buried the letter in the back of one of the drawers in my dresser.

It was fine. *Everything would be fine.*

I just needed to get my ass into gear and come up with a way to get the hell out of here to someplace my father would never be able to find me. I had no fucking idea where that was or how I planned to do it, but anywhere was better than back with my father.

Taking a few deep breaths to calm my trembling nerves, I grabbed my book bag and the keys to my new car and headed for the garage.

Sitting by the door, gleaming in perfect gold, was my brand-new Bentley. The gold was a little too gaudy for my taste, but I wasn't about to complain about a free car worth more than most people made in a year.

Sliding into the buttery leather seats was an absolute dream. It smelled brand new, the scent wafting over me as I brushed my hands across the steering wheel, taking in the sleek and shiny interior.

"Holy shit," I muttered to myself, still not quite grasping that this was mine.

I slid the key into the ignition, waiting for the purr of the engine.

But I was met with… *nothing.*

Turning the key a second time, the same dead silence greeted me.

What the hell is going on?

"Wow, looks like your new daddy bought you a lemon," Dacre said from where he leaned against the garage wall, arms crossed over his chest.

My eyes instantly narrowed on him. "What did you do to my car?"

He huffed a laugh. "I didn't do anything to your car. Byron doesn't know the first thing about buying them. He probably didn't even check it once it got delivered. It clearly needs some attention."

It was brand new, how had it broken down already?

Presley strolled into the garage looking like the football-playing prom king he probably was. "You look good in your new ride, D."

"Shame she can't drive it. Won't start."

Presley chuckled. "Oh yeah? Looks like you're riding with us then."

I jumped from the car, slamming the door shut behind me as every impure thought I'd dreamed about these two played in my mind. "I can walk."

Pushing a button on the remote on my keys that I hoped was for one of the garage doors, I walked towards it. Only the door two archways over opened. *Damn it.*

"It'll take you more than an hour to walk to Triple C from here," Dacre called and I halted. "Wouldn't it just be easier to ride with us?"

I sighed, swivelling on my heel. "Okay, well... Thanks, I guess."

Dacre inclined his head to the bright orange Lamborghini Spyder parked beside him.

The car was *hot*, there was no point denying it. And Dacre would look even hotter in it. No point denying that either.

"I'm riding shotgun!" Presley called.

"Dude, it's a two-seater car," Dacre clapped back, opening the door for me. "You're driving yourself."

I slid into my second buttery leather seat of the day, immediately dropping the lighted mirror to swipe on some of my favorite peach lip gloss.

Dacre and Presley both watched, eyes trained on my lips.

When I was done, I twisted the cap and tossed it back in my bag, glancing between them.

Presley winked at me as he made his way over to a bright blue sporty-looking Mercedes.

"See you on campus, Sass."

CHAPTER 6

We made our way along the winding, tree-lined roads that snaked through the Cape Canyon College campus. Scanning the manicured lawns and giant oaks, I couldn't deny that I was impressed.

I'd seen pictures of it online, but the images didn't do it justice.

The campus was beautiful.

Clearly Byron had spared no expense when he'd started this school, determined to offer a level of prestige few other schools could match. It was a playground for the truly wealthy and just like my new stepbrothers had tried to claim, I was apparently one of them now.

Dacre pulled into a parking spot in front of an ivy-clad building with gorgeous arched walkways. Groups of people milling about on campus turned to stare as he cut the engine.

Being an Aston was like being a celebrity.

"Want me to show you where you need to go?" he asked, assessing eyes burning over my skin.

I stared back, meeting the challenge. Given the muscle stacked on muscle covering his body, he could probably end me with his bare hands. But after life with my father, I didn't scare easily. The only thing I was afraid of was the man himself.

When it came to Dacre, the only person I had to worry about was me. Especially after he'd comforted me over my mother's scrutiny this morning.

Why would he be so nice to me?

And why couldn't I just hate these guys liked I'd planned?

I climbed out of the car, chastising myself. I *had* to keep my distance.

"I don't need a tour guide," I said flatly in an effort to push him away.

Dacre got out of the car on the other side, glaring at me over the top. "Wow, someone has her panties in a fucking knot today."

Tossing his book bag over one shoulder, he rounded the car, his attention rooting me to the spot and making my heart pound in my chest. Images flooded my head of him stalking towards me like that, pinning me to the side of the car and sliding a hand up my skirt.

I clenched my teeth, forcing the image out of my head.

You're sick, Dempsey. He's your stepbrother.

I couldn't work out if it was the wealth, the power, or the fact all three of them were walking sex dreams in very different ways that had me fantasizing about them while I was awake and asleep.

"You have no business thinking about my panties," I challenged Dacre.

I swallowed at the way his eyes roamed over my body and down my bare legs in my skirt.

"Sorry Bambi, but you have no control over where my mind goes."

Presley's car roared up into the space beside us, drawing even more attention to us. Dacre moved in, not quite close enough to be improper, but close enough that my traitorous body noticed.

Fuck. Wanting him—or any of them—was a one-way ticket to hell. My mother would end me. Byron would no doubt lose his shit. I'd be locked inside that house for life. Or worse, sent back to hell.

So I shoved past Dacre to the path. "Enjoy fucking me in your mind. It'll be the only place you ever get me."

Lies. All lies.

I just hoped they believed me, because the second I gave in to these feelings of need and pure recklessness, it would ruin all of us.

Presley called my name and I glanced back to find Dacre's hard gaze locked on me. His expression morphed into a scowl a moment before a heavy arm landed on my shoulders, startling me.

"If it isn't my favorite fuck," Trenton said, grinning down at me like a smug asshole.

Between my mother, my stepbrothers, and now Trent, I really couldn't catch a damn break today.

Dacre and Presley watched me walk away with Trenton until we were out of sight.

"Have a good weekend, babe?" Trenton asked, his arm like a deadweight around me.

The urge to shove him in the bushes lining the walkway burned hot and strong inside me. But I was new here, I needed to bide my time and work out the pecking order. Clearly the Astons were at the top, but I got the feeling Trenton wasn't all that far behind. I couldn't afford to make enemies for the sake of it. Even if the guy was a raging asshole.

Normally I was partial to a hot guy calling me babe, but not this one. Given his less than impressive skills when it came to getting a woman off, I'd be happy for him to never utter my name again. Being with him had been the most lackluster ninety seconds of my life.

"It was fine, thanks."

He gave my shoulder a squeeze. "Well, your week is looking up, because I'm here to show you around. All the best dining halls to hit, the right clubs to join…" He stopped short, pulling me with him and winking at me. "The best places to hook up between classes."

I forced out a smile, extricating myself from him now that we were far enough away from Dacre and Presley. "I'm good on my own, I've got it covered."

Trenton's face clouded with annoyance. "You're not really getting how this works." He closed the space between us, my back brushing the bricks of the archway to the building. "We hooked up. That means you're mine now."

I had to resist the urge to snort at his fucking audacity. "*Yours?*"

He straightened, smiling that smarmy fucking smile again. "I claimed you that first night at your mother's wedding, which means all other guys will back off. You may as well embrace it, babe. You and I are a thing now, no one else will touch you."

Anger surged inside me. Was this really how things worked in his world? "I licked it, so it's mine"?

Only he hadn't licked it. He'd rubbed at my left flap for ten seconds and asked me if I was close. There was no way in hell I was committing myself to spending any more time with him than I already had. And I definitely wasn't going to let people think we were together. Screw the pecking order.

I put a hand to his chest. He clearly thought I was about to pull him close and suck his face off, because his eyes heated with lust.

"Let me be really clear, Trenton." I paused for dramatic effect. "I'd rather be paddled by a pack of laughing monkeys until my ass is red raw than hook up with you again."

His lust evaporated in an instant, replaced by a dark rage.

"What did you just say to me?" His tone was low and vicious, but there was no way I was going to be intimidated by a guy who didn't know how to find the clit. "Who the fuck do you think you are?"

I smirked at him, stealing the move from my stepbrothers. "Oh, did you forget? I'm an Aston now."

Not waiting for his reply, I shoved past him, strolling away.

I'd only made it ten steps when a slow clap sounded from behind me to the right. Instantly on edge, I glanced over my shoulder.

The girl walking towards me looked like a damn bikini model. Striking brown eyes, dark skin, long black hair, and the most perfect curves I'd ever seen. If I played both ways, I'd definitely flirt with her. Maybe beg her to sleep with me.

"I've never seen someone shut that date-rapist-in-training down like that. That sorry sack of shit has had it coming, but all the girls around here are too scared to piss off him or his daddy."

I frowned. "I don't even know who his daddy is."

"Be thankful for that. The apple really doesn't fall too far from the tree there."

I tried to picture Trent with a bigger ego, a bigger bank account, and a few more decades of self-entitlement, and a shudder ran through me.

The girl picked up on it, letting out a laugh that showed off a set of straight white teeth.

"Exactly. It's a terrifying sight." She linked her arm with mine and we started walking. "I've heard about the famous new lady of Aston house, and now that I've seen just how well you can handle these assholes, I have to tell you something."

I shot a sideways glance as we walked, waiting.

"We're going to be friends."

I chuckled. "First of all, the new lady of Aston house is my mother. Second, don't I get a say in who I'm friends with?"

She stopped, looking around, her eyes alight with humor.

"I don't really see anyone else volunteering for the position, do you?"

I tilted my head side to side like I agreed. "Okay, so you've got me there. But they just haven't met me yet."

"Oh, trust me when I say they won't be able to handle you. Nor will they be as amazing as me. The personalities around here are *dry*."

I couldn't help my laugh. "Dempsey." I offered her my hand.

She took it, giving it a firm shake. "Arena Afia."

"Looks like I can check making friends off my list."

She gave me a blinding smile.

"It's amazing how quickly one asshole can bond two women together."

CHAPTER 7

I t was past midnight and I couldn't sleep.

Again.

It was finally the weekend and I'd survived a crazy first week at Triple C, thanks mostly to Arena. The workload was intense and I was already weighed down by reading and assignments. Not to mention the endless politics of their insane community.

I should be sleeping like a damn rock, but instead I was staring up at the ceiling like an insomniac.

The letter from my father was weighing on me more than I was willing to admit. I'd tried to push it aside every time that undercurrent of anxiety twisted in my stomach at the idea that he could turn up here any day and drag me back with him.

Would my mother put up a fight? She'd always been useless at standing up to him. Besides, did she really need me now? She was so wrapped up in Byron and her new life as Mrs. Aston that she'd probably let him have me. I was little more than a prop that she could parade at parties to prove what a loving mother she was. Her husband was all she truly cared about. Another few weeks and she and Byron would jet off via his private plane for the most elaborate European honeymoon known to man, and there'd be nobody standing between me and my father.

A swirling ball of stress formed in my gut at the thought. Which was how I found myself at the outdoor pool in the dark. It was still warm outside, the sounds of the ocean in the far distance filling the silence. Like the rest of the Aston estate, the pool was enormous, with several interconnected sections, a large grotto and waterfall at one end, and three different water slides over near the outdoor kitchen and cabana that had a swim-up bar attached. Every day that I lived here I was blown away by just how cashed up the Astons truly were. Not that I'd ever seen anyone use this pool, let alone appreciate its grandeur.

Tossing my towel on a lounge chair, I slipped into the pool, dropping under the water and letting the silence consume me. The stress rolled off my back instantly.

No one and nothing can touch me here.

I'd loved swimming since I was a kid, according to my mother. She claimed she'd struggled to keep me out of the pool. Neither of my parents were surprised when I made the swim team in high school. I planned on joining the team at Triple C eventually, if they'd have me.

I waded to the edge of the pool and pushed off, completing lap after lap of freestyle strokes, working my muscles until they ached.

Forty laps in, my lungs were on fire and my body lagged with fatigue. When my fingers scraped the wall, I pulled up, gripping the edge and dropping my forehead against it to catch my breath.

"Impressive."

My head snapped up at the voice, all the tension I'd just worked out of me filling my body again, putting me on edge.

Presley sat at the side of the pool, his legs dangling in the water. He was dressed in nothing but a pair of sleep shorts, his athletic body a mouth-watering sight.

Get a fucking grip, Dempsey. He's not yours to look at.

"I knew your body was too toned for you to be a couch potato, but I'd pegged you as a cheerleader."

I sniffed a laugh, turning towards him and pressing my back to the wall.

"Funny, from the look of you, I pictured you as a boring vanilla sex type of guy, not a raging exhibitionist."

My gaze purposefully ran over him, as though I were picturing him partaking in the mundane sexual position I'd just named.

He smirked back at me. "First of all, you know firsthand that there's nothing vanilla about the way I fuck. And I like an audience—so what? Plenty of people like to watch."

I rolled my eyes. "And second?"

"Second…" he said, eyes trained on me as he slid into the pool.

He made his way through the water like a shark tracking a seal. Only I was the seal, helpless against the strength and raw, dominating power of the shark.

Stopping in front of me, my back pressed to the side of the pool, he leaned in close, our slick bodies meeting in the water.

"… I'm obsessed with that smart mouth on you."

He tilted his head so his lip brushed my ear when he spoke, sending a shiver over my skin.

"We expected you to be meek. To fall in line, or at our feet, whichever you preferred. But so far, you haven't done either."

I swallowed, trying to hide the way my body was reacting to him. "And I won't."

The words fell from my lips with more confidence than I felt. My body was betraying me. I was enjoying being this close to him and wanted more.

Stop it, Dempsey. You can't have this and you know it.

He smirked at my words. "You know, I'd almost believe

you. But the way your chest is rising and falling fast right now, I know you're a fucking liar, Sass."

Sass.

The way he said the word was filled with heat.

His hand pressed against my stomach, his finger tantalizingly close to the top of my swim shorts. "You'll be moaning my name eventually, we both know it." I bit the inside of my cheek, forcing down the need unfurling inside me. "And what would our daddy say about that?"

Not only Byron. But my mom and this whole damn community.

There was no way any of my stepbrothers would risk ruining the Aston name, one that would open door after door for them the second they graduated from Triple C. Sinclair had already established himself in the tech world, and no doubt his name had helped him get there in some way. Presley wasn't about to risk his future for the chance to fuck me.

He pulled back, his lips no longer lingering and sending my head spinning, but he still towered over me.

"You're right. It would be a fucking scandal." He lowered himself so we were eye to eye. "But you just might be *worth it.*"

His blue eyes sparked with trouble as he pulled back, dipping under the water and resurfacing near the edge he'd been seated on. His back muscles rippled as he hauled himself out of the water.

Fuck. He was even hotter wet.

"Sweet dreams, Sass."

He strolled back towards the house like a soaking sex god.

CHAPTER 8

swiped my peach gloss over my lips, smacking them together, as I stared out over the open grounds of the Cape Canyon College campus. The sun was shining, which meant the lawns were full of students trying to soak up the rays while they studied or ate lunch.

Arena sat beside me, both of us opting for spicy salmon poke bowls from the nearby dining hall. She'd been talking my ear off about some petty drama between a couple in one of her classes that were always having public arguments. On any other day, I'd be deeply invested in the latest update, but I was still rattled by the letter the maid had handed me on my way out this morning.

Another note from my father.

No more games, Dempsey. Time to come home.

Home.

That house had never felt like a home. He'd made sure of that. There was no way in hell I'd ever willingly go back there.

"Hey, isn't that one of your smoking hot brothers?" Arena

pointed towards the parking lot, pulling me from my own head.

Despite claiming she rarely spoke to the Aston brothers, Arena knew them well. Knew a crazy amount of detail about each of them, the same way most people at Triple C did. Because of their near-celebrity status, I'd fallen into some strange kind of notoriety thanks to who my stepbrothers were. More than a few people had tried to befriend me in my first few days here, purely because I was an Aston now. Others had given me a wide berth and some of the bitchiest glances I'd ever received.

I squinted across the lawn to the parking lot. Sinclair was leaning against the hood of a shiny red Porsche. He looked mouth-wateringly good in tailored pants, dress shoes, and a white button-down shirt that was rolled up to his elbows. His piercing green eyes were hidden by dark sunglasses, his hair a perfectly dishevelled mess like he'd spent the morning sitting at his desk running his hands through it.

"God, he's so fucking hot. How do you live under the same roof as that without accidentally-on-purpose walking in on him in the shower?" Arena asked, practically drooling.

I rolled my eyes. "Because he has arrogance seeping from his pores."

She stared at me like I'd lost it. "So does every guy at this college and in this damn town. At least the Aston brothers can back up the arrogance. They're the richest family in the state and they're all fine as hell. They can be as arrogant as they want, if you ask me."

When I glanced back at Sinclair, he was looking in our direction. His sunglasses were tipped down and he stared at me, those green eyes unsettling me even from across the lawn.

Movement to our left distracted him, and he pushed his glasses back into place, moving to greet the girl who ran over, throwing herself at him.

He pulled her against him for a hug and I went back to my lunch. It was the same girl he'd been huddled up with on the couch after the wedding.

"Who is that?" I asked Arena, fighting to keep my tone casual.

"That's Veda Posey. Sinclair's girlfriend."

My gaze snapped to hers. "His girlfriend?"

I didn't think guys like the Aston brothers did girlfriends.

"Yup," she said, popping the 'p' as she toyed with her rice bowl. "Lucky bitch has been dating him since he was a junior at Triple C. Snapped him up nice and early."

Sinclair was twenty-two. He was two years out of college and already running a successful company. And it also meant he and Veda had been dating for three years.

My eyebrows crept up my forehead. "Wow, that's a long time."

Arena took a bite of her food, both of us watching Veda and Sinclair with their arms wrapped around each other, deep in conversation.

"Yeah, it was weird. Because before her, Sinclair had never really been with the same girl for more than a few weeks. But then he just started dating Veda, like, overnight." She shrugged. "They've been together ever since."

She leaned closer, expression serious. "I asked her once when we were alone together in the bathroom at an event how she managed to bag an Aston and could she write the rest of us a cheat sheet. She just laughed that perfect hot girl laugh of hers."

I gave her a tight smile.

I had no idea why Sinclair having a girlfriend annoyed me so much. He wasn't anything to me and I didn't want him to be. So why would it matter if he was taken?

Veda and Sinclair broke apart, going to separate sides of his car to get in. Sinclair gunned the engine and sped out of the lot.

Who my stepbrother chose to date was none of my business. And that feeling creeping into the pit of my stomach definitely wasn't jealousy.

That would be a level of crazy that I didn't have time to deal with.

CHAPTER 9

For the next three weeks, I rode to Cape Canyon College every day with one of my stepbrothers. Sinclair kept claiming he'd get my car looked at, but it would take some time.

Every morning was the same: Dacre and Presley played power games to see who could get me to ride with them, and I played into it far more than I should, enjoying the feeling of being wanted that slowly crept up on me.

When Presley had pissed me off with his display in the pool, I'd chosen to ride with Dacre the following day.

When Dacre had called me a princess over dinner when I'd said I didn't want to eat the crappy chain store pizza they'd ordered in because Byron and my mom had gone out and given the chef the night off, I rode shotgun in Presley's sporty blue Mercedes the next morning.

I'd barely seen Sinclair since that day he'd picked up Veda at Triple C. Whenever he failed to show at the family dinners my mother insisted on forcing upon us, Byron said Sinclair was busy running his company. Dacre said it was because he was busy boning his girlfriend in his fifteen-million-dollar penthouse apartment in the city.

I didn't care, I had to remind myself. I could do without those intense green eyes constantly assessing me

Despite my determination to escape before my father could get close to me, I loved it at Triple C. Arena was an incredible friend to have, helping me navigate the vultures of the social scene and introducing me to the professors in the classes we had together. The course work was engaging and motivating and the campus was even more beautiful than I first thought. And I'd made it onto the swim team at try-outs, the coach praising my breathing and stroke work, two things I'd worked hard on for the last year.

Even if it was against both my will and better judgment, I was starting to build a life here. There were only a few down-sides, all of them male.

"Dempsey!" someone barked my name as I made my way out of the library.

I glanced over my shoulder, cursing when it was Trenton jogging up behind me.

"What do you want, Trent?"

His jaw clicked at my dismissive tone.

Well, suck it, frat boy.

I wasn't interested in him, and he needed to take the fucking hint.

He stepped in front of me, intentionally blocking my path, his eyes hard. "Your new stepdad may have money, but you don't seem to understand who I am and what my name means around here."

I sighed. "I know who your Daddy is. That doesn't mean I'm going to sleep with you again."

He moved in closer, practically snarling at me. "I've tried playing nice with you, Dempsey. But maybe it's time someone taught you some manners so you learn how to fall in line like the rest of the women around here."

Anger boiled my blood, my bag slipping from my

shoulder and hitting the ground. Arena was right, Trenton was an abuser in the making if he continued to go unchecked.

He crowded me against the wall. I'd be happy to tell him exactly where he could shove his pencil dick. And it sure as hell wasn't anywhere near me.

But before I could open my mouth to do just that, a body slipped between us, and Dacre was staring down at me with his back to Trenton.

"What the fuck do you think you're doing?" Trenton snarled at him.

Dacre threw a look over his shoulder, his large body shielding me from view and slowly edging me away from Trenton. "Talking to my stepsister. Do you mind, bro?"

Dacre turned to face me, one hand pressed against the bricks above my head. He had me caged in, his voice low so only I could hear.

"When I step back, I want you to pick up your bag and walk."

I opened my mouth to argue but his free hand closed around my throat. Shock flooded me, my heart pounding in my chest.

What the hell was this and why did I like it so much?

His proximity. His scent. The power and possession radiating off him. All of it was like a drug and I wanted to get high.

I am so screwed up for liking this.

"Don't fuck around this time, Dempsey. Just do as you're told."

He leaned closer, our bodies pressed together, and inhaled deeply. "What is that?"

My brow pinched in confusion. "What do you mean?"

"That scent that haunts every one of my senses when I'm trying to sleep at night."

He lifted a piece of my hair, twirling it around his finger

and giving it a firm tug. The sensation sent a jolt of pleasure through me.

"I use coconut shampoo?" I squeaked.

It was the only thing strong enough to wash out the stench of chlorine after swim practice. It was potent, so it was a good thing I loved the smell. Evidently, I wasn't the only one.

He stared down at me, those blue eyes penetrating my fucking soul in a way I didn't consent to. There was no way I could let this happen. My mother would throw the shit fit to end all shit fits if she could see us right now. And this whole community would crucify us, regardless of the Aston's money and power. Status had become the most important thing to my mother. More important than me. And the fastest way to ruin it would be to fuck my stepbrother on a walkway at Triple C with Trenton watching.

"Don't look at me like that," Dacre said, the command in his deep voice making my core clench.

"Like what?"

His eyes filled with heat. "Like you're thinking what a better choice I'd have been to rail you in the garden at your mother's wedding."

I sucked in a breath. I hadn't been thinking that exact thought, but it was close enough.

"Fuck," Dacre swore, closing his eyes for a split second, before they snapped open again. "Let's go."

He backed off me an inch and I bent to scoop up my bag.

"Sorry Trent, but we've got to bail. Better luck next time," Dacre said, with a shrug that only stoked the angry fire in Trenton's eyes.

"Dempsey, we weren't fucking done!" he called after me, his voice hard with anger.

Ignoring him, I let Dacre throw his arm around my shoulders, sending my senses into overdrive. My body was so confused right now. Only a few nights ago I'd wanted to ride

Presley in the pool, now I was ready to screw Dacre in the front seat of his car.

I let him lead me out to the parking lot that looked more like a luxury car dealership. We hadn't made it far when a low whistle startled me, and Dacre's arm dropped from my shoulders.

"Only been here a few months and she's already getting herself into a jam," Presley said from where he and Sinclair sat against the hood of Sinclair's red Porsche, looking like every rich princess's dream.

Presley has clearly come from football practice in his black fitted Under Armor shirt and grey sweatpants. The backwards cap was like Dempsey cat nip. Sinclair was suited and booted like always, making him a walking, talking distraction for any woman within a ten-mile radius.

Why did they have to be so goddamn hot? It was *beyond* inconvenient for me.

I knew Presley and Dacre weren't fucking around when they said they would have been better choices than Trenton. I'd witnessed Presley's prowess with the way he'd made that waitress whimper. And from the way Dacre had my pulse racing against the wall, there wasn't a doubt in my mind that he'd be just as dangerous.

Sinclair was a wildcard. There was no way to tell what he was thinking with that deep stare and perfect chiselled face that never gave anything away. The guy was made of stone, which probably meant he'd be the freakiest of them all.

Too bad he had a girlfriend.

It should be that it's too bad he's your damn stepbrother.

Presley pushed to his feet and moved to his bright blue Mercedes which was parked next to Sinclair's Porsche. Dacre's orange Lamborghini sat on the other side, like a leprechaun had shit its rainbow all over the parking lot.

"So... who are you riding home with?" Sinclair asked,

those serious green eyes penetrating me. It was a simple sentence, but coming from Sinclair, it felt like a challenge.

I glanced at the cars, then at each guy.

Presley was the logical choice. His casual charm was easy to be around, the car ride would be flirty and fun.

Dacre was a dangerous option right now, given the spark of heat that had just ignited between us. He was still staring at me like he wanted to strip me down and worship me with his mouth. Riding with him would put my willpower to a test it was likely to fail.

I swallowed hard, gaze landing on Sinclair.

The enigma.

The one who gave nothing away.

The one I was least likely to do something reckless with, given we could barely hold a conversation without sniping at each other.

He also had a girlfriend, which meant he was the safest, most platonic option right now.

"You," I said with a nod to Sinclair.

I didn't miss Presley's muttered "mother fucker" at having lost the minor contest. But I couldn't tear my eyes away from the ghost of a smile tugging at the corner of Sinclair's mouth. The most he'd ever given me.

Dacre's arm slid around my shoulder for a second time, setting my skin alight. "I save you from Trenton—" His lips brushed the shell of my ear, his tone more playful than angry. "—and you're going to ride home with Sin?"

I shrugged like his touch had no effect on me, pulling away and striding around the Porsche to open the door. "What can I say? I really like red."

Dacre shook his head, fighting his smile as he slid into the Lamborghini. "We'll see who would've gotten you home the fastest."

———

When I walked in the door twenty minutes later, the maid approached me with a timid smile.

"Miss Dempsey, this came for you about an hour ago."

I stared at the envelope in her outstretched hand, dread pooling in my stomach.

It hadn't even been long since the last letter from my father. Was he really moving this quickly?

The maid frowned at me, patiently holding the envelope out.

I took it, shoving it in the side pocket of my book bag and bolting up the stairs. I locked the door to my room, tossing the bag aside and pacing back and forth.

Maybe it wasn't even from my father. Maybe it was an invitation to a society event?

Arena clearly worked fast given how quickly we'd become friends. It could be from her inviting me to some fancy function.

Deep down I knew I was fooling myself. But I couldn't imagine away the letter.

Stop being such a frightened little brat and open it.

Marching across the room, I snatched the envelope from the side pocket of my book bag and tore it open.

Inside was a thick piece of stationary, the same personalization as the first two.

Only this time the words were far more ominous.

The longer you play these games, the worse it's going to get.

———

I hit the outdoor pool that night.

The indoor pool made more sense, given it was designed for training, with diving blocks and lane ropes, but I loved the outdoor pool. It was my favorite place in Byron's entire compound. Granted, I was yet to see half of it, like the nine-hole golf course, the outdoor basketball court, or the indoor running track, but none of those would top this pool for me. It was peaceful, secluded, and usually... totally abandoned.

I finished up my standard forty laps, hauling myself from the pool and heading over to the lounger where I'd left my towel and phone. Scooping the phone into my hand as I dried myself off, I frowned at the message notification from an unknown number.

I clicked into the message, my heart racing as a video played.

It was grainy, like it had been taken at a distance, and shot from the roadside of the Triple C parking lot.

Sinclair and Presley were sat on the front of Sinclair's car like they had been only hours ago after Dacre had saved me from Trent. The video was taken from the side, my face and Dacre's were both half-obscured at this angle.

The grin on Presley's face as he spoke to me made my stomach flip.

God, he was gorgeous.

It was clear the moment I chose to ride with Sinclair. Presley swore good-naturedly, and I got to experience Sinclair's ghost of a smile all over again.

Then Dacre's arm came around my shoulder, and the camera zoomed in on the way he tugged me against him to murmur in my ear.

The way I leaned into him as he spoke.

The way he gazed down at me, waiting for my response.

Nothing about it looked brotherly. Or even platonic.

The video cut out and a text message appeared beneath the video.

You and your brothers look like you're getting close. Don't get too close, Darling. You know who you belong to.

· · ·

I tossed my phone across the pool deck like it had burned me. It hit the lounge chair three spaces over with a thump, bouncing off it and tumbling to the ground.

My father was closing in.

And he was threatening to expose a secret that could ruin all of us— one I wasn't even willing to admit to myself.

CHAPTER 10

"Dempsey!" my mother called from the hallway, pulling me from the book I was reading.

I glanced at my bedroom door, calculating whether I could make it across the room from where I sat at my desk, lock it, and pretend I was in the shower before she made it to the other side.

The chance of success was slim. I was going to have to talk to her, something I'd no doubt regret as soon as she opened her mouth. These days she only spoke to me when she needed to parade me around at some sort of event to uphold our new image of the perfect family. Perfectly fucked up was more like it, given I was having thoughts of riding at least two of my stepbrothers.

Too late to hide from her.

A knock sounded on the door and my mother swung it open, letting herself in.

I tossed my pen down on my textbook, abandoning the assignment I'd been working on. It didn't matter that my new stepdad owned Triple C. I still had to study if I had any hope of passing, earning a degree to get a decent job, and putting myself in a position where my father couldn't come for me.

"Sweetheart, I'm not interrupting, am I?" My mother forced a smile, her expression encouraging me to give the answer she wanted, just like it always did.

I sighed. "Not at all, Mom."

"Excellent, I need to talk to you about something extremely important."

It always was these days. But my definition of *important* and my mother's were vastly different. I didn't need to hear the words to know that I was going to hate whatever she needed from me.

"This weekend is the annual Cape Canyon Charity Gala at the country club. It's to raise money for survivors of a natural disaster on the other side of the world."

This was mom-speak for a charity she didn't care about after a disaster she had never heard of. She was only attending the event with my stepfather to be seen and uphold their standing as the ultimate 'it' couple in Cape Canyon. When did my mom become so shallow? She'd adapted to being a billionaire's wife a little too easily if you asked me. Not that anyone was asking. Least of all my mother.

"They need volunteers for the charity auction." My mother's expectant gaze held mine, and I frowned.

"So… you want me to help with the auction?"

Her smile widened. "That would be amazing, sweetheart."

"Okay…" My eyes narrowed, suspicion coursing through me.

This request sounded way too simple. She wanted me to show up and hold up some nice antiques beside an auctioneer in a tux while the uber rich bid on them so they could feel like decent people who gave to charity by accumulating more shit?

Sounded riveting.

"Thank you, darling. I'll find you a dress for the evening and organize someone to come and do your hair and makeup.

Byron thinks you'll be an excellent drawcard to get the Triple C students involved."

Drawcard? How would me assisting with an auction be a drawcard for the students at school?

"I don't have a lot of experience with auctions, but I'm pretty sure anyone could hold up an old vase so people can bid on it."

If my mother could frown, she would have. Instead, she tilted her head, peering at me.

"Old vase? Darling, *you* are the auction item."

My stomach and my expression dropped at the same time. *What the fuck…?*

"You want to auction me off? What the hell does that mean?"

My mother let out a small laugh. "Oh darling, only one night with you."

"One night?! You want to sell me off to some old dude to have his way with me?"

My mother's expression sobered. "Dempsey, don't be so crude. It's a companionship auction to raise money for those in need. Someone will bid on you and you spend the evening with them after the auction. I'm sure you'll get a nice dinner out of it."

Oh, so long as I get some fancy food, it's okay then. Had my mother lost her ever-loving mind?

"There's no way I'm doing that. Count me out, Mom."

She let out a heavy sigh. "You will be doing it, Dempsey. This is our home now and we've been welcomed with open arms. I gave up everything for you, now you'll do this for me."

The words clanged through me. There it was. Again with the *sacrifices* she'd made. It didn't matter that she was my mother and taking care of me was what she was supposed to do. It didn't matter that she'd come out of those sacrifices with a brand new, shiny life with more wealth, privilege and status than she could have ever dreamed of with my father.

She acted like saving me from what my father would have done to me was something she gifted me, and now I had to repay my debt.

If this was what love was supposed to be, I was better off without it.

"We need to earn our place here," my mother went on, completely unaware of the anger rolling through me. "And we do that by participating in the practices of the community we're now a part of. You will participate in this. All daughters of the families in Cape Canyon will be."

I ground my teeth. "Not the sons?"

My mother gave me a tight smile. "Not this time, darling."

Of course not. That would be far too progressive for these people. Sons were to be revered like gods. Daughters were only good for breeding and auctioning off to the highest bidder.

"I'll make sure the details are all arranged, all you need to do is show up. Saturday at two o'clock. Make sure you're on time, sweetheart."

Satisfied she'd successfully forced me into an event I wanted nothing to do with, she left, closing the door behind her.

I fell back on my chair, letting out a long breath.

This was going to be fucking hell.

———

I showed up to the country club on Saturday to find it a flurry of activity.

The place looked more like the backroom of a cotillion or beauty pageant than it did a charity auction. Benches with tall chairs and lit mirrors were lined up in row after row, girls surrounded by teams of people priming and primping them to within an inch of their existence.

Making my way down the aisles, I scanned the empty spaces for my name, spotting it down the end of the second row. A man and a woman waited for me: the guy with platinum blond hair, the woman with long blue waves and dark eye makeup.

They both smiled at me as I approached.

"You must be Dempsey?" the woman asked. "I'm Lyla, this is Gray. Your mother has arranged for us to get you ready today."

I forced a smile. "Nice to meet you both."

Gray motioned to the chair in front of the mirror and I took it. "Ready to join this circus?" he asked in the mirror, standing behind me.

"Not even a little bit."

Two hours later, my hair was styled in perfect waves down my back and my face was a glowing, highlighted, shining version of my real self. Lyla and Gray were absolute wizards and there was no denying I looked good.

Shame about the ever-growing pool of dread in my stomach. Who the hell was going to buy me? What if he was old? Or even worse... some arrogant asshole who tried to impress me with how much money he had? My mom had said this was just for dinner or companionship, but what if this dude tried to kiss me at the end of the night? Kneeing him in the balls and hightailing it out of some fancy-ass restaurant wasn't going to endear me to this community the way my mother hoped.

The hours I'd spent in the makeup chair had given me time to come up with a plan, though. The second this ridiculous event kicked off, I'd make a beeline for my stepbrothers and hopefully have all my problems solved.

Shoving out the dressing room doors, I wandered down the hall of the country club in search of a server or vending machine; anything or anyone who could supply me with some food. I hadn't eaten since breakfast and maybe if I looked bloated in the skin-tight gown my mother had selected, nobody would bid on me and I'd get out of this unassaulted, both emotionally and physically. To these people, being bloated was probably a cardinal sin, one that should involve doctors and multiple medical procedures to rectify.

I turned left, making my way towards the staffing quarters. They were just about guaranteed to have vending machines there. It's not like the staff were allowed to eat actual food. They were there to serve, not be served.

"Jackpot," I muttered to myself, when a glowing vending machine came into view.

I fed my money in, selecting a bag of chips and an energy drink to keep me sane and highly caffeinated.

"What a nutritious dinner," came a voice from behind me.

I swiveled, almost dropping my loot, to find Sinclair staring down at me.

He looked incredible in a fitted black tux that had clearly been tailored to his body. His bowtie hung untied and loose around his neck on either side of his unbuttoned crisp white shirt.

What the actual fuck. Was this guy created by the gods? He was so damn hot I was in danger of panting right in front of him.

"Interesting that you care what I eat. I thought you didn't like me?" I challenged.

He raised a single brow like he was deeply unimpressed with my comeback. "I don't remember saying that."

He didn't need to. It was clear in the way he only spoke to me when forced to. Or how, unlike his brothers, he avoided me wherever possible. The day I'd chosen to ride in his car was the only remotely friendly reaction I'd ever had from him and even then, the car ride had been adrenaline-fuelled silence the whole way back to the Aston estate.

I was about to cut back with exactly that when I remembered I needed his help.

"So, you're going to this thing today?"

He glanced down at his tux. "Looks like it."

"Maybe we can help each other out."

He offered me one of his signature brow quirks.

"Maybe you, Presley, or Dacre bid on me. Maybe you win. And maybe you save me from whoever else might be inclined to purchase me for the night to do fuck knows what."

Sinclair stared down at me in stoic silence.

I sighed. "Come on, Sin. Do me this one favor."

It was a solid plan. The charity would get their money, I would have done my duty and kept my mother happy, and I wouldn't have to spend the night with some lecherous creep who'd *purchased* a nineteen-year-old girl. I didn't need to spend it with my stepbrothers either. They could afford the fee, but that didn't mean we had to follow through and hang out.

"Is this you begging?" Sinclair asked, his gaze roaming over me. "Because I like it."

I rolled my eyes. Of course the arrogant asshole liked it. I bet making women beg was a hobby of his. Along with kicking puppies and pushing grannies down the stairs. But I kept my mouth shut, no need to snap back and piss him off. I needed him right now.

He moved closer, and I retreated until I felt my shoulder blades pressed to the cool glass of the machine. My gown was nearly backless, so the glass felt cool against my skin.

"I thought you didn't need anything from us?" Sinclair said, the low timbre of his voice making me shiver.

I stared at the collar of his shirt, refusing to look up at him.

"You made that pretty clear the night we met when we tried to warn you about Trenton. How's that decision working out for you, little sister?" His tone had an edge of amusement.

Forcing a saccharine smile on my face, I tilted my head up. "Just dandy."

He slid his hands into the pockets of his suit pants. "No need to worry about us bidding on you. Not when you've been so adamant that you can figure this place out yourself."

He moved back, taking the heat of his body with him.

"Enjoy your time up there, Dempsey," he called, not even glancing back in my direction as he strolled down the hall. "And enjoy your night after."

Fuck, fuck, fuckity fuck.

It had been a flawed plan, but the only one I had. Now it was up in flames because I had to go and get mouthy on my first night in Cape Canyon.

CHAPTER 11

"Do I hear five thousand?"

The auctioneer's voice boomed out across the room as the girl before me was auctioned off. She was gorgeous, like a walking doll in her sparkling blue gown, her chestnut hair shining in the stage lights.

Nerves trilled through me like the bracelets tinkling down my arm. I licked at my lips, the familiar taste of peach from my lip gloss doing nothing to calm me.

How the hell had I let my mother rope me into this? It was going to be a complete fucking disaster.

I glanced behind me at the line of girls still waiting to be sold like cattle, then to the open door behind them. I could make a run for it. Bolt like a spooked horse and tell my mother I got sick.

Only she'd never buy it and I'd never hear the end of it, and the consequences of skipping out on this event meant the next thing she asked of me would be three times as heinous.

Fuck, fuck, FUCK.

"Sold!" the auctioneer shouted into the microphone, polite applause breaking out in the room.

The girl before me stepped off the stage and my name was called. When I didn't immediately race forward, the girl behind me gave me a not-so-friendly shove into the spotlight. I stumbled over my dress, righting myself and forcing my shoulders back as I strolled across the stage to stand beside the auctioneer.

I caught my mother's eye at a table in the center of the crowded room. She motioned for me to smile and I willed one onto my face.

We hadn't even started and I already hated this with the fire of a thousand suns.

"Next up, we have the new jewel of the Aston family, Miss Dempsey Aston."

It was Dempsey Falconer actually, but I wasn't about to correct him and have one of these rich chumps send a direct line to my father about what his missing daughter was up to. He'd made it clear with his notes and the stalker video that he knew where I was and how to find me. The thought sent a shiver of fear through me, but I pushed it aside and lifted my chin.

I had to get through this insane event. I didn't have time to think about my father right now.

"We'll open the bidding on a night with Miss Aston at five thousand dollars."

My gaze cut to the auctioneer. Was he crazy? That's how much the girl before me had sold for in total. Why the hell did he think I could pull in more than that? These people didn't know me, they weren't going to part with their money that easily.

"Five thousand!" came a voice from the left side of the room.

I squinted through the stage lights to find Trenton in all his arrogant, confident glory. He gave me a smug nod and, if I wasn't all too aware of just how terrible he was in bed, it might have worked for me.

A voice came from the back of the room, pushing the bid to seven. Then another to the right moving it up to eight.

These people had more money than sense if they thought a night with me was worth that much. Especially when I planned on sitting at dinner like a mute.

A man to the left of the stage near the front raised his hand.

"Ten thousand dollars."

I tried to mask the way I was cringing on the inside and stop it showing on my face. He was a balding, sweaty, leery type of man. He looked like someone who couldn't keep his hands to himself and acted like it was an accident every time his hand brushed your ass or your breasts as you spoke to him.

Oh, hell no.

Glancing back at my mother's table in panic, my stepbrothers stared back at me on the stage, a picture of nonchalance and disinterest. Dacre was slouched back in his chair, drink in hand. Presley was flirting with the girl seated beside him, while Sinclair twirled his glass on the tabletop. Veda sat at his side leaning into him, but his eyes stayed trained on me.

Bids went up around the room, pushing the auction price higher and higher, but the balding leech just kept bidding.

I stared back at Sin, allowing my desperate pleading to bleed into my expression.

If he wanted me to beg, I would. I'd take back every word I'd ever said to him and get down on my knees if that's what it would take for one of them to save me from my fate right now.

But none of them moved to raise a hand or place a bid.

I bit my lip, glancing down at my shoes and accepting that this was destined to be a long night from hell.

"Twenty thousand!" came a voice from a table near the front on the other side of the auctioneer.

I bent forward to glance around the auctioneer's podium. The guy had to be pushing sixty, the same age as my stepfather. While he smiled back at me and appeared to be a much more appealing option than the balding leech, I still didn't want to spend the night with a man old enough to be my father who got off on bidding on young girls for sport.

"Come on," I muttered to myself, pleading with my stepbrothers even though they couldn't hear me.

Dacre sat forward and muttered something to Sin, but he shook his head, his eyes never leaving me. The bastard was loving this. He was making me pay for the standoffish way I'd treated them since I'd arrived. I'd need to remind myself to key his precious car the minute I got home after this disaster of an evening.

The balding leech and the man to the right went to battle over me, pushing the bids so high that everyone else bowed out.

"Twenty-eight thousand I have now, a record price so far tonight," the auctioneer called. "The bid is back with you, sir." He motioned to the balding leech who'd somehow grown even sweatier than when we'd started.

He eyed me like a steak he wanted to devour for dinner.

Please, no.

"Thirty thousand," Mr. Sweaty and Sinister called.

My eyes landed on my stepbrothers again. Presley had finished flirting with the girl beside him and was now staring up at the stage. He still made no move to bid, though.

I glared at Sinclair. Whether the others were willing to admit it or not, they deferred to him. He was the leader of their little hot brother trio.

A smirk spread across his stupid mouth, and I cursed under my breath.

It didn't matter how much I pleaded or begged with my eyes, those boys weren't going to lift a hand to help me.

"Fifty thousand dollars," called the man to my right, and collective noises of surprise went up around the room.

What the actual fuck...

"Wow, that's quite a price tag for a night with the lovely Miss Aston!" the auctioneer said, clearly delighted that the two men had made his job so easy by fighting it out amongst themselves.

He appealed to Mr. Sweaty once more, who bowed out with a shake of his head. The auctioneer banged his hammer down on fifty thousand dollars to the man who was as old as my stepfather, and my shoulders slumped as I rushed from the stage.

This was going to be a heinous night.

———

An hour later when the auction had wrapped, along with the fundraiser where I'd been forced to sit through a meal with the same stepbrothers who had refused to buy me, I received a message from a waiter.

He approached me as I got up from the table to leave.

"Miss, I have a message from Mr. Sensewell," he said quietly, aiming for discreet.

I frowned.

"The man who purchased you at auction, Miss Aston."

"Oh... right... yes. What's the message?"

The waiter smiled politely. "He'll meet you at the valet drive in fifteen minutes." Then he disappeared back to wherever he'd come from, most likely to continue to serve his master. Mr. Sensewell really couldn't have come over and told me that himself? He had to pay someone to do that for him?

My mother stood from her seat beside Byron and glided over to my side, brushing my hair back over my shoulder. "That gives you enough time to change and freshen up."

Freshen up? What the hell did she think I needed to be

fresh for? Some old guy to feel me up in the front seat of his Mercedes?

"I thought you said this auction was about my company for the night, nothing else?"

My mother frowned. "Of course it is, Dempsey. Whatever are you implying?"

"That he paid for the privilege of railing her without having to care about her feelings afterwards," Presley offered from across the table with his most charming smile.

"Presley!" Byron snapped. "Speak like that about your sister again and I'll cut off your credit card for six months."

I shot Presley my best 'screw you' smile.

"Go and get changed. I bought you another dress for tonight," my mother said, shooing me towards the dressing room.

I complied, mostly because it would give me a moment to breathe without a million eyes on me. I'd need to psych myself up for this heinous life experience. Only the wealthy would think auctioning off their daughters to their friends was a good idea.

The dressing room was mostly deserted with only a few makeup artists and hair stylists packing up, along with a few girls who had clearly been sent back here with the same directive as I had.

I gripped the edge of the counter with both hands, dropping my head and taking several deep breaths.

I could do this. It would be fine. I had to do this.

Did I though? I could bolt.

No, my mother would murder me seven ways to Sunday and send the pieces of me back to my father. There was no escaping it. And my mother's punishment would likely be worse than whatever this man had in store for me.

"It feels heinous, right?" came a voice to my left.

My head popped up and I eyed the girl two seats over, dabbing at her lips in the mirror.

"Excuse me?"

"This whole event. It's a bullshit excuse for a charity event. It's just a chance for creepy old men to force themselves on young girls." She rolled her eyes, turning back to the mirror.

"Glad I'm not the only one who thinks so," I offered. "Any tips to get me through it?"

She smacked her lips together, assessing her reflection with an approving nod.

"Don't blow him for less than three thousand and don't sleep with him for less than ten. These assholes can afford it. Oh, and always get payment upfront. I learned that one the hard way my first year."

With that she turned on her heel and sauntered off towards the door.

She was joking, *right*?

There was no way in hell I was sleeping with the old guy who'd bought me. Not even for ten thousand dollars.

Blowing out a long breath, I moved to the racks at the end of the room. I unzipped the garment bag on mine, eyeing the dress my mother had chosen for me.

"Are you fucking kidding me?"

It was a glorified milk maid dress, albeit a modernized version of one. It was white, with thin straps at the shoulders, a balconette chest with a drawstring that would completely expose the shape of my breasts. It was coupled with a corset around my ribs and a draped angled skirt that stopped mid-thigh. It was cute. A little too cute though, in a sexy, come-and-get-it kind of way. My mother had paired it with white strappy heels I'd nearly broken an ankle getting into.

Anger flooded me as I stared at the outfit. Did she think I was just some doll she could dress up and pimp out to her new husband's friends? I was her damn daughter. Was this really all I meant to her now? *This* was how she wanted me to repay my apparent debt to her?

Begrudgingly, I pulled the dress from the bag and slipped it on, because what fucking choice did I have? I had no money and nowhere else to go, which meant I was forced to go along with my mother's outrageous expectations of me.

Maybe if I took too long getting changed, Mr. Sensewell would grow bored and agitated and leave me behind.

A girl could dream.

Except when I stepped outside to the circular valet forecourt there were several cars still idling, along with a black stretch limo with dark tinted windows.

"Excuse me?" I asked the valet. "Do you know which car belongs to Mr. Sensewell?"

The valet motioned to the stretch limo, because of course it was. Nothing said filthy rich quite like a car three times longer than standard, that was a bitch to park, took up half the road, and came with a driver in a stupid hat.

But the sooner I got in that car, the sooner I could get out of it.

I'd go to dinner, smile politely, say as few words as possible, then when I got home, I'd lock myself in my room and take a long scalding shower to scrub this entire night from my skin.

If he dared touch me, I'd scream. I didn't care about fancy restaurants or impressing other rich families like my mother did. I'd scream the building down if that's what it took to keep this man away from me.

Squaring my shoulders, I approached the limo. As I drew close, the back door opened, but it was too dark inside to see much of anything.

I hesitated, indecision warring inside me. I wanted to bolt, the voice inside my head screaming at me to run. But another part, the small obedient part of my brain, told me I had nowhere to go.

Before I could decide, a suit-clad arm reached out, fingers closing around my wrist and yanking me forward.

I ducked, narrowly missing being decapitated by the roof of the limo as I was pulled inside, landing in a heap on the plush-carpeted floor.

"Damn it!" I rubbed at my elbow and ass bone that had both collided with something on my way in. "What the hell is wrong with you?"

I glared up at the suit who'd man-handled me, expecting to find Mr. Sensewell.

My eyes widened as Dacre smirked down at me.

"You were taking too long. If I had to watch you weigh up whether to climb in or cut and run for a second longer, I was going to fucking expire from pity or boredom."

Chuckles sounded behind me and I glanced over my shoulder to find Presley and Sinclair sprawled on the seats, legs splayed like the arrogant assholes they were.

I glared at each of them. "I didn't know people like you were capable of normal human emotions like pity."

Climbing off the floor, I slid into the seat beside Dacre, facing forward. Presley was in the long bench seat that ran along the right-hand side, while Sinclair was at the far end, facing us and half cast in shadow.

"Is that the thanks we get for saving your fine little ass?" Presley said, eyes running over me. "And that's quite a fucking dress, Sass."

I crossed one leg over the other to ensure I didn't flash them again. They would have seen enough of me when I tumbled into the car at their feet.

"Thank you, I guess? Although you've just ensured my mother's wrath by stealing me away from Mr. Sensewell."

Chuckles again. I hated being the butt of a joke I didn't understand.

"What the hell is so funny?"

The limousine started moving, the lights we passed slanting across Sinclair's face down the far end. "Rowan Sensewell was my mentor at my dad's company before I went out on my own." He smirked wider than he ever had. "I asked him to buy you."

I froze, surprise ebbing through me. Their relaxed stances at the table. Their less than interested glances during the auction. They knew Mr. Sensewell had it covered, that's why they looked like they didn't care. That was why my pleading looks had been ignored.

"Why would you do that?"

"Because you looked like a desperate little lamb being led to slaughter up there, Bambi," Dacre said, handing me a tumbler with ice and what smelled like whiskey inside.

I took an extra-large gulp. I'd just gone from thinking I was going to have to spend hours fending off an old guy who thought he was going to pay me to service him, to learning that my stepbrothers had saved me.

I now had to grapple with the idea that maybe these three weren't actually as bad as I thought? That maybe they were actually pretty decent?

"It was ridiculous of your mother to suggest you participate in that glorified sex ring," Sinclair said, his expression hardening.

His eyes locked on mine, something passing between us. Some kind of understanding, maybe? Whatever I'd felt towards them before, all I felt right now was a deep sense of gratitude.

"We told you at the wedding," Presley said, leaning forward so I could see his face clearly. "You're one of us now, whether you want it or not."

Not, not, not.

Part of me wanted to scream the word at them. But another smaller, more secret part of me liked the sense of belonging they were offering me. It was something I'd never had.

From the outside my parents and I had appeared to be a normal, loving family. But my father had used me like bait, while my mother turned a blind eye to it. I'd never felt like I belonged or was worthy of being loved. While my mother may have saved me from my father, now it was her turn to treat me like a pawn to be used.

So, yeah… a sense of belonging wasn't something I had ever felt before. It was something I had no idea what to do with.

I said nothing, taking another sip of my drink and letting the alcohol burn down my throat instead.

Silence filled the car, nothing but the rumble of the engine.

"Thank you," I said eventually, glancing at each of them.

Presley grinned back at me. "Don't mention it."

"No, really, don't mention it," Dacre added. "Sin doesn't like being reminded that he has a heart."

I smiled to myself. "Consider it forgotten."

The world moved by fast outside the window, taking me to God knows where, but at least it wasn't to get railed by an old dude… I didn't think.

"Where are we going?"

Presley pushed back in his seat, legs spreading wide. "We're going to do what we do best."

Dacre knocked his glass with mine. "We're going to party."

CHAPTER 12

"Please tell me Arena is here?" I called to the guys over the thumping music.

The party was in some kind of warehouse, a pretty low brow location given the wealth in the room. But it wasn't just Cape Canyon offspring here either. They were mixing with the normal people tonight, too. The ones whose daddies didn't make eight-figure paychecks.

Dacre rolled his eyes. "Yes, your girl crush is here. Presley made sure of it."

My gaze landed on Presley, surprised. Were he and Arena friends or had he actually been thoughtful in considering what would make this fun for me?

He waggled his eyebrows at me, cutting from the group to head for the bar, just as Arena spotted me. She squealed and threw herself at me, both of us wrapping the other in a hug. "Thank God you didn't get sold into a life of sucking wrinkly dick!"

I grimaced, playing it up. "Right? I might have choked and died."

"Bit dramatic, don't you think?" Dacre said, leaning in close. But I was distracted by the blonde head that had appeared at Sinclair's side, her tongue suddenly trying to bond with his in a permanent way.

"Have you ever sucked wrinkly dick?" Arena asked Dacre, unfazed by the show Sinclair and Veda were putting on.

Veda was beautiful and Sinclair was definitely kissing her back. But there was something off about their vibe. Or maybe I was looking for a problem with them when it didn't exist. They broke apart, Sinclair taking her hand and towing her along behind him as they threaded their way through the crowd towards the bar.

Next to me, Dacre screwed up his face in response to Arena in a way that might have been adorable if I felt some kind of way about him.

Which I didn't. *No way.*

"Can't say that I have." Dacre chuckled, the sound making my core tighten.

Even his laugh was hot.

I shook my head, trying to rid myself of these insane thoughts.

Presley and Dacre might flirt hard with me, that didn't mean they'd actually act on it. But they'd saved me tonight. In a way that had ensured no attention was drawn or scandal was brought down on any of us. As far as everyone else knew, Mr. Sensewell had bought me.

Yet that one caring act from my stepbrothers had shifted something inside me.

I'd been determined to push them away from the moment I arrived because life with my father had taught me it was easier to stay detached. Not to trust anyone.

And staying away from my stepbrothers stopped me from lusting after them. Although that wasn't entirely my fault, either. They didn't need to be so damn beautiful to look at.

But tonight wasn't about whatever weird attraction I had to my stepbrothers. Tonight, I was going to get drunk with my friend to celebrate escaping a night of wrinkle dick and see what other kind of trouble we could get into.

Presley's gaze landed on me from across the room where he was talking to a couple of guys at the bar. He excused himself, making his way over to us, a shot in each hand.

"Ladies." He handed one to me and the other to Arena.

She grinned at me, clinking her glass with mine. "Down it goes."

Presley's gaze was trained on me as he watched me swallow.

"You girls have fun tonight." He took the glass from my hand, our fingers brushing. I swallowed hard as a spark shot up my arm. "I'll see you later."

The words hung between us like a promise, his eyebrow quirking at me with loaded suggestion as Arena tugged me onto the dancefloor.

Another two shots and two gin and tonics later, I was more than a little buzzed. Arena and I had been dancing our asses off, and my skin was coated with a light sweat, my voice hoarse from singing along to the music.

I couldn't remember the last time I'd had a night of carefree fun like this. Coupled with the alcohol, the devil in me was ready to play.

A warm body appeared at my back, moving with me to the music. I smiled to myself, the drinks I'd consumed warming me from the inside out and had a part of me hoping it was one of the three someones it shouldn't be pressed against me.

Warm hands landed on my hips, fingers brushing over me, as we swayed.

I turned in his arms to look up at them, a kernel of disappointment unfurling inside me.

It wasn't any of my stepbrothers.

Which is a good thing, you idiot, I warned myself. None of them would risk being seen grinding me on a public dancefloor.

The guy was still cute though. He towered over me with blond shaggy hair that fell in his brown eyes. He smiled, hands tightening on my waist as we moved together.

For three songs, our bodies swayed, making my pulse pound in my veins as the music filled me. We were getting each other all worked up. I could feel it when he pressed closer, his heart beating under my palms when I smoothed them up his chest.

After another two songs, I was ready to combust. Only... he wasn't who I wanted to do it with.

Glancing to my right across the room, Presley was propped up against the bar, surrounded by women. He'd ditched his tuxedo jacket and tie in the limo, his white shirt unbuttoned to expose his tanned chest, and his sleeves rolled to his elbows. He was so fine it made me falter.

We'd been catching each other's eye all night, heat spreading through my body every time I caught him watching the sway of my hips to the beat.

His effortless confidence, coupled with his lean body, the sharp cut of his jaw, and the near-constant amusement dancing in those brown eyes... the boy was like a beacon. And impossible to ignore.

I kept my eyes locked on him as I grinded with my cute dance partner, our pelvises brushing together and turning me on even more. Then the girl beside Presley leaned in and he ducked his head so she could whisper something in his ear. A seed of jealousy took root in my stomach, slowly unfurling.

"Everything okay?" Arena called over the music, following my gaze. She tried and failed to hide the tilt at the corner of her mouth.

"I'm fine, I don't have a care in the world!" I called back, dragging my eyes from my stepbrother and throwing my hands in the air to sway to the music. The move made my dress creep even higher up my legs, almost exposing my ass cheeks, but right now I didn't care. My dance partner's hands roamed over my ass in appreciation.

I was drunk and I'd escaped a night of being forced into sex by a man old enough to be my father, which in my eyes was a reason to celebrate. I was determined to have a good time.

Another two drinks later, I couldn't stop my eyes from straying to Presley as I danced. I was still hot and turned on by all the grinding with the blond. But Pres hadn't glanced my way again once, seemingly too distracted by the small army of gorgeous women surrounding him. It was driving me to madness in a way it definitely shouldn't.

Pres was the most dangerous kind of playboy. The kind who would sell you a dream with sweet words and a killer smile... then drop you the minute the high of winning you wore off.

But I couldn't help it. After all the grinding, my body was aching for release and my tequila-buzzed brain didn't care that he was my stepbrother, or what scandal it would cause. All the weeks of flirting, the way he'd pushed his body against mine in the pool, the fact that all three of them had saved me tonight...

I wanted this. *Badly.*

I pushed from the arms of my dance partner, throwing him an apologetic smile.

"I'll be back in a minute," I called to Arena.

She smiled, shaking her head.

I shrugged. "What? I need the bathroom."

"Bathrooms are that way!" She pointed over her shoulder, when I started edging through the crowd in the opposite direction.

"I can't hear you!" I called back with a wave, slipping between writhing bodies towards Presley, until I was standing right in front of him.

I edged between the girls crowding him, ignoring their noises of outrage and protest. I resisted the urge to grip his shirt in my fist and tug him down to me so I could whisper in his ear about all the crazy hot things I wanted him to do to me. There were too many eyes on us.

Those sparkling blue eyes landing on me with a grin. "You need help with something, Dempsey?"

His tone was teasing. Playful. *Suggestive.*

I didn't dare break eye contact. "Yes, actually. I need to speak with you."

His grin never faltered, even when his eyebrows crept up his forehead in surprise at my bold move.

He leaned forward. "I love *talking*." He motioned to a hallway to the left. "Lead the way, Sass."

Edging around the gathered girls shooting me daggers with their eyes, I threaded through the crowd of revellers to a hallway at the back. If I'd been sober, I might have listened to the voice inside my head telling me to stop, to backtrack, to bolt in the other direction. But I wasn't sober and right now I didn't want to do any of those things.

I sauntered down the deserted staff hallway, throwing a glance over my shoulder to find Presley following me, biting his lower lip as his gaze ran over my legs and ass.

"In here," he said, gripping the handle on a door to the left, and swinging it open.

He motioned for me to go in and I obeyed. He followed, closing the door behind him.

It was some kind of supply closet, shelves lining three of the four walls, the only light coming from the glowing exit sign above the door.

I rounded on him. "Wow, classy. You really know how to woo a girl, Pres."

"Says the girl who was ready to bone me in the bathroom," he said, shifting closer.

His hand closed over my hip, giving it a possessive

squeeze and I shivered, the pressure of his touch like an instant promise of what was to come.

"Besides, we both know slumming it is your sad little attempt at rebellion. You should be loving this right now. Getting railed up against the detergents instead of in the back of some stranger's limo like Mommy's good little girl."

My eyes narrowed, but there was no way he could see it in the dark. And what exactly was I annoyed at? That he was right? Rebelling against my mother behind closed doors was exactly what I'd done with Trenton.

"Does the sound of your own voice get you off? Because you're doing a lot of talking right now." My hands tightened in his shirt and I tugged him towards me. "I knew you had an ego on you, but this is something else."

I could hear his smile in the dark. "That's it, Sass. Rip into me. That mouth of yours turns me on." He dipped his head, his lips grazing my neck. "You sure about this?"

I nodded and he pulled back, my lips brushing his in the lightest touch. It was all the permission he needed, and his mouth fused with mine in a claiming kiss.

Fuck. I knew Presley would be good at this, but not *this good*.

"I knew that lip gloss you're always swiping on your perfect fucking mouth would taste good. Like peaches."

I tugged his mouth back to mine.

His kiss was like a fucking drug, invading my senses from the jump. His hands smoothed over my waist and down to cup my ass, groaning into my mouth when his fingers brushed the bare skin where my skirt rode up.

Presley pulled back from the kiss. "Remind me to thank my new Mommy for buying you this dress."

A laugh escaped me, and I slid my fingers in his hair, reaching for him again, our tongues going to war for dominance. We were already going to hell for this, may as well make it count.

His hand grazed my thigh, sliding up my side, to cup my breast. His thumb brushed slow circles over my nipple and it instantly hardened.

"Fuck me, this is the perfect handful," Presley said, a little breathless. It was good to know I wasn't the only one affected right now.

He pulled back, using both hands to massage my breasts and sending shivers shooting down my spine when he thumbed both nipples at the same time. He tugged at the string keeping the top of my dress together and it fell open. Dragging it down to free me, he dipped his head, taking my nipple in his mouth, swirling circles with his tongue.

My head fell back on a moan, and I gripped his head to keep him right where I wanted him. "I could die happy right now."

He chuckled, the sound vibrating against my skin. "We've barely gotten started. Who knew you were so easy to please?"

His teeth closed around the hard bud, biting down, and I cried out. When his hand crept under my skirt, shoving my lace panties aside, I jolted at the contact. He switched his mouth to the other side, tongue swirling around my hardened nipple before sucking it into his mouth, while his fingers worked over my clit, making my entire body heat with need.

"God, how are you so good with your tongue? And why hasn't it been on my body from the minute we met?"

He pulled back, tongue flicking my nipple like a fucking tease. "I offered. You were too stuck up and sulking to accept."

I opened my mouth to reply when his fingers slicked over my wet center and I let out a moan.

He gripped the back of my neck, tugging me to him, his mouth closing over my exposed throat. "You're so fucking sexy like this, panting and dripping wet all over my fingers." He thrust a finger inside me and I cried out again.

He pumped in and out at a torturously slow pace, his

thumb creating friction against my clit while he thrust his fingers inside me. "You going to come for me, Sass?"

I nodded, too worked up and close to the edge to form a coherent sentence. It had taken a matter of minutes for Presley to have me close to the edge. It had taken Trenton a minute tops for me to realize there was no way in hell he was capable of getting me off.

Pres ducked his head again, sucking my nipple into his mouth like the fucking pro that he was. The dual sensation of his finger pumping in and out of me and his tongue swirling over me while he played with my clit, pushed me closer and closer.

"Oh my god, Presley, I'm going to…"

His thumb pressed down on my clit and the words died on my tongue. I exploded from the inside out, my body flooding with sensation. I clung to his shoulders, riding the wave of my orgasm hard. He didn't slow down, his fingers working me over, his tongue still swirling against my skin, until my body was trembling and spent.

When he pulled back, he lifted his head and pressed his mouth to mine in a kiss that stole the breath from my lungs. "The sounds you make are so fucking hot."

I smiled in the dark. Everything he'd just done to me was so fucking hot. But I wasn't about to tell him that and fuel his already rampant ego.

"It was okay," I said, through panted breaths.

I could hear his smile. "Liar. You've probably never come so hard in your life."

It was the truth. But that was the last thing Presley needed to hear fall from my lips.

"Someone thinks highly of themself." I stepped into him, my hand sliding between us to his waistband. "Time to return the favor."

He gripped my wrist, stilling me. "No."

I pulled back. *What the fuck?*

"No? Why the hell not?"

"Because sex isn't transactional, no matter how hard assholes like Trenton try to convince women it is. You don't owe me anything because I got you off. I got the pleasure of watching you come undone and soak my fingers."

I stilled. "Are you being a really decent guy right now?"

Another smile in the dark. "I am a decent guy, Sass. You just don't know me yet."

Guilt flooded me. I'd been so busy hating on my new life and trying to stay as far away from my stepbrothers as possible, that he was right. I hadn't bothered to get to know them at all. I had no idea what kind of men I was surrounded by now.

"So what you're saying is, deep down you're a decent guy with a fetish for public sex?"

He laughed this time. "Nothing wrong with a little thrill of getting caught." He moved in close, one hand sliding along my jaw. The other cupped my breast, his thumb brushing over my sucked and sensitive nipple, making me squirm in his arms. "Besides, you fucking love it, too."

He wasn't wrong. The thrill of getting off in a public place you're not supposed to, the high of knowing someone could walk in at any moment — it turned me on.

His mouth closed over mine, our tongues instantly tangling. "See you at home, Sass. Don't do anything I wouldn't do."

"That doesn't leave much," I murmured, as he moved for the door.

His chuckle filtered back to me, along with the pounding music from the party.

He disappeared out the door, leaving me thoroughly satisfied and even more screwed than ever.

———

I slipped from the supply room, but instead of heading back to the party, I headed for the bathrooms. Locking myself in one of the stalls, I leaned against the back of the door, blowing out a long breath.

Presley wasn't all talk. He definitely delivered on his promise to show me a good time, my body was still trembling from the comedown.

I took a moment to clean myself up, then made my way back out to the party.

"And where have *you* been?" Dacre asked, a knowing grin playing at the corners of his mouth. Did he know I'd been with Presley? Or just know I'd been gone for a while with someone?

He was standing by one of the bars with several guys from Triple C, who all glanced my way.

"None of your business," I said, but there was no bite to it.

His laugh followed me as I pushed through the crowd of people searching for Arena. I guess there was no hiding the flush in my cheeks and the thoroughly satiated look on my face. I felt like I was floating on a damn cloud after the earth-shaking orgasm Presley had just given me.

When I found Arena on the dancefloor pinned between two man-mountains, a grin stretched across her face as she took me in. "I'm not even going to ask."

I couldn't help my smile as I shook my head.

Was hooking up with my stepbrother in a supply closet monumentally stupid? Yes.

Did I regret it? *Hell no.*

Arena didn't ask for details and I didn't supply them. Instead, we danced together for the next hour, letting a rotating door of guys buy us drinks, offering them nothing more than the privilege of rubbing up against us for a song or two.

Presley was no longer propped against the bar

surrounded by a gaggle of fawning girls, a fact that made me infinitely happy in a way it probably shouldn't.

I didn't know where he was, but he wasn't flirting with anyone in front of my face, which meant the jealous little beast inside of me from earlier could stay in her cage.

I was buzzed and happy when Sinclair pushed through the mass of writhing bodies on the dancefloor towards me, his usual hard expression on his face.

"It's time to go."

I screwed up my nose at his tone. "I'm having a good time."

"*Now*, Dempsey."

Arena's eyes widened at the biting words. "Imagine him using that voice in the bedroom." She fanned herself with her hand, and I fought my laugh.

Sinclair turned and took off without waiting for me, shouldering people out of his way. I rushed to hug Arena goodbye and followed after him.

"What's the damn rush?" I asked, having to work double time to keep up with him.

He ignored me, stalking out of the club, the cool night air hitting my heated skin.

He moved to the left, the limo parked up the street. Dacre had the door open and was trying to haul a *very* drunk Presley into the back.

"Is he okay?" I asked, as Sin helped Dacre with their stumbling brother.

"He will be," Dacre grunted.

Presley's face lit up when he saw me and I couldn't help the way my stomach flipped at the sight. Nobody had ever looked at me that way before and while I could try to fight it all I wanted, as part of me liked it that Presley was grinning at me like I meant something to him. Even if he was drunk off his ass and that look was probably sex-induced.

"Sass!" He shoved Dacre with an unexpected level of

strength only the truly drunk can pull off, and Dacre stumbled into the side of the limo with a grunt and a muttered 'fuck you, bro.'

Presley ignored him, taking my face in his hands and closing his mouth over mine. I instantly grimaced. His tongue was wet and sloppy, like I was being lapped at by an overeager puppy. And we were on the sidewalk where anyone could see us.

I placed two hands on his chest and shoved him off. He stumbled back, laughing, his back hitting the car door.

"What the fuck are you doing?" Sinclair asked, getting in his face.

Presley kept laughing. "Relax, Sin. She'd never hook up with you anyway."

Of course I wouldn't hook up with Sinclair. He had a girlfriend. And why the hell would Sinclair even care? He'd sooner set me on fire than invite me into his bed.

"We're on a public fucking street. Are you trying to get yourself sent into exile by Byron? Because sucking her face off —" Sinclair thrust a finger in my direction, but didn't take his eyes off his brother. "—will get you there."

Presley's face fell, a darkness clouding his eyes.

"Get in the car, Pres. Now."

Dacre glanced at Presley, then me, some kind of judgment clear in his eyes.

Presley ducked his head and climbed in the car, Sinclair following.

"That's an interesting development," Dacre said.

I didn't respond, because he wasn't wrong—it *was* an interesting development. One I probably never would have acted upon if I'd been sober, but one I couldn't find it within me to regret. Presley and I had a good time. More than a good time. And he had been sweet and giving. Caring, even.

That didn't mean it would happen again or that anyone else needed to find out.

Dacre tore his gaze from me and turned to climb in the car. I blew out a long breath and climbed in after him.

Presley was sprawled on the bench seat along the side, Sinclair taking up the same seat he had on the way there, down the end near the driver. I slid in next to Dacre, pulling the door shut behind me and the car pulled away from the sidewalk.

"I've seen you do some stupid shit, bro," Dacre said to Presley, shaking his head. "But kissing our fucking stepsister on the street where anyone could see was a dumbass move."

Presley's gaze slid to mine and I silently prayed he was going to keep what we'd done tonight to himself.

"How do you think they're going to react..." he staged-whispered to me. "...when they hear that I got you off in the supply closet at the club?"

I sucked in a sharp breath, bracing myself for the fallout.

"What the fuck is wrong with you?" Sinclair snapped, his voice deathly quiet.

I bit the inside of my cheek, forcing myself to stay silent.

Dacre scrubbed a hand over his face. "You know what Byron's planning, Pres. He's not fucking around when he says that if you screw up you're gone again. Is that what you want?"

Gone? What the hell did that mean? And why hadn't I been told about whatever Byron was planning? He'd stressed over and over what a valued part of this family I was now. Clearly not valuable enough to share the family secrets with.

"I don't give a shit what *Byron* wants," Presley said, anger clouding his expression.

Sinclair shot him a dark look. "Only because you're fucking drunk. In the sober light of day, we both know you'll feel differently."

Silence fell over the car as we raced along the road towards home.

Dacre's tone gentled as he stared at his brother. "It's

serious this time, Pres. Byron won't hesitate to bury you if you become a problem again."

My face twisted with confusion. I had no idea what they were saying, but asking would be pointless. They were already speaking like I wasn't there. So I stayed silent.

Presley tipped his head back against the seat with a sigh. "Fucking Byron."

A loaded look passed between Dacre and Sinclair.

"It's the fourth time this month," Dacre said as though Presley couldn't hear them.

Sinclair's jaw tightened and he stared out the window. "I know."

Presley got this drunk often? The guy was loaded, smoking hot, and could likely get anyone he wanted. What the hell did he have to drown his sorrows about so heavily?

"Why does he do it?" I asked, my voice cutting through the quiet car.

"Because I'm a pretty little rich boy, what problems could I possibly have?" Presley said, offering my own words back to me, his arm flung over his eyes.

I flinched at the accusation, given I'd just been thinking exactly that.

He let out a humorless laugh. Forcing himself to sit up, he leaned back against the seat. "Maybe you nailed it the first night we met and my mommy never loved me enough."

I stared at him, this beautiful boy who had it all. Charming, athletic, great kisser and great at... *other things*. Whenever I saw him on campus or at events, he was surrounded by people, always laughing and living it up. But right now, as I watched him tip his head back against the window of the limo and let out a drunken, loaded sigh, I realized just how broken he was.

Which mom was he talking about? The one he shared with Sinclair and Dacre? Or his birth mom?

My own mom had told me the story of the boys before the

wedding. Sinclair was the only biological child of Byron and his ex-wife. Together they'd adopted Dacre, then Presley. But my mom hadn't shared any details about how or why they'd been adopted. Or why their mom and Byron had ended things. Most would look at their life and think they'd won the lottery with a dad as wealthy as Byron. But no amount of money could cover emotional wounds. Particularly those inflicted as a child. My own father has given me enough to last a lifetime.

Presley sighed long and heavy. "Fuck, I need a drink."

He leaned forward, reaching for the bottle of vodka in the bar across from him.

Dacre snatched the bottle away. "No, you fucking don't."

Presley's gaze locked with his brother's, a silent conversation passing between them.

"Fine. I won't have another drink." His gaze slid to me. "So long as Dempsey comes over here and sits in my lap."

I opened my mouth to decline, but Sinclair cut me off. "That won't be fucking happening."

Presley rolled his eyes. "Captain Buzzkill is back again. What a fucking surprise."

Sinclair sat forward. "Look around, Presley. The party is over. There's no one here to fuck or flirt with or help you drown yourself in alcohol. It's just us and we're not buying the little bitch routine."

Dacre cleared his throat and Sinclair sat back in his chair, anger radiating off him.

"What Sin means, Pres…" Dacre shot Sinclair a hard glance. "…is that you need to cut this shit out. How long are you going to keep doing this?"

I stared at Presley, his head tipped back against the window once more.

"For as long as it takes to stop feeling so fucking empty."

And if that wasn't the saddest thing I'd ever heard from the poor little rich boy.

CHAPTER 13

My chest heaved with exertion, my pulse pounding behind my eyes from intense strain.

Pulling myself from the water, I moved around the pool to where I'd left my towel at the front of the stands.

"Good effort today, Dempsey," my swim coach said as she passed, giving me an approving nod.

"Thanks, Coach." I picked up my towel, eyeing my best friend who was seated beside it. Her legs were crossed, a book open in her lap and a pen in her hand, but she'd spent the majority of the last hour definitely *not* studying.

I'd tried out for Triple C women's swim team last month and made it. Since then, I'd had three weekly practices, and my times had already improved. It helped having an Olympic-size lap pool at Byron's house to use any time I wanted a workout.

"Thanks, Coach," Arena mimicked as I joined her. "Isn't someone a good little team player?"

I laughed. "Are you bitter because we all know you don't play well enough with others to join a team?"

Arena levelled me with a look. "Bitch, I play very well with others."

"Just not when clothes are involved." I bit down on my teasing smile.

Her mouth fell open in mock outrage. "I told you about my threesome in confidence! Not so you could casually brandish it about on the Triple C pool deck!"

I shook my head, grinning. "You really should have known better than to trust me with your secrets."

Her eyes narrowed on me. "You're a vault, don't play with me."

She was right. I'd never spill her secrets for the sake of it. Betrayal really wasn't my thing. Especially when friends in this place were in short supply for me.

Luckily, Arena was all I needed.

"You know there are two libraries on this campus you could choose to study in?"

A shrill whistle filled the pool deck. The guys' swim coach was signalling the end of their practice. A buffet of near-naked male bodies climbed out of the pool and paraded past us in a steady stream of dripping wet muscle.

"And miss the catwalk of abs going on in here?" Arena said, her eyes trained on them as they went. "You can keep your stuffy libraries where everyone is fully dressed. I'm more than happy where I am, thanks."

I leaned over and swiped at her lower lip. "I think some drool escaped, you creep."

She swatted at my hand, laughing. "You're such a jerk."

I'd left my phone with the rest of our stuff, and it vibrated against the bleacher seat.

I answered the call, holding it to my ear. "Hello?"

"Miss Dempsey, it's Gretel, Mr. Aston's household manager."

Gretel and I had become well acquainted in the months since my mother and I had moved into the Aston estate.

There was nothing the woman couldn't organize, procure, or create from scratch to satisfy every whim or desire my mother or Byron could come up with.

"I could never forget you, Gretel, how are you?"

"Well, thank you, Miss Dempsey. I wanted to let you know that we've had a delivery arrive for you at the house. I was wondering where you'd like us to put it."

My stomach dropped and dread bled through my insides. The only deliveries I ever got were from my father.

"Is it a letter?" I tried to keep the fear from my voice. "You can just put it in my room."

"It's not a letter. It's twelve boxes addressed to you."

My brow pinched. "Twelve boxes?"

"Yes."

"What's in them?"

"I'm not sure. Would you like us to open one?"

"Yes, please."

The sound of a knife running across packing tap echoed in the background as one of the maids no doubt opened the box.

"It's Portadillo granola, Miss Dempsey."

It's... *what*? There was no way my father was sending me twelve cases of my favorite gluten-free granola... which meant this delivery definitely wasn't from him.

"That's weird, especially given I didn't order it. I'm sorry it's taking up space; is there room in the kitchen to store some of it?"

"Yes, Miss Dempsey. I'll have the rest put in the storage room and instruct the kitchen staff to keep it restocked for your breakfast."

I thanked Gretel and hung up. I highly doubted my mother would have thought to do this. She definitely hadn't stopped trying to force eggs on me in the mornings. Maybe Byron had ordered the granola for me? If he had, I was touched by the thoughtful gesture. I'd have to remember to thank him for it.

Arena snapped her textbook shut, shoving it in her book bag. "So, what are we doing for the rest of the day? Hanging out at your place so I can drool over your incredibly fine stepbrothers?"

I rolled my eyes. "Sure, they're hot if you're into fuckboys who only care about themselves."

I felt a pang of guilt in my chest at the lie. Fuckboys who only cared about themselves didn't save their new stepsister from charity sex rings. Or, in Presley's case, get them off hard in dark storage rooms.

But if anyone—even Arena, although she probably suspected after I'd disappeared at the party—ever found out the filthy things I'd been dreaming about them, or the scandalous acts Presley and I had committed together, it would be a fucking disaster. Better to exaggerate my disdain for them and really sell it than fall short and raise any kind of suspicion.

Arena leaned back on her hands, a dreamy expression on her face. "You've just spelled out my type exactly. And there's three of them. Do you think they've ever had a foursome with the same girl or do you think if I propositioned them, I'd be the first?"

Now it was my turn to swat at her. "Seriously, Arena, get a grip on your libido and stop drooling over my family."

Good thing Arena didn't know that her exact scenario had played out in my dreams more than once. But the idea of them doing it with Arena—or anyone else—had that crazy jealous creature rearing inside me. Which was stupid for many reasons.

I wrapped my towel around my torso, tucking it in under my arms and staring at Arena. I was so thankful for the way that she'd crashed into my life on my first day at Triple C. Being able to stay for Arena was almost enough to have me going to Byron and my mother for help about the threatening letters my father had been sending.

But my mother had made it *very* clear that our new life here—her precious new existence that meant more to her than anything else—wasn't to be tainted with the darkness of our past. What she really meant was that she didn't want Byron to ever learn how beneath him my mother actually was. She put on a good show of playing the role of the perfect society wife, and had fooled him enough to get him to marry her. She was living her dream and wanted to keep it that way.

My problems—these threats against me—would be an inconsequential thing of the past for her.

Arena eyed me warily. "Why are you staring at me like that?"

I shrugged. "I can't appreciate how hot you are and what a good choice I made for my best friend?"

She snorted a laugh. "Bitch, I chose you. You had no choice in the matter."

I rolled my eyes good naturedly, waving goodbye to her as I headed to the locker room to shower.

By the time I was done, the locker room was deserted. I dressed fast, towel drying my hair and tying it up in a half-wet bun on top of my head. Once I threw on some underwear and a hoodie with a pair of Triple C sweats and some slides, my fashionable ensemble was complete. I'd call this one homeless chic. Or standard swim team post-practice attire.

The pool deck was empty when I strolled out, one of the coaches moving around in their offices at the top of the bleachers, likely packing up to leave for the day, but the blinds were drawn.

A voice stopped me mid-stride.

"You've been avoiding me," Trenton said as I passed where he was leaning against the wall between the male and female locker rooms.

I stopped short, swivelling to face him in surprise. "I'm not avoiding you, Trenton. I just have nothing to say to you. We have nothing to say to each other."

There was a calmness to him that was unnerving when he pushed off the wall and casually moved to close the space between us. "I disagree. We have a lot to talk about."

I rolled my eyes, opening my mouth to answer him, when his hand shot out and closed around my neck and my back slammed against the tiled wall.

"Don't fucking mouth back at me, Dempsey. I've had enough of your disrespect. You're making me look weak and unwanted in front of the other families."

My hand closed over his wrist, trying to tug his hand free, but his fingers closed around my throat, squeezing the breath out of me.

"I spelled out the rules your first day at Triple C."

I smacked at his wrist, trying to dislodge his fingers as I fought to draw breath. My fingernails dug into his skin but his hold didn't falter.

Trenton ducked his head so we were eye to eye. "I've claimed you, and it's time for you to fall in line."

My voice rasped in my throat as I tried and failed to tell him where the fuck he could go. Then I pulled up my knee directly into his groin.

He groaned, his hand loosening from my throat as he bent in half, cupping his balls. I sucked in a desperate breath.

"What the fuck is wrong with you!" I rasped at him, pushing him aside.

He fell to the tiled floor, still clutching his tiny dick, but I didn't hang around to make sure he was okay.

I bolted for the door as fast as my feet would carry me. My throat burned and my eyes watered with tears.

No, you will not cry. Not here.

I wasn't going to fall apart in the parking lot of Triple C over a fucking psycho like Trenton.

There were only a handful of cars left for the night, and I scanned the lot for Presley's bright blue Mercedes. He was supposed to give me a ride after he finished football practice and I was done in the pool.

Where the hell was he?

Brushing a hand over my aching throat that was sure to bruise, I slid my phone from my hoodie pocket and checked it for messages.

There was nothing.

I dialled his number, listening to it ring until his voicemail picked up. I immediately hung up and sent him a text.

Dempsey: *What the fuck, Pres? You're supposed to be giving me a ride? Where are you???*

I tapped the send button just as my battery hit zero percentage and my screen went black. Fuck! Why was this happening to me right now?

Sucking in deep breaths in an effort to hold myself together, I glanced around at the nearby buildings. Surely one of them was still open and would have a phone? Or maybe I could try the dorms? But the thought of standing outside, dialling room after room in the hope that someone answered, listened long enough to let me explain myself, *and* let me come up to use their phone was enough to make me dismiss that plan. And I really didn't want to answer questions about why I was struggling to speak or the finger-shaped marks that had no doubt started to appear on my neck.

"Dempsey!" a voice called from across the lot.

I glanced over my shoulder to find Trenton coming for me. *Oh, hell no.*

Hitching my bag higher on my shoulder, I started across the lot in the other direction, making it to the path and hurrying along.

"Dempsey!" Trenton called again, his voice further away than before.

There was no way in hell I was going to let him close enough to touch me again. The guy was a sociopath.

Cursing Presley's name every step I took, I made it to the edge of campus, glancing each way down the sidewalk of the main road.

I had no phone. No one knew where I was. And I had no way of getting home, other than walking. For miles. In the dark. In fucking slides.

But what choice did I have?

I started in the direction of the Aston estate. It would take me more than an hour to get there, Dacre had said as much on my first day when I'd tried to walk instead of riding with them.

Several cars passed me as I walked, all in a rush to get home. Each time the shine of the headlights lit up the road, I prayed none of them were Trenton. I didn't think I could keep it together through another altercation with him. I'd crumble.

I'd been walking for at least twenty minutes, the slides starting to rub painfully against my feet, when a giant grey truck with blacked-out windows drove past so close the rush of air almost bowled me over.

"What the hell is your problem?" I called, knowing full well they'd never be able to hear me.

Only maybe they did.

Brake lights lit up the road and the truck slowed. Then turned around.

Fear unfurled in my stomach as the truck drove by me at half-speed going the opposite way this time. The windows were so dark it was impossible to see inside.

I kept moving, watching the truck out of the corner of my eye. It moved further down the street, back the way it had come, and I relaxed... but then the brake lights lit up again and it pulled a U-turn, heading back my way a third time.

"The universe is really trying to screw me over today," I muttered to myself, hoping if I acted like I wasn't freaking the heck out right now I might actually start to believe it.

Walking as fast as I could, I tried to make it to the corner.

And then what? Did I really think I was going to out-walk a damn truck? Was it Trenton behind the wheel?

From the corner, I glanced down both streets. The truck was gaining on me. I opted for left, cursing when the street led to an open field and not houses. I must have pissed off the karma gods good and hard in a past life.

Glancing back at the corner, I tried to convince myself that I was just being paranoid. The person driving the truck was lost, that was all. It wasn't following me. It was going to drive right by this street and continue on the main road.

Only it stopped and so did my heart.

The wheels turned in my direction, the engine revving as the truck sped towards me.

Oh, fuck.

I turned back around and bolted along the sidewalk, my book bag thumping against my back and my slides barely staying on my feet. The truck's engine revved harder, the sound getting closer and closer until it was right on my heels.

"What the fuck do you want with me?" I called out, but my voice was still a hoarse whisper.

Ripping my bag from my back, I tossed it at the truck. It landed on the hood with a thud. What I thought my damn book bag was going to do against a three-ton pickup truck, I didn't know, but I was panicking, and the bag was the only weapon I had.

The truck revved harder, gunning for me, and my heart was instantly in my throat, fear rocketing through me.

I turned and ran, the slides slipping from my feet as I veered right into the open field praying they wouldn't follow me since there were no roads.

No such fucking luck.

The truck followed, careening across the grass like it was trying to get in front of me, trying to herd me like cattle to cut me off.

Pulling a one-eighty, I bolted back towards the road.

Whoever it was behind the wheel, they could easily catch me. Instead, they were toying with me. Playing a torturous game of cat and mouse to wear me out.

If it was Trenton behind the wheel and he was trying to scare me, it was working.

My heart was thundering in my chest and adrenaline pumping through my veins, fueling my already fatigued muscles. I was going to lose this game, and I had no idea what the heinous prize would be when they caught me.

I reached the road, praying to any deity who would listen to let me get out of this alive.

A car screeched to a halt in front of me in a blur of red, and I pulled up fast to keep from slamming into it. My hands planted on the hood, my upper half sprawling across it.

The door opened. Dacre was in the passenger seat and Sinclair was behind the wheel. Relief flooded me so fast I could cry.

"Get in," Dacre ordered, his eyes hardened with anger.

He didn't need to ask twice. I threw myself into his lap and he slammed the door behind me.

My whole body trembled, my chest heaving as I tried to get my breath back.

"What the fuck happened?" Sinclair snapped, eyes darting between me and the truck.

I shook my head, eyes glued to the truck which had stopped at the edge of the field. Sinclair pulled a U-turn just as the driver's door to the truck opened.

My stomach lurched, fear instantly flooding my body at the sight of the tall, broad, dark-haired man staring back at me.

Algor.
My father's right-hand man.
He'd finally come for me.

CHAPTER 14

"Dempsey, tell us what happened. Who was that?"

Dacre tried for about the nineteenth time to get a response out of me, but I shook my head.

I could feel the tension radiating off him from beneath me, but I couldn't speak. Not with the amount of fear running through my body. Or with my voice wrecked from Trenton's greedy little hands.

I thought I'd have more time. Yes, my father had sent me letters. *Warnings*. But I didn't think he'd act upon them so soon. Not yet.

Sinclair glanced between me and the road. "What the fuck is that on your neck?"

I stiffened. Trust Sin to notice the remnants of psycho Trent, even while behind the wheel of a speeding Porsche.

Dacre's touch was gentle when he moved my hoodie aside, swearing at the marks. "Did the guy in the truck do that to you?"

I shook my head, but didn't utter the name I knew I so easily could. I didn't know what would happen if I told them it was Trent who'd attacked me.

The adrenaline ebbed from my body, replaced with a mix

of devastating anxiety and exhaustion that left me trembling. Unable to get my breathing under control, I focused on pulling in air through my nose and blowing it out of my mouth.

"What is she doing?" Sinclair glanced at Dacre.

"Deep breathing." Dacre's arm tightened around my waist, his other hand rubbing small calming circles over my back with his knuckles. "You're okay," he murmured in my ear, his words soothing me more than I would have expected. "Close your eyes, I've got you. Nobody can get you here with us."

I knew he believed it, but it wasn't true. My father could reach me anywhere, he'd just proved that. Nowhere was safe. He was determined to force me into a life that would break me. All for his own gain.

My father *always* got what he wanted.

Dacre's arms tightened around my waist and he leaned forward, his lips gently brushing against the marks on my neck. I shuddered at his touch, but the move successfully distracted me from my thoughts for the briefest moment.

I leaned back, letting my body melt against him. The feeling of being held, being comforted, wasn't something I was used to. It sure beat comforting myself while I sobbed in the shower, my usual coping mechanism.

I still planned on doing exactly that the moment I was out of this car, but having Dacre's solid body at my back, his arms around my waist, and his lips gently caressing my throat brought me momentary comfort.

Sinclair gunned the Porsche through the gates and into the giant garage. He stopped the car, turning in his seat to glance at me, then at Dacre, another one of their silent conversations passing between them.

"I want to go inside," was all I managed to rasp out.

Dacre opened the door, helping me from the car before sliding out after me.

I made a beeline for the doors to the house, Dacre and Sinclair behind me.

"Dempsey, tell us what the hell that was about..." Sinclair started, before Dacre cut him off.

I ignored them both, heading straight for my room and locking the door. I slid down it to the floor, the tears I couldn't hold back any longer falling down my cheeks.

This was pointless. All of it.

Trenton was a violent asshole who was always going to get away with it because his father had money and influence in a community that was all too willing to turn a blind eye to that kind of *criminal* behavior.

As for Algor and my father... my body trembled and I dropped my head to my knees, hugging myself tightly.

A small part of me had believed my mother when she'd said that our lives with Byron would be a fresh start. That we'd be protected. And maybe that was true for my mother, but it didn't apply to me. My father had never seen me as a daughter, only ever a chess piece in a game I'd never agreed to play, but could never stop playing either.

He'd never let me go. Not until he'd gotten what he wanted.

Swiping at my cheeks, I forced myself to my feet and into the bathroom. I refused to look in the mirror at Trenton's handiwork. It would only cause more angry tears to fall.

I turned the shower to scalding and stripped down, stepping under the pounding spray. I let it soak me. Let it wash away the dirt and sweat and fear of running from that truck. Let it wash over my neck, stripping the feel of Trenton's malicious fingers from my skin, even if it wouldn't remove the marks he'd left behind.

But I couldn't outrun my past or my future. And when I pulled my face from the water so I could breathe, the fear was still there. Still pulsing through me like a living, breathing thing.

Tears slid down my cheeks again, mingling with the hot water falling over me. Curling in on myself, I dropped to the floor, pressing my back against the wall and pulling my knees up to my chest once more.

My head dropped to my knees.

How was this my life? Why had I ever thought doing anything with Trenton was a good idea? Why was mine the father I'd been given? How different would my life be if I'd gotten someone else to call Dad?

The door to the bathroom opened, someone stepping into the fogged space and closing the door behind them. Quiet footsteps sounded across the tiled floor, along with clothes being discarded, then a body slid in beside me.

"I'm so sorry, Sass," Presley said. His voice was gentle. Torn. Quiet.

Quieter than I'd ever heard him.

It made the tears fall faster.

"I'm so sorry I wasn't there."

He wrapped an arm around my shoulders, tucking me against his side, and I lifted my head. "Where were you?"

His expression twisted with remorse. "I... I had a bad day. I hit a bar not far from campus and I lost track of time."

I pulled away from him and his expression crumbled. "Would you have been able to drive even if you had remembered?" I demanded, eyes brimmed with tears.

Anguish filled his own and he shook his head. "I should have been there for you." He pulled me against him again and I let him, my head falling to his shoulder.

He was still wearing black boxer shorts, the material soaked from the showerhead raining down on us.

"I'll never let you down like that again. I swear it, Dempsey. I'm so fucking sorry."

I nodded, knowing he meant it. I lifted my head, my gaze locking with his.

"I promise you, I'll always be there." His hand came up to cup my cheek, his palm warm against my skin.

I shifted closer and his brow pinched, eyes searching mine in question. But I didn't want to answer. I didn't want to talk at all. Right now, I wanted to feel anything but the anxiety and fear overwhelming me.

Tilting my chin, I angled my face towards his. He didn't hesitate, his mouth dropping to mine, his soft lips caressing me. Our tongues met, sliding against one another and Presley groaned, pulling back. "We can't do this right now."

I pulled back just enough that I could slide my leg over both of his, twisting my body until I was straddling him. His hands landed on my bare back, eyes dropping to the rivulets cascading down my chest.

"You sure about that?" I asked, leaning in to kiss him again. He kissed me back with an eagerness that took my breath away.

Until he pulled away again.

"I can't take advantage of you with what you've just been through. I'm a stupid, selfish asshole, but I do have some boundaries."

I slowly leaned in until my mouth closed over the sensitive flesh at his throat. "I want you." I sucked hard, making him shudder. "Help me forget, Pres."

His name falling from my lips in a way that was borderline begging was his undoing. He hardened beneath me, the head of his cock brushing against my core and making me moan.

His hands tightened at my waist, before reaching up to cup my breast.

"Fuck me," he muttered to himself, staring down at my chest as he toyed with my nipple.

"I'm trying."

The grin that tugged at the corner of his mouth was

ruinous. His hand slipped between my legs, groaning again when he realized I was slick and ready for him.

"Are you sure?" he mumbled against my skin, lips brushing over my collarbone like he couldn't resist.

I nodded, arching my back so my breasts were in his face.

"Fuck, Sass, you're killing me."

I rocked my hips over his hard cock once. Twice. Three times. Enjoying the delicious shudder that ran through us both. "So let's die happy together."

It was all the permission he needed, his resolve shattering in an instant. He wrapped an arm around my waist to lift me off him slightly. Just enough to tug his boxers down, his hard cock springing free. Lowering me back down, I grinded my hips over him, the sensation twice as satisfying now there was no barrier between us.

"Should I get something?" Pres asked, his expression tight with need.

I shook my head. "I'm on the pill. And I'm clean."

"I'm clean too. I get tested."

Leaning in, I kissed him again, long and slow. His cock lined up at my entrance and I stilled, tilting my hips so he slid inside of me.

He tipped his head back against the wall and groaned long and low.

"You feel incredible," he muttered, wrapping his arm around my waist again and tugging me closer so my breasts were pressed against his chest, the water still raining down on us.

The proximity meant my clit brushed against his pubic bone with every tilt and thrust of my hips, both of us panting in unison.

"God, you're such a hot little bitch, Sass. So damn tight."

I shuddered at his degrading praise, the sound of it only heightening the sensation between my legs.

The water soaked us, running in rivulets over my skin, as

we rocked together. Every rock and thrust pushed me higher and higher until I was teetering on the edge.

"Pres…" I said, breathlessly. "Pres, I'm going to come."

He gripped my hips tighter, holding me down on his cock. Then he lifted me up, sliding out, only to thrust back in. The sound of my pleasure echoed around the cavernous bathroom.

I couldn't hold on, my body overwhelmed with sensation, and my orgasm exploded inside me. Presley's fingers flexed at my waist, then he was groaning his release along with me.

When we were both spent, I lifted myself off and Presley slipped out of me. Then he wrapped his arms around me and I fell against his chest, letting his comfort wash over me along with the water.

CHAPTER 15

T he following day I leaned against the wall of the garage, Sinclair's head buried under the hood of my Bentley.

"I really wouldn't have pegged you as a car guy."

He stood tall, eyes pinning me in place. "Because you know me so well?"

Jesus, this guy was pricklier than a fucking cactus in the Nevada desert. Those green eyes locked on me, completely disarming me like they always did. And I fucking hated it.

"Just wouldn't have thought you were the type to get your hands dirty."

"And what *type* do you think I am?" Sinclair asked, reaching for a tool from the rolling cabinet beside him.

He was wearing a pair of jeans that sat low on his hips, a black long-sleeve t-shirt hugging his chest and arms. It was the most casual I'd ever seen him dressed. Usually it was all dress pants, fancy leather shoes, and button-down shirts for the oldest Aston brother. Suited and booted Sinclair was a sight, but roughed up, greased-stained Sinclair was something else entirely. Especially bent over an engine, the hood propped above him.

Which means he's good with his hands.

I really needed to get a grip. It wasn't like my stepbrothers were the only hot guys I'd ever seen in my life. It was just annoying that we were forced to live under the same roof and I had to see them every day. At least, with Sinclair I felt that way. Since Presley and I had fucked each other in the shower, he was all I could think about. And how desperately I wanted to do it again.

I shrugged in response to Sinclair's question. "A sexual sadist."

It was a joke, but then again… it could be true.

He didn't react, those careful, calculating eyes watching me. He turned back to the car, disappearing under the hood again. "Didn't realize you'd given so much thought to my sexual preferences."

From anyone else, I might've considered it flirting. But not Sinclair. Everything about him was so matter-of-fact. It didn't surprise me one bit that he'd managed to grow the company he'd started in college into a multi-million-dollar empire two years out. He was ruthless, unfeeling, and deliberate with every move he made and every word he uttered.

If I were the wagering type, I'd put money on odds he didn't even like me. There was no way he was going to flirt with me.

"Sometimes the mind wanders where you can't control."

He stood tall again, closing up the hood of the car. "Does it? My brother not keeping you satisfied?"

His gaze ran over me, making my brow pinch in confusion. What the fuck was that look for? And he was just going to bring up me and Presley hooking up so casually, like it meant nothing? He was a mindfuck and a half.

"What happened yesterday?" he asked. "Why didn't you head into one of the buildings on campus and call someone when Pres wasn't there?"

I pushed off the wall, tugging up the neckline on my high-neck shirt to cover the finger-shaped bruises. "Who was I going to call?"

"Dacre. Your mom. My dad." He halted for a beat. "Me."

Our gazes locked, silence passing between us.

I shook my head, resigned. "I was going to, but Trenton showed up and my phone died."

I stopped before admitting that he was the one who'd put the marks on my neck. After the shower, Presley had bundled me in towels and ushered me to the bed, where he'd held me tight and tried more than once to get me to talk about what had happened. But I'd kept my mouth firmly shut.

As much as I'd love nothing more than to see Trent get what he was most definitely owed, it didn't need to be at the hands of my stepbrothers. I wasn't allowed to make waves in this community.

Sinclair's expression pinched with irritation. "We warned you about the guy. You should have listened." He reached for a rag on the tool cabinet beside him, wiping at his hands.

I rolled my eyes. "Let me just go grab my time machine and go back and heed your advice."

"You could have just taken it in the first place."

I leaned against the side of Dacre's car which was parked beside mine. "I didn't know you at all. I had no reason to trust you."

Silence hung between us again.

Sinclair discarded the rag, slowly moving between the cars so he was in front of me. "But you do now?"

My brow pinched. "Do what?"

"Trust us."

He shifted forward, leaving only the smallest space between us.

What would it be like to have his body pressed against mine? He was dominant and commanding in every aspect of his life, surely he'd be the same in the bedroom. A small part of me willed him to come closer so I could find out.

He stared down at me, those green eyes trapping me as we gazed at each other in a standoff. Would his fingers tangle in my hair when he angled my mouth to his? If I tilted my hips and pressed them against him, would he be hard? My mouth watered at the prospect.

I'm sure his girlfriend likes it when he gets hard, too.

The thought was like a bucket of ice water over my head and I dropped my eyes, clearing my throat and moving around the front of the car.

"Is my car roadworthy again?" I asked, avoiding looking at him.

"It always was."

My head snapped up and he shrugged. "We knew you'd put up a fight about riding with Presley or Dacre, so we gave you no other option."

Irritation flooded me. They'd messed with my car so I'd be forced to ride with them?

"You're a real controlling asshole, you know that?"

A smile twitched at the corner of his mouth, but he didn't let it break free.

He glanced down at me as he made his way to the door back inside.

"Yeah, I do know that." His gaze dropped down my body like a promise. "It's what makes me so damn successful at anything I focus on."

CHAPTER 16

had two hours to kill between my classes every Wednesday so I decided to hit the gym on campus.

Credit to Byron, the facilities at Triple C were incredible. The gym itself was decked out with white marble polished floors with thick mats under brand new machines. There was a reformer Pilates room, a hot yoga room, and a dance studio off the main floor, as well as a boxing ring taking up pride of place in the center of the room… And it was currently occupied by Dacre and Presley.

I acted like I hadn't even noticed my stepbrothers sparring in the ring, their toned and sweat-slicked torsos drawing the thirsty gaze of every girl in the room. It was particularly hard to ignore Presley's glistening skin, knowing my hands or mouth had been pressed against almost every inch of it while I was riding him in the shower.

God, what I wouldn't give to do it again.

Ignoring them, I made my way to the treadmills, pulling my headphones out of their case as I went. I was so focused on not focusing on Presley and Dacre that I didn't notice Satan's spawn at the squat rack with two of his fucking sidekicks.

It had been two weeks since he'd attacked me on the pool deck, and the bruises he'd left on my throat were almost completely gone.

"The new girl is obsessed with me," Trenton said, staring at himself in the mirror, clearly pretending he couldn't see me. "I can't go anywhere without her showing up."

There was no way in hell I was going to rise to that bait. It wasn't worth an ounce of my energy, and I wouldn't give him the satisfaction of the reaction he was so desperate for.

"My dick is just that good. It makes the ladies crazy."

His friends laughed at their master like good little minions and I tried not to throw up in my mouth. God, he was disgusting.

I should have listened to Sinclair, Dacre and Presley when they warned me about him at the wedding reception. Except I'd been too busy trying to prove that I had nothing to prove. That, despite my mother forcing my position in her new perfect life, I wouldn't be a good little girl who did what she was told. Least of all from my stepbrothers.

If only it hadn't come back to bite me in the ass this hard.

Trenton was a tool, and I was riddled with regret for ever going near him.

I stepped onto the treadmill, putting my earbuds in and cranking my music loud enough to drown out the sound of the dickwad nearby.

Just as I'd gained a rhythm, my phone rang, the sound echoing in my headphones.

"Hello?" I didn't slow my run, whoever it was could deal with my panting breaths.

"Miss Dempsey, it's Gretel, Mr. Aston's household manager."

I fought a smile. "I know who you are, Gretel. You're unforgettable."

"Thank you, Miss Dempsey. That's very kind. I'm calling

to let you know another delivery arrived for you. Six cases this time."

Another one?

"More granola?"

"One moment, we'll find out."

There was silence down the line while someone cut open one of the boxes.

"Coconut shampoo, eight bottles to a box, Ms Dempsey."

"Shampoo?"

Who the hell was sending me shampoo? Whoever it was, I'd take that over another ominous missive from my father.

"Yes, Miss Dempsey. Shall I have some placed in your bathroom and move the rest to the storeroom?"

"Yes, thank you, Gretel."

I hung up, focusing on my run and not my surprise deliveries. I still hadn't managed to thank Byron for the granola. Maybe the shampoo was from him, too?

Twenty minutes later, my skin was slick with a thin layer of sweat and my legs were fatiguing, but I wasn't ready to stop.

Running didn't bring me the same solace and silence that swimming did, but I still loved the feeling of my muscles aching, my chest heaving, and fatigue taking over my body.

Focused on my strides, I didn't feel it when my earbud dropped out until it hit the empty cup holder. Propping my feet on either side of the speeding running pad, I picked up the earbud. I was about to put it back in when Trenton's obnoxious voice carried across the gym.

"It was worth it. Dempsey is one freaky slut."

My stomach dropped, anger coursing through me. Did Trenton really just call me a slut for sleeping with him?

"What the fuck did you just say, DeGrossi?"

I didn't turn around, but I caught the fury on Dacre's face in the mirror from where he stood in the boxing ring, his knuckles blanched white from his death grip on the ropes.

If Trenton was concerned about being called out by a raging Dacre, he hid it well as he turned casually towards the ring.

"Heard that, did you, Dacre?"

"Yeah, I fucking heard it, so get in the ring. Because you don't get to trash a fucking Aston and walk away with your face intact."

I'm not a fucking Aston.

I bit down on the words threatening to climb up my throat, because it wasn't important right now. Instead, I pretended I couldn't hear them at all. I dropped my gaze and stepped back onto the treadmill to continue my steady rhythm. Unfortunately, I couldn't seem to stop myself from watching the drama unfold in the gym mirror.

Trenton sauntered towards the ring, his face hard with disdain. "For fuck's sake, Dacre, you're always such a thug."

God, what had I ever seen in that wet noodle? I deeply regretted the fourteen-point-four seconds he'd spent inside of me. And probably would for the rest of my damn life.

"I wonder if your real father was a bruiser just like you," Trenton went on, crossing his arms over his chest with smug satisfaction at the way Dacre's gaze was locked on him, his body coiled with barely contained rage. "Maybe he banged up your birth mom and that's why she dumped you in that group home where Byron found you. Just so she could get away from her shitty life of raining fists."

Rage flooded me, and I slammed a hand down on the emergency stop on the treadmill, swivelling in an instant. I whipped the remaining headphone from my ear, tossing it with the other one, then marching across the room to the boxing ring. "What the hell did you just say to him?"

Trenton glanced my way like I was nothing more than an annoyance. "Oh, hey Dempsey. Didn't see you there."

His obnoxious little friends who'd been watching this whole thing play out snickered from behind him.

Fucking sheep.

"Don't talk to her," Presley said casually, moving to the edge of the ring to lean against the corner ropes, as though the mounting tension in the room was a total bore to him. "How about you stop acting like the total pussy that you are and step into the ring like Dacre asked?"

The briefest hint of apprehension flashed in Trenton's eyes.

Not so brave when he's being called out, instead of skulking around pool decks offering unwanted neck accessories.

He scoffed with false bravado, reaching for the lowest rope and swinging himself up onto the mat. He ducked, dipping between the ropes, bringing him face to face with Dacre.

"You want to talk shit about our family, you'd better be prepared to back it the fuck up," Dacre spat.

He was mean when he was angry. It was a side I hadn't seen from him yet. He'd been surly on my mother's wedding day when I'd first met him, but this outright rage was something else. And the fact he was acting this way in my defense was all kinds of… well, *hot.*

"Do you really think you can take me in a fight?" Trenton said with a laugh.

But Dacre wasn't laughing. His hard gaze was locked on Trent with a seething intensity that would have me shaking in my sweats if it was directed at me.

"I know I can, pretty boy. Now fucking hit me." Dacre motioned to his jaw.

Trenton turned back to his friends with a look of mocking disbelief. But without warning, the comic expression dropped, his eyes hardened, and he swung at Dacre in the most cliché fucking fake out.

"Cheap shot," Pres called out, but it was more a heckle than a protest.

Dacre didn't dodge the hit even though it was clear to

everyone and their grandma what Trenton had been about to do. Dacre tested his jaw, eyes locked on Trent.

"Good. You got a hit in. Now you can't run to Daddy crying about how I wiped the fucking floor with you."

Dacre's fist moved faster than lightning, whipping out to hit Trenton clean in the mouth. He stumbled back, hitting the mat and clutching his face. Dacre was on him in a second, throwing his weight at Trent like a seasoned pro. Dacre swung punch after punch at Trent's jaw, alternating his hands.

"Dacre, Dacre, he's our boy," Pres sang like a cheerleader from his spot in the corner. "He'll fuck Trent up like an old dog toy."

Blood spilled from Trent's nose, splattering against the mat, but Dacre didn't let up.

"Stop!" I shouted, finding my voice.

Dacre stilled, both he and Presley staring in my direction.

"That's enough, Dacre. Let him up."

Dacre relented, raising both his hands and pushing to his feet.

Trenton rolled to his side, coughing up a mouthful of blood that he spat on the mat. "You're a fucking snake, Aston."

"The only snake here is you, you little b—" Dacre lunged for Trent, but Pres held him back with a firm arm across his chest.

"Let's go," I called, backing away from the ring and hoping my stepbrothers had the sense to follow. Dacre needed to cool off and distill some of the fury still clearly rattling him. And that wasn't going to happen with Trenton mouthing off at him from his bloodied position on the floor.

The fucking audacity of that asshole.

"Listen to your new Mommy, Dacre," Trent called, sitting up and wiping blood from his face with the back of his hand.

Dacre made a move back to the ring, but both Pres and I grabbed him this time, hauling him back.

I rounded on him, getting in front of him. "Outside. Right now."

He glanced down at me, those blue eyes locking with mine. They were laced with a mix of fury and something else I couldn't name.

Shaking us both off, Dacre marched for the door.

"Fuck!" he shouted once we were outside.

He ran both hands through his hair, leaving them there. His biceps rippled, his t-shirt riding up to show a strip of toned stomach. Coupled with the masculine rage coming off him, the whole look was mouthwatering.

Dacre swivelled, looking at me, then Presley. Another one of their silent conversations passed between them.

"I'm out of here," Dacre said, still vibrating with anger.

He took off down the path towards the parking lot before either of us could protest.

Presley pulled his phone from his pocket. "Sin? Dacre's out of it." He glanced my way, phone pressed to his ear. "Trent was shit-talking Dempsey at the gym so he hauled him into the ring and beat the shit out of him."

He paused, listening to whatever Sinclair was saying.

"Nah, Dempsey called him off, got him outside, but he just took off."

He paused again.

"Can do. See you later."

Presley hung up and slid his phone back in his pocket, a broad smile spreading across his face. "So, should I walk you to class?"

My face contorted. "Are you serious right now? What the fuck just happened in there?"

A part of me loved that Dacre had come to my defense like that, and I knew better than anyone that Trenton deserved it.

But raging out on someone like Trenton could have serious consequences.

Pres shrugged. "Dacre is a complicated guy."

An understatement. They were all fucking complicated. Presley with his chronic drinking and Dacre with his secret rage. Who the hell knew what Sinclair's issues were. He probably had at least seventeen of them, given his permanently icy demeanour.

"That's it? That's all you're going to give me? That he's complicated?"

He sighed, blowing out a long breath. "Dacre gets real protective of those closest to him. Especially family."

"I'm not your family."

Presley chuckled. "Well, whether you want to be or not, Dacre considers you family. Me and Sin do, too."

He wrapped an arm around my shoulders, jostled me against him in what I think was meant to be a hug.

"We meant it when we said you're one of us now, Sass. Assholes like Trent don't get to talk shit about you without D reconstructing their faces."

I mulled it over, trying not to get distracted by his body touching mine. Dacre's reaction had been protective, but his fury had levelled up the moment Trent mentioned his birth family.

"Was it because Trent talked about his mom?"

Pres ran a hand through his hair, looking more uncomfortable than I'd ever seen him.

I'd quickly learned that Pres was well practiced at masking any kind of discomfort with his panty-dropping grin and signature charm.

"Dacre is crazy protective of those close to him. It's just what happens when you've gone through the system." He glanced out over the campus, choosing his words carefully. "When you've been abandoned more than once, you learn how to protect the things that are important to you. Dacre just does it with his fists sometimes." He shrugged like what he was saying was nothing. But it was a whole lot of something.

He stopped on the path, looking down at his feet in a move that caught me off-guard. When he glanced up at me, the bravado was gone, replaced with a vulnerability that was edged with regret.

"It hits Dacre the hardest when I get shitfaced all the time. He takes it personally. Thinks he hasn't been there for me, or isn't being a good enough brother to stop me spiraling."

I stilled at his tone, my stomach clenching at the remorse lacing every word.

The bonds between the three of them ran deeper than I'd ever realized. The issues plaguing them did, too. I'd judged them from the first day I'd met them as rich playboys whose biggest problems were whether or not their father was going to gift them the latest Maserati or where they'd find a vacation villa big enough to house them and all their nepo baby friends for the summer. But Dacre, Presley, and Sinclair were the walking wounded, carrying a crazy amount of baggage around. Even if their problems were gold-plated.

I reached out and took Presley's hand, giving it a reassuring squeeze. I wasn't entirely sure how else to comfort him in this moment. Both Dacre and Presley were battling issues with abandonment, just in very different ways. Presley opted to write himself off on the regular, while Dacre's manifested as a fierce protectiveness that he could barely control. The altercation with Trent had started over me, but how much of it had really been about me and how much of it had been about his mom?

"Dacre had been ready to break Trenton's entire face."

Pres scowled. "He deserved it. The guy is a monumental douche."

I tilted my head at him. "Trent's a tool, no question, but Dacre looked like he'd kill him if I hadn't called him off."

I wouldn't have been opposed to the idea of Trenton being

severely maimed. But I was opposed to the idea of Dacre getting arrested because of me.

He shrugged. "I don't know what to tell you, Sass. You're in the inner circle now whether you want it or not."

CHAPTER 17

The sound of the cheering crowd filled my ears every time I tipped my head to breathe through my freestyle stroke.

I was half a body length ahead of the racers in the lanes either side of me, but I knew the swimmer from Pierson U over in lane two must be right up there with me; I just couldn't see her.

It was the final race of the meet and I'd already placed first and second in my breaststroke and backstroke races. The success made me push harder. I wanted to finish my first meet swimming for Triple C strong.

My stepbrothers were here. I'd seen them arrive and make their way up the stands to sit next to a stunned-yet-stoked Arena. Why were they even here? Years with my father meant suspicion was an in-built reaction for me. But if the last few weeks and the way they'd defended me, saved me, and had my back had taught me anything, it was that Presley, Dacre, even Sinclair, had meant it when they said I was one of them. Maybe their presence here was just another kind of support they were offering me.

It was a dangerous thought. I could get addicted to this feeling of belonging that flooded me as I propelled my body through the water. Whether I wanted it or not, I was an Aston now, and my stepbrothers seemed determined to show me what that meant. I'd seen them show up for Presley every time he drank too much. Maybe coming to my swim meets was a much more sober way of showing up for me,

Better make it worth their while, Dempsey.

I pushed my body harder, working it over and willing it to go faster. I glided through the water, only tipping my head to suck in a breath when I absolutely needed to.

It was so peaceful in the pool. Even with racers swimming on either side of me and the crowd roaring when I took a breath, it was still so quiet. Just me and the water.

Powering to the end of the pool, my fingertips met tile and I pulled up, chest heaving with exertion. I had to be close to taking out the win.

Glancing at my coach while we waited for the times to flicker across the board, she gave me a solid thumbs up. She was confident too.

I dared a peek into the stands, Arena smiling at something Presley said to her, Dacre joining in, their excitement evident. Sinclair was focused solely on me, his eyes burning down at me. I glanced away.

The board flickered as the times were displayed, my name sitting at the top. The Triple C section of the pool deck erupted in cheers and a grin split my face.

I'd done it. I'd successfully taken out my first college swim meet.

Ducking under the lane ropes, I hauled myself out of the pool, grabbing my towel and accepting a high five from my elated coach. I'd planned to make my way to the locker room and rinse off, but Arena and my stepbrothers bounded down the stands to cut me off.

"Way to freaking do it, superstar!" Arena said, grinning at me. "I'd hug you, but..." She screwed up her nose at the water dripping off me.

"I love getting wet," Presley said with a broad smile, scooping me into his arms and swinging me in a circle.

"Oh my god, Pres, put me down. I can hardly breathe." I choked out a laugh.

"Nice job," Dacre said with a nod, eyes trailing over my wet form.

I bit the inside of my cheek. "Thanks."

Things had been a little weird between us since he'd beaten up Trenton on my behalf.

Presley turned to Sinclair. "Sin? Anything you want to say to Dempsey?"

All eyes turned to him.

"Congratulations," he said flatly.

Presley chuckled shaking his head, and Arena rolled her eyes.

"It isn't often you see the Astons all together in one place that doesn't have a bar," a deep voice said from behind me and I swiveled.

A tall man, with broad shoulders, thinning dark hair, and a thick dark moustache offered me a greasy smile.

"Congratulations on your performance today. I'm sure your new stepfather will be very proud."

I pushed my shoulders back. "Thanks. Do we know each other?"

Presley offered the man his hand to shake. "This is Robert DeGrossi."

"Trenton's dad," Arena added, and my brow twitched in surprise before I could stop it.

That totally tracked. He was creepy as fuck.

Trenton pulled up at his side with a smarmy grin I'd love to wipe off his stupid face, despite the purple bruising still evident around his eyes. "Nice effort, Dempsey. Shame about the loss in the backstroke."

"She came in second," Dacre cut in. "She didn't lose."

Something swelled in my chest at Dacre coming to my defense. Again.

Trenton smirked. "She definitely didn't come first."

"Now, now, Trent. Credit where it's due. Dempsey swam beautifully." There was a hard glint to Robert's eye as he uttered the compliment, making it clear that some kind of sucker punch was about to land. "Talent clearly runs in every adopted member of the Aston family."

My jaw clenched at the clear slight on Sinclair and the reminder that Presley and Dacre were additions to the family. As though they weren't true members.

The guy was a snake and I was ready to tell him as much, when Sinclair cut in from behind us.

"We'd be happy to spend some time with Trent in the hopes some of our family talent rubs off on him, if that's what you're angling for, sir."

Robert's gaze cut to Sinclair, eyes pinching at the corners.

"I doubt there's anything you could teach him that he couldn't already learn from me." He moved to leave. "You all have a lovely rest of your day and be sure to say hello to your mother and father for me."

The two of them moved past us, poolside, and I had to hold back the urge to shove Robert DeGrossi in the damn pool.

"We could teach him how to be a decent fucking human being," Dacre muttered.

Presley clapped him on the shoulder. "That's a lost cause, bro."

"Let's go," Sinclair said, staring back at me. "Do you need to shower?"

I nodded and the guys wandered off towards the exit,

telling me they'd meet me out front to take me home. I'd have to let the coach know I wouldn't be taking the bus back to Triple C.

Arena linked her arm with mine. "See what I mean about Trent's dad? Total asshole, just like his son."

CHAPTER 18

groaned, letting my head flop to the side against my pillow and my eyes flutter closed.

"I really can't go, Mom. I'm not feeling well."

Before she'd come into my room, I'd splashed warm water on my forehead and bolted under the covers in order to sell my lie that I was too sick to go to yet another party at the country club. This week had kicked my ass and there was no way in hell I wanted to face Trenton and his bullshit right now.

I was feeling vulnerable and on edge. I needed some downtime to regroup and get my shit together.

My mother frowned down at me, her skepticism evident. She reached out, pressing her palm to my forehead. "Oh my, you're burning up."

I nodded solemnly, really trying to sell it.

She glanced at her watch. "It's such late notice to cancel, but I guess it can't be helped." She strolled for the door. "Rest up. We'll be back before midnight."

I scoffed at her truly loving and motherly response to her only child being sick. I could really feel the nurturing just rolling off her.

An hour later I heard the door slam, Byron and my mother leaving with my stepbrothers. I flung the covers off and pushed to my feet.

All alone in this big house. What was I going to do with myself?

I needed to swim but I couldn't be bothered getting into my gear, then washing my hair afterwards. Settling on a run on the treadmill, I changed into my navy running shorts and matching crop top and made my way down to the gym.

I strolled in, stopping short at the grunts and clanging of weights. My heart ratcheted up several notches, thinking someone had broken into the house, until my gaze landed on a figure across the room.

Dacre was at the squat rack, an insane amount of weight on each end of the bar. His skin was covered in a sheen of sweat, the dark green tank top and small black shorts showing off the muscles of his biceps and thighs. Coupled with the strain on his face and the sounds he was making, the whole scene was weirdly erotic to witness.

"Hey," I said.

Dacre dropped his weights, his gaze sliding over to me then away again as he reached for his water bottle and took a long drink. I tried not to stare at the way his Adam's apple bobbed as he swallowed.

I tried… and failed.

When he'd finished drinking, he went straight back to his weights as if I wasn't even there.

I shouldn't be hurt by it, but I was. Sinclair was always the one who acted like my presence was a major inconvenience. Never Dacre.

My mind snapped back to that day I'd been attacked by Trenton and chased down by Algor. Fear shuddered through me, followed quickly by something else. The feel of Dacre's hands drawing slow, soothing circles across my back. And the touch of his soft lips brushing over the marks on my throat. How could someone who looked so lethal be so gentle?

"I can let you know next time I'm in here," he said flatly, squatting low with the bar across his shoulders and pushing up tall. "That way you can come stare at me every time."

I hadn't realized I'd been staring. Clearing my throat, I dropped my water bottle and towel on the mat at my feet and walked to the machine a few feet away from him.

I tried not to think about him. Or even glance his way.

But there was no ignoring Dacre.

Presley was always friendly. Sometimes a little too friendly. Sinclair was as cold ice, and Dacre usually landed somewhere in the middle. I'd thought we'd bonded after he and Sinclair had saved my ass from Algor. But something had shifted between us after the fight with Trenton at the gym, and it had been there at the swim meet. It was like Dacre was permanently mad at me and I didn't understand it.

Watching him through the mirrors lining the wall, I pretended to stretch. How was I supposed to focus on working out with him so close by, sweaty and straining and gorgeous?

It was torture.

Twenty minutes passed in silence, save for the clanking of the squat rack, as I contorted my body into different stretches. I'd be lying if I said part of me wasn't enjoying the way Dacre's eyes kept landing on my ass when I was bent over. It was better than the broody silent treatment.

He scrubbed a hand over his face, still slick with sweat, and I couldn't help the way I swallowed at the idea of getting sweaty with him. All three of them had incredible bodies worth drooling over, but Dacre was the fittest, hands down. He was slightly shorter than Presley and Sinclair, and broader, the defined muscles on his shoulders and arms a warning everywhere he went. I imagined all too often what it would be like to have him toss me around a room.

Eventually, he slotted the bar back in the rack, scooping to pick up a towel. He wiped at his face while facing the mirrors, stealing glances my way when he thought I couldn't see.

"Enjoy your workout," he said coldly, gaze narrowed in my direction.

I pushed out of my stretch and got to my feet, the gnawing feeling in my stomach reaching an unbearable level now he was leaving. "Is everything okay between us? You seem… I don't know what."

"Sure," he grunted without meeting my eyes.

I glared at him. "Look, I know I crashed into your lives and turned shit a little crazy, but I didn't ask to be here. And I definitely didn't ask you to beat Trenton's face in on my behalf."

"I know that."

"So… why are you so mad at me?"

He stilled, half turning to face me. "I'm not."

I bit the inside of my cheek, at a loss for what to say. I couldn't force him to talk to me.

He started across the room again, headed for the door, then he paused again and turned to face me, his expression stormy. "You know what? Fuck it. Yeah, I'm fucking mad at you."

"Great," I said, throwing my hands up in the air. "So now that we've gotten that out of the way, maybe you can tell me why?"

He tossed the towel to the floor, slowly stalking towards me. His gaze was locked on mine, anger burning there. "Trenton was the one who put his hands on you and marked up your neck, and you never said a fucking word."

I stiffened, dread filling me. If he'd beaten Trenton for speaking badly about me, what would he do knowing it was Trent who had hurt me?

"How do you even know that?"

His voice was low and tight, like he was trying to leash his feelings. "The prick told me all about it when we were in the ring. Trying to rile me up. He asked me if I liked the hand necklace he'd gifted you. Right before I beat the shit out of him."

I forced myself to breathe through my nose to stem the rising anger in me. That fucking asshole had *bragged* about assaulting me to my stepbrother. Used it as a means to goad Dacre in the ring.

There was no way someone that callous—that *calculated*—hadn't done this before. No one was that confident they could get away with something like that unless they already had.

"Why didn't you tell us?" Dacre growled. "Why the fuck did you let him get away with doing that to you?"

"Pretty sure he didn't get away with it. You broke his face."

"And I want to fucking do it again!" Dacre shouted, his anger getting the better of him. "Nobody gets to put their fucking hands on you."

It all made sense now. Dacre had shown Trenton up by allowing him to get a punch in, so Trenton had fought back with his words. It hadn't been enough to insult his birth mom, he'd tried to use me against Dacre a second time too. The thought simultaneously broke my heart and filled me with a deep-seeded rage. Breaking his face wasn't enough. I wanted to hurt him the way he'd hurt someone I cared about.

Because I did care about Dacre. Watching him now, trying to keep control of the emotions roiling inside of him at the thought of Trenton hurting me, changed everything. Nobody acted like that if they didn't care.

I already cared about Presley. The night in the pool and at the club, the things he'd shared in the limo even if he had been drunk, and the shower when he'd comforted me after the truck attack, had all meant something, no matter how hard I tried to fight it.

And realizing now just how protective Dacre was of me…

"I'm sorry I didn't tell you," I said quietly.

He stared at me, hands on his hips, chest rising and falling as he worked to get himself in check. "I'm not your enemy, Dempsey."

"I know that."

At least, I was starting to realize that *now*.

His eyes pinched at the corners like he was trying to bury some unknown pain. "Don't ever keep something like that from me again."

I nodded. He scooped up his towel and moved to the door. With one last look back at me that I couldn't decipher, he turned and walked out, leaving me alone to finish my workout.

For the next forty minutes I ran hard on the treadmill until my lungs were ready to give out, trying to outrun the feelings I couldn't get a handle on.

I'd been determined to stay as far away from my stepbrothers as possible, but I'd failed. I'd hooked up with Presley twice and I was all churned up at the idea that I'd hurt Dacre by keeping things from him. I had no idea he cared so much.

Pres had tried to tell me that Dacre was fiercely protective of the people close to him, yet I hadn't really understood it until tonight. Staring into the hurt and anger in those blue eyes had almost broken my heart.

Smacking the button to stop the treadmill, I wiped the sweat from my face as I headed to my room to shower, feeling like absolute shit. Changing into a pair of soft shorts and a fitted white t-shirt, I made my way to the kitchen, pulling carrot sticks and a tub of hummus from the fridge.

The house was unusually quiet. The staff often made themselves scarce when Byron and my mother were out, busying themselves in other parts of the house.

But where the hell was Dacre?

I hadn't heard anything coming from his room when I'd passed it on my way down here.

The doorbell rang and I wandered through the house in that direction. When I reached the entry hall, one of the butlers was closing the door, an envelope in his hand.

"For you, Miss Dempsey." He handed it over.

I took it, the sense of dread I'd become so accustomed to lately filling every part of my body. My hands trembled as I gripped the envelope, sliding a finger under the flap to pop it open.

You can't run forever. You know better than anyone that I always get what I want.

I leaned against the side table in the entryway to keep myself upright.

How the fuck was he doing this? The letters weren't post-marked, but I wasn't stupid enough to think my father was hand-delivering them himself or sending Algor to do it. He only sent Al when there was serious dirty work to be done. Mail drops were beneath him. That had to mean my father was handcrafting his threatening little letters and sending them via courier. That's surely the only way he could get them past Byron's gatehouse.

Pulling in short, sharp breaths in an effort to keep my rising anxiety at bay, I opened the draw to the sideboard, burying the letter inside it where I wouldn't have to look at it. I was gaining quite the unwanted collection and I hated that my father could affect me like this. One letter from him and I was a mess.

I had to calm down. I had to get my head on straight.

I had to find Dacre.

Heading towards the part of the house that housed the gym and swimming pool, I hurried down the hall, searching each room. When I turned into the second hallway, classical music filled my ears.

What on earth was that? Did Dacre play an instrument?

Treading quietly towards the door, I paused, listening intently. The music was so loud my quiet approach was pointless. If Dacre was in that room, there was no way he'd be able to hear me coming.

Trying the handle, it twisted in my palm and I gently pushed the door ajar, glancing inside. It was some kind of studio, with canvases leaning against every wall, some blank, some beautifully, intricately painted. Others hung from hooks in the walls, filled with splashes of color or dark, sombre pieces staring back at me. There were several easels in the room, some with blank canvases, others half-painted like they'd been discarded mid-thought or the inspiration had died before they could be finished. Brushes and paint tubes and palette mixers were scattered on every surface in the room, including the two enormous benches running along the middle. And two large sinks sat at the back of the room.

"You may as well come in and close the door, since you've invited yourself in already."

Dacre's voice cutting through the music made me jump, glancing to the right where he stood at one of the large tables, mixing out paints on a palette.

He was shirtless, wearing nothing but a pair of jeans that hung loosely on his hips. His feet were bare, a streak of red paint marring his dark brown hair. A streak of black was smeared across his right pec. Heat flooded me in a rush at the sight of him. My god, I'd never wanted to climb someone so badly. Who knew tortured artist did it for me?

Gym rat Dacre had been hot. But dishevelled painter worked for him even more.

Like, really fucking worked for him.

He smirked at me, shaking his head like he could read my thoughts, then turned his back on me to face the canvas he was working on, switching the music off with a remote. I closed the door as directed, walking between the tables to the back section of the room where the canvases were set up on clear plastic that covered the floor and the back wall.

"So... you're an artist?" I asked, stating the damn obvious.

But I was still riddled with surprise at this secret revelation. I'd already been surprised to learn just how soft Dacre was with those he cared about, but to learn that the boy who looked like a bruiser on the outside was actually a gentle artist on the inside was something else.

He shrugged, still assessing the canvas and I stared at the works on the walls and on the nearby easels. "You're really talented."

It was the truth. I could see any one of these pieces hanging in a gallery or any number of the giant mansions in our neighborhood.

"Not sure my father would agree with you," Dacre muttered, and I didn't miss the bitterness in his voice.

I moved closer, wanting to be able to read the expression on his face, but he was still facing away from me.

"He doesn't support your art?"

He scoffed, turning to discard the palette and brush in his hands on the table. "The only thing my father supports is making money. Why do you think Sinclair is the favorite? He's proven how good he is at it."

So, Sinclair was the favored son. I'd always wondered if it was the case. Part of me had assumed that Byron was just an asshole who had adopted two boys only to favor his biological son. But if Dacre was right, it was his business success that made Daddy love him more. It also made me really sad for Presley, who was clearly already so fucked up about his birth mom and had to work to prove himself to his adopted dad, too.

"I guess all of us are screwed up by our parents…" I muttered more to myself as I stared at a canvas on one of the nearby easels.

It was mostly black with streaks of navy and blues through it. It was moody and deep and made me feel things I didn't quite understand.

Dacre was really fucking good at this.

He turned to gaze at me. "Your mom seems pretty decent."

I scoffed a laugh. "She puts on a good show. I'm more of an accessory than a part of her life."

Dacre nodded, staring at the ground beneath the easel in front of him. "I get it. It used to feel like that with Byron, too. He got so caught up in what he had, what he wanted, what else he could achieve, and how he could teach us to get those things, too. Sometimes he forgot what we really needed him for."

I nodded, surprised at the way he was opening up to me.

When I'd first met Dacre, I'd labelled him as angry and broken. Turns out that was Presley, who hides it so well behind his easy smiles and a quick comeback. But Dacre's love of art, him opening up about his relationship with his dad, the way he'd protected me with Trenton… there was a much deeper side to him.

And it shattered the defenses I'd been so determined to have up around him.

"Have you ever thought about putting on an art show? You could sell these, especially in this community, where everyone is flush with cash. You should capitalize."

He leaned against the table, crossing his arms over his chest, his biceps bulging and his toned pecs making my mouth go dry. It should be criminal for someone to be that hot. He really needed to put a shirt on.

"Byron would never let it happen."

"Do you always do what your dad wants?"

He huffed a laugh. "Byron Aston always gets his way. You don't know that by now?"

Sounded familiar. My father was the same but worse.

"I haven't really had a lot to do with Byron."

Dacre pushed off the table, turning to face it and gripping the edge. He leaned back, the muscles of his forearms contracting. "That's the way it always works with him. Everyone loves him, thinks he's so charming and agreeable. Presley's just like him in that way."

His tone had a protective undercurrent when he talked about his youngest brother.

"But everyone has a dark side," Dacre went on, turning his head to look at me.

"Even you?" I asked, curiosity getting the better of me.

Now that I understood just how little I really knew him, I wanted more.

"Especially me. Sin and Pres, too."

I bit the inside of my cheek. For the first time since I'd arrived here and they'd told me I was one of them now, I wanted it to be true. When they declared it at the wedding, I'd resented it. Promised myself there was no way in hell I'd let these guys control me or tell me what to do. But now I could see, it wasn't about that. They were loyal, they looked out for each other. They cared about each other. And I wanted to belong to that, too.

"Can you show me?" I nodded to a blank canvas on a nearby easel.

A slow smile spread across Dacre's face. "Yeah, I can show you. But do you want to change first? You're going to get paint all over your clothes."

I let my eyes roam over his bare torso, drinking in every inch of his toned body and smooth skin. Then I reached for the hem of my t-shirt and tugged it over my head. Dropping it to the floor, I stood there in my shorts and magenta balconette bra.

Dacre's brows quirked. "Okay, then." Picking up the palette from the table, Dacre motioned to the canvas, handing me a brush. "Choose a color."

I swiped the brush through a dark purple he'd mixed up.

He discarded the palette on a small table nearby, moving behind me where I stood in front of the canvas.

"Close your eyes," he murmured in my ear, just like he had in Sinclair's Porsche that day.

I did as I was told, letting my eyes close, relishing the feel of him at my back.

"Now focus on a memory, something that brings up deep emotions. The best way to paint is to feel something first."

Cycling through my memories, they were all negative. Times my father had been anything but a loving parent, and my mother either turned a blind eye or couldn't stop him. The feeling of being completely alone in a room full of people at my mother's wedding. The fear of being chased by Algor's truck. Trenton's hands at my throat, cutting off my air.

A shudder rolled through me and Dacre's warm hands landed on my arms. "Breathe through it. You okay?"

I nodded, eyes still closed, enjoying his warm, capable hands on my body.

"You want to try painting through it? Press the brush to the canvas in whatever way feels right."

My eyes popped open and I pressed the brush to the canvas, slashing diagonally across it in fast, vicious strokes. When the brush ran dry, Dacre held out the palette. I dipped the brush in black this time, using the same aggressive strokes to paint what I was feeling.

We repeated it several times over, until the canvas was covered in dark slashes, and my chest heaved with exertion. "Who knew painting could be so physical?" I said through jagged breaths.

"That's one of the things I love most about it." His voice was deep and sensual, and I glanced at him over my shoulder. His eyes blazed with a heat he was clearly trying to leash. "You have to feel everything and let it all out. You can't hold anything back."

I stilled, closing my eyes and letting the feel of his warm body at my back wash over me.

"Dempsey..." his voice was low and quiet, like a caress against my skin.

His hands landed lightly on my waist, and I dropped the brush to the floor, turning in his arms.

I stared up at him, my fingers gliding over his shoulders and down across his pecs. "I don't want you to hold anything back."

His hand slid up my back to grip my neck, our bodies pressing together.

"Then I won't."

His mouth collided with mine, kissing me with a passion that nearly knocked me off my feet. His tongue lashed mine, making me moan into his mouth. I clung to his waist, pulling him against me, desperate to close the space between us.

The kiss was endless, our mouths fused, our hands roaming over every inch of exposed skin. Kissing Dacre was nothing like I thought it would be. It was better. He was so full of passion and wanting, it made my core tighten and my heart soar.

Presley flashed in my mind for the briefest moment, but I shoved the thought aside. I'd deal with the possible fallout of my actions later. Right now, all I wanted was Dacre's hands on my body and his tongue in my mouth.

His hands glided from my waist, over my ribcage, making me shiver. He moved to my back, reaching for the clasp on my bra and popping it open. I stopped touching him long enough to let it slide down my arms to the floor.

Taking my face in his hands, he tilted my chin to look at him.

"Don't ever keep something from me again." His gaze burned with an intensity that took my breath away.

I nodded, the hands that had been roaming over his delicious back muscles stilling as I pressed our bodies together. "I won't."

He kissed me again, this time slowly. The sensual feel of his tongue dancing with mine had me moaning softly in his mouth.

He pulled back and I whimpered, my mouth desperate for his.

"What's wrong?" I asked, trying to decipher the expression on his face.

He stared down at me, touching me with a reverence I'd never felt before.

"I've wanted you in here naked like this since the moment I saw you walking down the aisle at the wedding." He cupped my face, staring at my mouth as he brushed his thumb across my swollen bottom lip. "All my fucking fantasies are coming true right now."

A slow smile spread across my face and I wrapped my arms around his neck, my breasts pressed against his chest, our bodies fused. His hands landed on my bare back and he buried his face against my neck, kissing along my throat and making me shiver with desire.

"I want to paint your body. I want to brand you with my art."

My stomach swooped at his words, heat flooding my core.

I nodded, making him chuckle against my throat, my voice breathy and desperate when I spoke. "I want that. I definitely want that."

Our mouths fused in an endless dance and he gripped my waist, walking us backwards until my back hit the edge of one of the large paint-splattered tables in the middle of the room. His mouth left mine for the briefest moment so he could grip my hips and boost me up onto it until I was sitting at the edge. Nudging my knees apart, he stepped between them, his fingers tangling in my hair.

"Don't move," he ordered when he pulled away.

I couldn't, even if I wanted to. The reverent way he was touching me, the fierceness in his kiss, it rendered me useless.

Dacre returned with a mixing palette full of paint and several soft brushes. He kissed me again, his tongue claiming every inch of my mouth.

"Lift your hips for me."

I obeyed, leaning back on my hands and lifting off the table.

His thumbs hooked in the waistband of my shorts, dragging them down my legs along with my underwear, discarding them on the floor. He stared at my body, so focused on drinking me in. So attuned to my every move.

When his gaze lifted to mine, his eyes were tortured. "I've never seen anything as beautiful as you laid out naked on my table. You're a fucking masterpiece."

"Are you going to paint me now? It's something I want to experience at least once."

He smiled, cupping my cheek. "You think we're only doing this once? Now that you're letting me have you, I'm going to turn you into a walking masterpiece every chance I get."

Warmth spread through my body, pooling between my legs. Dacre gripped the backs of my knees, gently tugging me to the edge of the table and motioning for me to lay back.

He climbed up on the table with me, sprawling at my side and placing a loaded paint palette on the table just above my head. He swiped his finger through the red paint, then he trailed it over my collarbone, slowly making his way down between my breasts.

"You have no idea how fucking hard I am right now."

But I couldn't concentrate on the words, so consumed by his finger caressing my body, spreading the paint across my skin.

I swallowed, biting back the sounds that were trying to escape me.

"You didn't want me holding anything back, so don't you dare hold back on me either." He swiped his fingers over the paint palette again, this time choosing a bright orange. "I want to hear every damn sound you make when my hands are on you."

He swirled orange paint around my nipple, so close but not quite touching it. We'd barely started and already my body was lighting up like lightning in a storm with every swirl of his finger against my skin.

When he dipped his fingers in the paint again, they came away covered in green. This time he brushed them directly over my nipples, making me gasp. My back arched off the table.

"You're so fucking beautiful laid out for me like this, Bambi."

His mouth dropped to mine, our tongues meeting in a wet, open-mouthed kiss. His fingers caressed my breasts while his tongue explored, the needy feeling growing between my legs.

He pulled back, reaching for the palette, his fingers coming away red once more. He trailed a finger between my breasts again, grazing over my stomach and creating a swirling mark around my belly button, before trailing them lower. He dropped his mouth to my throat, lips closing over my sensitive flesh and sucking hard while his fingers dipped between my legs, finally touching me exactly where I needed him.

"I need more," I said breathlessly, clinging to his shoulder while his beautiful, artistic fingers tortured me in the best way.

My back arched again, my painted breasts brushing against his chest. His soft strokes over my clit, mixed with the hard sucks against my throat, were sending all kinds of sensations barrelling through me.

"I'll give you anything you want," he murmured against my throat.

Reaching between us, I unzipped his jeans, pushing them down his hips. His hard cock sprang free, resting against my hip. My mouth watered at the sight of it.

Raising my hands above my head, I reached for the palette. He pulled back, watching me with a half smile on his face as I smeared my hands in blue and green paint. I gripped his shoulders, imprinting on him, before moving over his pecs and doing the same.

I was desperate to mark him the same way he'd marked me. Brand him as mine.

Gliding my hands over his pecs, I lowered them, caressing the ridges of his abs until my hand wrapped around the hard length of him.

He let out a soft groan at the contact, his eyes closing. When I moved my hand, stroking him, he bit the edge of his lower lip. The sight of him weak for me only heightened my need for him.

"Dacre," I said quietly and he opened his eyes, staring down at me, his hands absently moving over my skin. "I need you."

Gripping my hip with one hand and wrapping an arm around my back with the other, he rolled onto his back, taking me with him. I straddled him on the table, his hard cock beneath me.

"Ride me so I can admire the most stunning piece of art I've ever created while I'm buried inside you."

Spurred by the heated desire in his gaze, I lifted up and he held me by the waist. I lined him up with my entrance and sank down on him, impaling myself.

We both moaned in unison at the feeling of utter fullness.

"Fuck, Bambi, you're so damn tight. You've got my cock in a chokehold."

I gave him a lazy, pleasure-induced smile and started rocking my hips, my fingertips digging into his hard pecs.

He gripped my waist, helping me rock against him. He lifted his head, staring down at where his cock was buried deep inside me.

"That's it, baby, ride me, my perfect fucking muse."

We picked up speed and the friction between our bodies intensified. I tipped my head back and moaned his name over and over, the words falling from my mouth against my will. The pleasure was so damn overwhelming I couldn't think or feel or see anything but him.

He reached out to cup my breast, his thumb teasing my nipple, making my pussy clench around him. "Tell me you're mine, Dempsey," he demanded through our panting breaths as we rocked together.

I nodded, the sensations he was drawing from my body making my head spin.

"I'm yours," I said breathlessly. "I'm yours. I'm yours."

His hand dipped between my legs, his thumb circling my clit, making me cry out.

"Dacre…" I breathed, the combination of his fingers on my clit and his cock buried deep pushing me closer to the edge. "I'm going to…"

An orgasm ripped through me so fast I barely had time to catch my breath.

"Fuck, you're so beautiful when you let go," he gritted out, thrusting hard several times before he spilled inside me, hot and fast.

He gripped the back of my neck, tugging my mouth to his as we rode out our orgasms chest to chest, our tongues tangled together through our comedown.

When we broke apart, I collapsed on top of him, my body needing more than a minute to recover.

I lifted my head, resting my chin on his pec. "People weren't lying when they said artists are the best lovers."

Dacre's face lit with a smile just for me, the sight so damn beautiful.

If I'd been as talented with a brush as he was, I would have painted that moment so I could keep it forever.

CHAPTER 19

strolled down the hall in the house I was supposed to call home—but still didn't quite feel like it—with my head bent over my phone, texting with Arena. She was regaling me in far too much detail about her hook-up with a drama major last night. She claimed the girl was not only dramatic on stage, but crazy dramatic in the bedroom, too.

Walking past the doorway to the theater room, I startled at the sound of my name.

"Dempsey, get in here."

Backtracking, I took a tentative step into the room to find Dacre sprawled on one of the plush recliners, the giant screen lit up in front of him.

"Are you watching The Great British Bake Off?" I asked.

I wasn't prepared for the sight of him in a plain white tee that wrapped around his thick arms or the loose red plaid pajama pants he was wearing. Shirtless in his paint-covered studio jeans would forever be my favorite outfit of his, but this one made my knees shake at the memory of his mouth on me last week.

He shrugged, a small smile creeping across his face. "I like the artistry of it."

Of course he did.

"Watch with me." He inclined his head to the seat beside him, and I didn't need to think about it. My feet moved on their own accord and I sprawled next to him, my body instantly relaxing into the cushions.

We watched in tense silence for a while, totally unsure on where we stood. Whether we'd been caught up in the moment in his art studio, eager to get each other off, or if it was the kind of intimacy we'd be repeating.

I definitely wasn't opposed to a repeat performance. The memory of Dacre reverently painting my body would stay with me for a lifetime.

There was also the giant, awkward issue that I was also sleeping with his brother. Or had slept with his brother. I had no idea where Pres and I stood either.

"Are you coming to my next swim meet?" I asked eventually.

He glanced my way. "I'll come to every meet if you want me there."

His words instantly disarmed me, melting any awkwardness between us.

I gave him a small smile. "I mean... you don't have to come to *every* one."

His hand brushed over my knee, resting there. "Whatever you want, I'll do it."

Heat crept into my cheeks at the sweetness of his offer and I turned my attention back to the screen. "Hopefully Robert DeGrossi doesn't come to every meet."

Dacre's expression hardened. "Fuck him, he's just bitter. All the DeGrossis are."

I sat up a little at his tone. "About what?"

"That DeGrossi money isn't the same as Aston money. At least not around here." He sighed. "Byron has worked hard for decades to solidify the Aston name and it's paid off. Everybody respects Byron, looks to him for leadership, wants him at their events, in their clubs, on their team. Robert wants all of it."

"That sounds like Byron earned his position and Robert wants it handed to him."

Dacre shifted, his leg brushing mine, making me hyper-aware of him, like I wasn't already. "Don't get me wrong, Robert has amassed an impressive fortune from his businesses, but he's not on Byron's level. It's created this weird rivalry between our families for years. Sin, Pres, and I couldn't care less, but Trent takes it seriously, and because of it he's fucking insufferable."

I swallowed. "So, I guess it didn't help when he and I..."

Dacre's expression shuttered. "I already hated the guy. That just made me want to kill him."

I bit down on the urge to apologize, because was I actually sorry? I was sorry that I'd ever done anything to hurt Dacre, but I'd been free, single and feeling deeply insecure about the new life I'd be thrust into. I made a choice, and God knew it had backfired hard, but I didn't want to go out of my way to apologize unless I really meant it.

"If it makes you feel better, you're a much better lay than he is," I said.

He tipped his head back and laughed, making me smile. "I already knew that, but hearing you say it really does it for me."

He grinned over at me and I wanted to take his face in my hands and kiss him stupid, but I held back.

His face turned serious. "Do it."

I frowned. "Do what?"

He shifted closer. "Whatever you were just thinking about, do it."

"And miss finding out who's going to take out this tiered themed cake contest?" I motioned to the screen. "No way."

We turned back to the screen, watching in silence for a beat.

"Do you ever call Byron Dad?" I asked, still staring at the screen.

"I used to. Not as much anymore."

"How come?"

He let out a sigh. "Because he stopped being a dad to me a long time ago."

Why?

The question burned in my throat and I so desperately wanted to ask it. Would he tell me? He'd told me only a moment ago to do whatever it was I'd been thinking.

"What did he do?"

His gaze locked with mine while he thought about how to answer.

"A lot of things, one being that he doesn't support my art."

I pulled a face. "You mentioned it in your studio, but I don't understand what kind of father doesn't back his child's dreams?"

"The kind that doesn't believe that artistic pursuits are a viable career path." He said the last part in a deeper voice like Bryon's. "Byron believes in making money, and thinks the only way to do that is to go into business like him. Or sports if you're Presley. He'll tolerate that."

I absently reached a hand out, tracing the pattern on the pants covering his thigh. His eyes followed the movements of my finger.

"Why don't you have an art show? Prove him wrong?"

He shrugged. "I don't feel the need to prove anything to him. He can think what he wants."

It had to hurt him though, having a father who didn't believe in him.

"How about we don't talk about Byron anymore?" he said, moving onto his side so he was facing me.

I fought a smile. "What should we talk about then?"

"What it's going to take for you to kiss me."

The smile won out and I chuckled. "Probably not much."

His eyes lit up and he shifted closer. "Oh, yeah?"

I nodded, and his hand slid along my jaw, tangling in my hair. He gently tugged my face towards his, pressing his lips to mine. The kiss was slow, and soft, and sensual, all things that I'd come to learn summed up Dacre. He was so much more than the hard-bodied exterior.

"Fuck, you taste as good as last time. Like peaches and my dream girl."

I couldn't help the way I swooned at his words. The sweet side of him was so unexpected, so at odds with his usual demeanor that it surprised me every time.

He kissed me again, tongue brushing over my lips and I opened for him. He swept into my mouth with dizzying strokes and I leaned into him, my body pressed against his. My leg hitched on its own accord, sprawling across his and he grunted in approval, our mouths never breaking the kiss.

"Dacre," a voice snapped and I rolled off him.

"Sinclair," Dacre said, shifting back up into a seated position and shooting his brother a dark look.

Heat flooded my cheeks at being caught out by Sinclair. Would he judge me for sleeping with both brothers? Try to warn them off being with me or convince one of them to give me up?

"Good thing I'm not Byron or Bea. I made it all the way into the room to find you two on top of each other without either of you noticing."

Dacre sighed. "Did you come in here just to lecture us, big bro?"

Sinclair glanced at me, his eyes hardening, then back to Dacre. "Oh, there's an us now?"

The two brothers glared at each other, another silent conversation passing between them.

"I've just come out of a meeting with Byron, and he'd like to see Dempsey." He ran a hand through his hair, messing it up in a way that was seriously fucking hot on an asshole like him. "Like I'm a fucking messenger boy."

Dacre tossed an arm around my shoulders, settling us back against the recliners. "Don't act like one if you don't want to be one."

Sinclair's jaw ticked, but he didn't snap back, just stalked from the room.

Dacre smiled down at me. "Where were we?"

"About to get busted by your hardass older brother."

He huffed a laugh. "Ignore him. He's all bark, no bite."

I totally disagreed, but I didn't want to talk about Sinclair right now. Not when Dacre's hand that wasn't slung around my shoulders was trailing down my stomach towards the button of my jeans.

"You seem tense," he said with a smug smile. "Why don't you let me take care of that for you?"

He unbuttoned my jeans, moving to the end of the recliner to tug them off, tossing them on the floor. He climbed over me, his mouth fusing with mine in a heated kiss.

When he pulled back, I screwed up my face, annoyed at the loss of his mouth on mine.

"Fuck, what I wouldn't give to have those pouty peach-covered lips wrapped around my cock right now."

I raised a brow in question, gaze dropping to his hard cock tenting his pants.

He shook his head. "I want to taste you today." Then he slid my black lace panties down my legs, slipping them into his pocket.

"You're not keeping those," I said, pointing a finger at him.

He grinned back at me. "I need a trophy to remind myself that you let me have you." He smoothed his hands down my legs, staring at me like I was the moon in the night sky.

"But those are my favorites," I whined, my mouth snapping shut the moment he gripped my ankles and split my legs apart. I barely had time to take a breath before his mouth was on me.

"Dacre," I said on a sigh, my head dropping back against the recliner when his tongue slid over me. "We can't do this here, we're going to get caught."

He looked up at me from between my legs, a grin pulling at the corner of his mouth. "You'll just have to be quiet then, Bambi."

CHAPTER 20

hurried to Byron's office, fixing my clothes and hair to cover the fact his son had just gone down on me in the theatre of his luxury house.

When I got there, Byron was seated behind his enormous mahogany desk, my mother seated on the other side shooting lovesick puppy eyes at him. I swear, Byron could tell her he'd just murdered a family of seven because he wanted to see how their blood would splatter and my mother would look at him like he was a gift to this world.

Part of me was jealous. Not because I wanted my mother's attention; I'd long given up on her the same way she'd given up on me. But I wanted to feel that all-consuming way about someone.

"Ah, Dempsey," Byron said with a smile as I stepped into the room. "Thank you for coming to see me. Please, take a seat." He motioned to the empty chair next to my mother, who gave me a forced smile.

I sat as directed, feeling like I was in a meeting with HR and was about to be managed out of the company.

"Your mother and I have called you in here today to share some news with you." Byron gave me an encouraging nod.

I glanced between them. "If you're about to tell me you're pregnant, I'll run out of here screaming."

"Dempsey," my mother chastised. It appeared playful but underneath I could see the agitation pinching at the corners of her eyes. "Stop being so silly."

Was it really that silly? My mom wasn't *that* old. It was likely still physically possible. And men like Byron loved producing heirs; it fuelled their egos.

Byron cleared his throat. "Thankfully, we've both had our children for this lifetime."

I nodded, waiting for the big reveal, my curiosity growing by the minute.

"Byron is considering a career change. Quite a significant one."

He grinned broadly. "I plan to run for Governor of the fine state of California."

I blinked back at him. "You're… going into politics?"

Looking to my mother, I found her beaming. Did she know these were his aspirations when they started dating? Had he chosen her for her potential as a political trophy wife? She had no aspirations of her own. Hell, I'd never heard my mother discuss politics even once, so she was no threat to him or his popularity.

Byron nodded once. "Yes, which is why we need to have a serious discussion."

Their smiles dropped along with the upbeat vibe in the room.

"A political tilt means scrutiny. More than we're currently used to," my mother said, as though she'd spent all her life in the wealthy society pages of the media just as the Astons had. "There will be many eyes on all of us."

"Which means," Byron added. "That everyone must be on their best behavior."

I take it back. This wasn't an HR meeting. Now it had taken a turn into stern school principal territory.

"Best behavior?" I asked, confused. When was I ever not on my best behavior? The only events I attended were the ones my mother forced me to. I didn't go anywhere other than Triple C and swim meets. I had exactly one friend—Arena.

"Yes," Byron said, staring back at me. It was easy to see where Sinclair got his intimidating gaze from. "I've always had high expectations from my family members, but now those standards will increase ten-fold."

My mother sat up straighter, her face more serious than I'd ever seen. "What Byron is too polite to say to you outright, Dempsey, is that you will not partake in any activities or behave in any kind of way that will bring shame or embarrassment to this family. Do you understand me?"

I nodded again, because what else was I going to do? Tell them to shove their demands and storm out? I had nowhere to go.

"Sure thing, Mom. I'll do my best to act like a lady." I tilted my head. "Was that all?"

My mother frowned at me. "Don't you have anything to say to Byron?"

I stilled. "Oh… congratulations?"

Congratulations on being such an ego-maniac that you want to run for public office.

Byron beamed back at me. "Thank you."

I pushed from my seat. They were worried about embarrassment for the family, yet had no idea that I'd let Dacre go down on me in the theater room only ten minutes ago or let Presley fuck me in the shower weeks ago. It had been bad enough when we only had the shame of this community finding out to worry about. Now that Byron was running for office, if our scandalous acts were ever discovered we'd be front page news.

I'd nearly made it to the door when Byron called my name. "Congratulations on making the Triple C swim team."

I paused, questioning his motive. "Thank you…"

"Astons excel at everything they involve themselves in, and I expect the same from you now that you're part of this family. I look forward to seeing more of those first place wins long into the future."

"Yes, Byron."

I left the room, an anxious undercurrent rippling through me.

Not only did I need to excel at every swim meet from now until eternity, but I had to stay the hell away from my step-brothers too before we created a scandal that would be splashed on front pages across the country.

CHAPTER 21

walked through the door after meeting Arena for coffee, greeted by the sound of arguing.

Not just regular arguing—an aggressive male shouting match.

The maid gave me a tense smile as she took my coat and purse, shuffling off to hang them in the entryway closest that was the size of most people's kitchens. But my mother needed somewhere to keep all her furs and designer coats now that she was *the* Mrs. Beatrice Aston.

"Fuck this!" came Presley's voice from further into the house.

A door crashed open, footsteps echoing along the hallway off the entryway. Byron's office was in that direction.

"Don't you walk away from me, boy." Byron's voice was hard, his words clipped with anger.

Presley came into view, stopping at the corner where the hallway intersected behind the grand double staircase. They clearly didn't know I was there. Should I make a run for the stairs up to my room and risk being seen? Or stay where I was and hope they didn't notice me? If Presley was headed for his room, he'd come straight past me.

Indecision kept me rooted to the spot.

And also the tea.

Always the tea.

"I'm not your *boy*," Presley snapped back. "And I don't give a fuck about your threats, or your future aspirations, *Dad*."

The way he said the last word made the disdain he had for Byron clear. Had they always been at odds like this or was it a new thing? Unlike Dacre, Byron was the only father Pres had ever known.

Yet out of the three of them, Presley seemed to have the biggest issue with Byron.

"Don't you fucking speak to me like that," Byron bellowed, making me jump.

Presley scoffed at him, then turned on his heel, heading for the stairs.

His eyes locked with mine when he spotted me, flaring with a hint of surprise mixed with the anger brewing there. But he didn't say a word, rounding the banister and taking the stairs two at a time. Byron sighed from the hallway, followed by footsteps and the slamming of his office door.

Well, clearly we aren't playing happy families today.

Taking the stairs up to my room, I glanced at Presley's door, two down and across the hall from mine. Music blared from it. Before I could second guess myself, I moved to knock on it.

There was no response, but he probably couldn't hear me over the music.

Twisting the handle, I cracked the door open, edging in and closing it behind me.

Presley was pacing the room, a glass of what looked like tequila on the table beside him, anger rolling off him in waves.

"Pres," I called over the music.

He glanced over his shoulder, his eyes darkening at the

sight of me in his room. He marched towards me, pinning me against the back of the door and slamming his mouth over mine. His tongue invaded my mouth, the taste of tequila overwhelming. We didn't utter a word, our mouths fused, his tongue wrestling with mine until my knees were weak.

His hand reached down, popping the button on my jeans and lowering the zipper in one quick movement. Then his hand was in my panties, his fingers brushing over me, making my gasp against his mouth.

"You're so wet for me, Sass."

"Yeah, well, that kiss was hot."

He smirked, but it had a hard edge to it, as though he got off on making my body react to him. Without warning he shoved a finger inside me, making me cry out. Gripping the back of my neck roughly, he held my mouth to his, his fingers pumping in and out of me.

It was angry and savage, things I wouldn't usually associate with Pres. But it was making me so wet, and I wanted more.

He shoved my jeans to the floor, kicking them away when I stepped out of them. Then gripped the backs of my thighs, he pulled my legs out from under me until I was wrapped around him. He didn't hesitate or ask for permission, just lined up his cock and shoved inside me. I let out a cry of pleasure at the invasion, loving every second of this with him.

"That's it, scream for me, Sass. Let your new daddy hear how good your stepbrother is dicking you down right now."

What the fuck?

This was nothing like Presley. Yet this show of dominance and ownership was so fucking hot I was in danger of coming all over his cock already.

I tilted my hips back and forth, meeting his thrusts and heightening the delicious friction between our bodies.

"Fuck yeah, ride me, Sass."

The sound of my desperate moans and our bodies moving together was drowned out by the blaring music.

"Are you going to come for me? You going to soak my cock like a good girl?"

His dirty talk pushed me so high, on the next thrust I was toppling over the edge, clinging to his shoulders and screaming his name. He groaned, thrusting harder and chasing his own climax. In a matter of seconds, he was coming, his cock pulsing inside me as he spilled into me.

Talk about a hot and dirty quickie.

A moment later he dropped his head to my shoulder. "Fucking hell, Dempsey."

"I should fuck you when you're mad more often," I said through panted breaths, making him chuckle. He held me while he pulled out, setting me on my feet.

"I need a shower," I said, reaching for my jeans and sliding them back on.

He smacked me on the ass with one hand, reaching for his drink with the other and downing it.

"There's no way I'm letting you run out of here. Shower with me. And then get dressed to party, because we're going out tonight."

Three hours later, we were in some nightclub not far from campus. It was packed, mostly with Triple C students.

Presley had pawed at me the whole ride here, kissing my neck, his hand sliding higher and higher up my thigh until I'd swat him away. Then he'd start all over again.

Sinclair had told him to "fucking cool it" more than once, but Pres had just pouted about how once we got there, he wouldn't be allowed to manhandle me anymore. Dacre had glanced at Presley's hand on my thigh once, then stared out the window.

Pres had downed another tequila in the car, but his brothers stayed quiet about it, so I did too.

"Try to behave yourself tonight," Sinclair said once we were inside the club, moving past me like I was a major inconvenience he was forced to tolerate.

Presley winked at me, a sly smile on his face, and Dacre slapped a hand on his shoulder, indicating he should follow Sinclair. Before Dacre went after them, he leaned down to whisper in my ear. "Make sure you behave yourself tonight too, Bambi."

He pulled back, quirking a brow at me, and I shrugged. "Can't make any promises."

His responding smirk made my knees weaken, and he shook his head, following after the others.

Arena appeared at my side, staring after them. "What's up with the trio of thirst traps today?"

"You mean Moody, Grumpy, and Horny?" I asked, rolling my eyes. "They're always like that." I grabbed her hand, towing her towards the bar and ordering us both a double vodka soda.

"Wait, which one is which?" she asked, clearly mulling it over. "Sinclair could be Moody or Grumpy. Dacre could be all three. Which means Presley has to be Horny."

I huffed a laugh. Not after what we'd done together earlier.

Although, just the thought of him taking me roughly against the back of his bedroom door had heat pooling between my legs and I was desperate for another round, so maybe it was true.

"Do we have to talk about my stepbrothers?" I reached for the drink the bartender placed in front of me. "I thought we were here to have a good time?"

"Oh, a good time is what you're after? Well, in that case, let's go, bitch!"

Grabbing her drink, we made our way to the dance floor.

The next two hours passed in a blur of drinks and dancing. A couple of girls from one of our classes joined us, all of us dancing our asses off, shouting out lyrics until we were hoarse.

"I have to go to the bathroom," I yelled in Arena's direction.

She nodded, shaking her hips to the beat and waving me off. Slipping through the crowd I made it to the bathroom and the thankfully short line.

I was making my way back to the dance floor, when a hand closed around my wrist, yanking me around the corner to a darkened hallway that led to an emergency exit.

"What the hell—" I started, when a hot, familiar mouth that tasted of tequila landed on mine. "Presley, we can't..." I pushed at his chest, worry flooding through me at the thought of getting caught.

Byron was going to announce any day now, which meant reporters and photographers would be everywhere. Anyone with a camera phone could make a huge amount of money off a video of me and Presley wrapped around each other.

"I can't help how much I want you, Sass." He held my face in his hands. "And I don't give a fuck who sees."

His fingers tangled in my hair, his tongue delving into my mouth like it had never left. I tried to protest, but lost the fight with myself as much as him.

"What the fuck is wrong with you?" Sinclair's hard voice cut through the moment.

Pres pulled back, expression dropping. "Well, if isn't the fun police." His eyes were glassier than I realized, his words slow and lazy.

"How many times do we have to fucking do this, Pres?" Sinclair demanded.

Dacre rounded the corner, took one look at me pinned against the wall, Pres up in my personal space and swore under his breath.

"Bro, come on." Dacre levelled Presley with a look that was a mix of disappointment and annoyance. I guess it probably got exhausting constantly taking care of your brother every time he got wasted. Which, for Presley, was far too often.

"Do you think I don't want to take her up against a wall right now?" Dacre asked Pres, his gaze running over me in a way that made it pretty clear what he wanted to do to me.

I bit down on my smile.

Presley tilted his head. "I didn't think about that."

"Maybe if you stopped drinking every damn day you'd realize what a stupid idea it is to kiss our damn stepsister in a fucking bar," Sinclair said.

Presley laughed, stumbling a little, and Dacre and I both reached out to steady him.

"Maybe if you had a girlfriend who actually fucked you, you might not be such a cockblocking asshole all the time."

My gaze shot to Sinclair, whose eyes flared with anger.

What did that mean? Veda wouldn't sleep with Sinclair? Why the hell not? He was sex in a damn suit every waking moment.

"Fuck you, Pres." Sinclair's expression was harder than I'd ever seen it.

Dacre slung Presley's arm around his shoulders to help him walk, at the same time Pres threw his head back and laughed at his older brother's ire. It caused him to stumble again, catching Dacre off guard and nearly taking him down too.

"We're going," Dacre said, glancing at both me and Sinclair.

I nodded once, pulling my phone from my bag to text Arena that I was leaving.

I hated seeing Presley like this and hated that it was always Dacre and Sinclair who had to take care of it.

I didn't know how to fix it or even help, really. All I could do was be there.

———

"I'm not going in there," Presley insisted, swaying backwards on his feet.

Dacre swayed with him, gripping him by the waist and holding on to Presley's arm that was slung over his shoulder.

"For fuck's sake, Pres, it's your own damn bedroom," Dacre grunted, trying to keep them both upright. Presley had half a foot of height on him, altering his center of gravity, but Dacre had the muscle.

Pres shook his head. "Nope, nope, nope. I'm not sleeping in there."

"Then where the hell do you plan on sleeping?" Sinclair asked from where his shoulder was propped against the wall next to the door, his arms crossed over his chest.

Presley's glassy gaze slid my way and he grinned, twirling his finger in the direction of my room. God, he really was off his face with the goofy way he was acting.

I quirked a brow. "You think you're sleeping in my room?"

"Come on, Sass, don't you want to snuggle?" He pouted, sticking out his bottom lip in a way that was beyond comical. He may look like a big, tall, imposing sports boy, but he was a damn puppy at heart. Or at least when he was wasted.

"I'll make you a deal," I said, crossing my arms to match Sinclair. "You walk to my room unassisted and I'll let you sleep in there."

Presley's face lit up at the challenge and he shoved Dacre off. Holding his arms out wide like he was walking a tightrope in the circus, he put one foot in front of the other, stepping the diagonal line from his room to mine.

"This isn't a curbside sobriety test, you can walk normally," Dacre said.

Pres ignored him, slowly and steadily making his way right to my door. He knocked on it, grinning at me over his shoulder like the happiest drunk in the world. "Let me in, Little Red. It's the big bad wolf."

Sinclair pushed off the wall. "If by big and bad, you mean drunk and ready to drool all over you." He glanced my way. "Good luck with that." Then he strolled down to his door, slamming it shut behind him.

God, he was a fucking delight twenty-four seven.

I opened my door and Presley strode inside, immediately stripping down to his boxers and flopping back on my bed, limbs splayed and making snow angels on top of the covers. Dacre followed him into my room, probably to make sure Pres didn't swallow his own tongue.

Jesus. Why had I agreed to this?

I grabbed my sleep shorts and shirt and headed for the bathroom. "I'll be right out."

Changing fast, I washed my makeup off and brushed my teeth. When I emerged from the bathroom, the room was dark, Presley snoring from the bed.

"He passed out about seven seconds after you went in," Dacre said, tossing pillows on the floor beside my bed. He opened the bench seat at the foot, taking out the spare comforter.

"You're sleeping in here?" I asked, watching him. "On the floor?"

He nodded. "Pres has a habit of waking up halfway through the night and deciding to go streaking through the house or think it's a good idea to grill steaks at four am when he's still wasted. I can keep an eye on him if I'm here."

I hesitated. I was nervous enough about sharing my space with Presley, I didn't know how I'd cope with two of them and becoming a Dempsey sandwich, but I couldn't let Dacre sleep on the floor.

"Why don't you sleep up here?" I climbed onto the bed and scooted under the covers. The second I did, Presley reached for me in his sleep, wrapping his arms around me and tucking me against his chest.

Dacre gave me a rueful smile and shook his head. "I'm good right here."

I stared back at him, trying to convey everything I felt. "Yeah, but I'm not."

He halted, our gazes locked. Then he reached for the collar of his shirt at the base of his neck, tugging it over his head in one swift movement. I was instantly mesmerized by the sight of his impeccable body. The same one that had been beneath me while I rode him hard in his art studio. The memory alone made my core ache.

Dacre's gaze never left mine as he flicked the button on his jeans, unzipping them and kicking them off, leaving him in nothing but a pair of tight black boxers. The outline of his semi-hard cock was visible and I swallowed.

I moved over as much as I could with a drunk Presley wrapped around me like a freaking pretzel. Dacre climbed in, lying on his side facing me.

"Did you have a good time tonight?" he asked quietly.

I nodded. "I'm having a better time now though."

He huffed a quiet laugh. "I bet you are, Bambi."

My eyes narrowed. "Why do you call me that? I don't get it."

He reached out to brush my hair back from my face, dragging the backs of his fingers along my cheek. "It was the sight of you walking down that aisle at your mother's wedding. You were trying to put on a brave face, but I saw you. You were like a damn baby deer walking into a world full of lions ready to rip you apart, and I saw the moment you realized it, too."

He was right. I had been trying my best to appear confident, like I didn't care that there were the eyes of hundreds of strangers on me as I was thrust into a new world and new life I'd never asked for.

But Dacre had seen through it all.

"Maybe I don't hate that nickname as much as I thought," I said, my eyes drooping as fatigue threatened to take over.

The sheets rustled as Dacre shifted closer, pressing his lips to my forehead in a soft kiss. "Sweet dreams, Bambi. You deserve them."

CHAPTER 22

woke up hot and content after one of the best night's sleep I'd ever had.

Blinking awake, my room came into view and so did the two hulking men asleep on either side of me. Presley was sprawled on his back, taking up two-thirds of the mattress, while I was wrapped in Dacre's arms, the two of us huddled together in what little space was left.

Glancing between their sleeping forms, I gently lifted the covers, slipping out of Dacre's arms and doing my best to climb over him without waking him.

"Don't even think of sneaking out on us in your own bed," Dacre muttered with his eyes still closed, a smile playing on his mouth.

His arms wrapped around me where I was half-straddling him in my efforts to climb over him, and he pulled me back down to the bed, rolling on top of me.

I laughed, trying to wriggle free. "I'm not sneaking anywhere. I need a drink, my mouth is like the desert, and I didn't want to wake you."

He stilled, pressing a quick kiss to my lips. "I'll allow it."

He rolled off me, his arms loosening from around me, and

I climbed from the bed, hustling into the bathroom and closing the door. Quickly cleaning my teeth and downing two glasses of water, I strolled back out. I barely made it within two steps of the bed when Dacre reached for me, tugging me down on top of him, his hands landing on my ass and palming it like it was his favorite toy.

"We slept in the same bed the entire night and you didn't get this handsy," I said with a smile, pressing my mouth to his.

Now that the tension was gone, it felt so easy between us.

"That's because I'm a gentleman," he offered, giving my ass a smack.

"Oh? And this morning you're not?"

He shook his head, rolling me over so he was on top of me again. "Not a fucking chance. Spending the night with you in my arms has me so fucking hard. I need you to take care of it for me, Bambi."

He pouted and the sight of it from a six-foot, muscled man baby made me laugh. I glanced at Presley who was still snoring lightly on the other side of the bed. "Does he…?"

"He knows about us, but I didn't give him any details. Those are just for you and me," Dacre said, staring down at me like I was precious and important to him. "Sin, too."

I reached up, threading my fingers in his hair and tugging his mouth down to mine. His tongue instantly invaded my mouth and I moaned against him.

He kissed along my jaw and down to the neck of my t-shirt, where he pulled back long enough to lift the material from my body, exposing my stomach and breasts.

"My new favorite place to be." He dropped his head, but paused. "Well, it'll be my second favorite place soon." He glanced down between my legs and when he looked back up at me, his eyes were filled with heated promise that set my body alight.

Before I could respond, his mouth closed over my nipple,

causing me to suck in a sharp breath at the sudden sensation flooding my body. He worked me over, swirling and sucking until I was hot and ready. Then he released my nipple with a wet pop, moving to the other side.

God, everything he did to me made my body sing with desire.

My hips bucked off the bed, desperately searching for the friction of his body, but he kneeled over me, withholding it while he focused his hot mouth on my hardened nipples.

Glancing up at me, he smirked with satisfaction at the state he'd already put me in, kissing his way down my body with his eyes still locked on mine.

He slid my sleep shorts to my knees, kissing between my legs. I squirmed with need.

"Don't tease me," I said, breathless.

He hummed a chuckle against my skin, parting me, his tongue delving between my legs. The feel of his tongue running over me stole the breath from my lungs and my back arched as I moaned at the pleasure.

In an embarrassingly short amount of time, Dacre had me teetering on the edge, and me quietly begging him to let me fall over. He upped his pace and my eyes screwed shut, my fingers tightening around the bedsheets. His muttered name fell from my mouth over and over as pleasure ripped through me.

When I was done, Dacre lifted his head, wiping his chin with the back of his hand, an endless grin stretched across his face.

"That was quite a fucking show," Presley said from beside me, and my gaze snapped to him.

He was lying on his side, head propped with his hand. He stared back at me with a heated, desperate gaze.

"She's probably in need of some dick now though." He looked to his brother. "How about I give her that while she takes care of yours?"

Dacre pushed up so he was kneeling over me, brushing his fingers over my swollen clit one last time in a possessive touch and making me gasp. Then he swung from the bed, standing beside it, his hardened cock in his hand. He stroked it lazily, right at my eye line and my thighs clenched.

"Roll over, Sass."

I did as Presley asked, rolling so I was face down and he was behind me. He gripped my hips, pulling me back towards him so my ass was in the air and I was on all fours on the bed.

Dacre stood in front of me, still stroking his hard cock as he watched Presley position me to take them both.

Presley's fingers delved into my slick center from behind. "Fuck, Sass, you really fucking want this."

I nodded, glancing up at Dacre who was staring down at me with his usual reverence. I loved the way he looked at me, like he'd set the world on fire if I asked him to.

The thought of taking both of them at once had my insides turning molten.

Presley palmed my ass. "You're glistening. Such a fucking good girl."

He rubbed the tip of his cock along my seam, coating himself in my wetness. Then he lined himself up and thrust inside me, my body jolting towards Dacre.

He was waiting for me, holding my chin in his hand and running the tip of his cock over my bottom lip. "You ready for me, Bambi?"

I nodded up at him, opening wide and taking his thick cock in my mouth.

"Holy shit," Dacre swore, tipping his head back.

"What's her mouth like?" Presley asked, doing shallow thrusts inside me.

I wanted more. No, I *needed* more than this. I was coiled so tight, ready to combust at all the sensations pinging through me.

"Like a fucking vacuum," Dacre ground out, staring down at me. "I could shoot my load just looking at her taking me down her throat."

The moan that escaped me was completely involuntary. This whole thing was driving me crazy and we'd barely started.

Presley held my waist and drew me back onto him. "What would your new daddy say if he saw you getting fucked by both your brothers, Dempsey?" His tone was teasing, chastising. Like I'd been a bad girl and he was determined to teach me a lesson.

Dacre smirked above me. "Better yet, what would Mommy say about her good little girl taking two cocks at once?"

Their dirty mouths heightened everything, wetness gushing between my thighs.

"Fuck, she loves it," Presley said, increasing his pace. He thrust into me, sending me shooting forward so fast Dacre's cock hit the back of my throat.

"God damn it, Bambi." Dacre's fingers tangled in my hair, pulling tight.

My eyes started to water, but there was no way in hell I was going to stop. I was already so close to coming and I knew when I did it would be a full-blown fireworks display inside of me.

They alternated their thrusts, Presley railing me from behind and Dacre jolting his hips into my mouth. We moaned together every time he hit the back of my throat, Presley matching me every time he bottomed out inside me.

I hummed around Dacre and he stroked my cheek. "She's going to come."

"That true, Sass?" Presley's grip on my waist tightened and he thrust inside me harder and faster.

I nodded with my mouth still full, the heightened pace sending my vision white at the edges. I came with a scream, muffled by Dacre's cock in my mouth, and he came down my throat a moment later. My pussy convulsed around Presley as I came and he groaned in response, his fingers tightening at my waist as he spilled inside me.

Dacre slipped out of my mouth, Presley pulling out from behind and I collapsed on the bed on my front.

Dacre reached out to stroke my hair. "That was the hottest thing I've ever seen. You took us so well, Bambi."

I nodded, too spent for words. Presley's warm body landed at my back as he lay down beside me. His lips pressed to the bare skin at the top of my spine.

"You're fucking dynamite, Sass."

CHAPTER 23

Another day in Cape Canyon, another event at the damn country club.

Only this one was particularly bad because not only had my mother forced me to wear a hideous green dress she'd chosen for me and was cut to make me look like a nun, but Arena was away with her family in Greece on a luxury vacation. She'd taken to sending me pictures daily of "Greek hotties"—girls and guys—that she'd hooked up with while living her best life over there. While I was stuck here with the same boring people at the same inane events.

But the very worst part was I couldn't touch Dacre or Presley because we were out in public. It was a special kind of torture, given how incredible they looked in their suits tonight. Presley's was all black, with a crisp white shirt and thin black tie that made him look like Clark Kent. Dacre had opted for a navy suit that brought out the blue in his eyes, tailored perfectly to his incredible arms.

I watched Presley talking to two girls I'd seen around at Triple C, and who used any excuse to touch him as they spoke to him. They were gorgeous and I hated it every time they gripped his bicep or swatted his forearm, that jealous little monster inside of me resisting the urge to claw their eyes out.

The image of it had me laughing to myself—me flying into a fit of possessive rage over my stepbrother and jumping on one of the girl's backs, hauling her away from him and down to the floor to claw at her face. The drama of it. My mother would be scandalized. I'd be disowned, disavowed, and shipped off to a remote mental health facility. This community would be talking about it for years to come.

I took a sip of my drink, eyeing their interactions. Presley liked the attention, that was easy to see, but I got the sense he didn't particularly care about it coming from them. Or maybe that was wishful thinking on my part. Maybe I was giving more meaning to us sleeping together than was actually there.

"He had a threesome with them last year," came a voice from beside me.

Sinclair appeared at my left, taking a sip of his champagne, and I scowled. I could have lived without knowing that.

"Did you just stop by to *ruin* my day, big brother?"

Those intense green eyes locked on me. "Did you move here to ruin mine?"

I stared back at him, trying to sort joke from reality, but there wasn't an ounce of humor on his handsome face.

He shifted closer, his cologne invading every one of my senses, and I resisted the urge to let my eyes flutter closed as I breathed him in.

"You've got both of them half in love with you already." He nodded in Presley's direction, but I knew he meant Dacre too. "And I want you to know that if you fuck with them, I'll fuck with you."

I studied him again, assessing the threat. There wasn't a doubt in my mind that he meant every word. A part of me respected him for it. He was protective of his brothers; the three of them were bonded in a way I hadn't seen from other siblings. But he needn't have bothered with the warning. It was far more likely I was the one in over my head and would be the one left in pieces if it fell apart.

Or maybe it was *when* it fell apart. I had no idea where I stood with either of them, and I was too scared to find out.

"Come on, Sin, if you're jealous just say that," I taunted, trying to hide the effect his words had on me. "If you want the chance to fuck me for yourself, all you have to do is ask. We can go find a quiet place right now and I'll choke on your cock too."

His eyes pinched almost imperceptibly at the corners and it was his turn to study my expression for the lie.

I smiled sweetly back at him. Although if he called me on it, would I say no? Sinclair was a walking fucking promise that any kind of sex with him would be mind-blowing.

I'd been trying to fool myself into thinking I wasn't attracted to him, but it was a damn lie.

I wanted him. Wanted all of them.

A blur of blonde hair in a blue dress appeared at his side, fracturing the moment.

"God, my mother is such a pain in the ass, she's all over me about when you're going to propose." Veda rolled her eyes, slipping her hand into Sinclair's.

His fingers tightened around hers, just as she glanced my way.

"Oh, my bad. I'm interrupting."

Sinclair shook his head. "Not at all."

The look he gave her was almost affectionate. More than I'd ever seen from him with anyone, and something a lot like jealousy burst through me.

Why her? It was nearly impossible to penetrate Sinclair's outer armor, yet she had done it well enough to become his girlfriend. What did she have to offer him that no one else could?

She was beautiful, that much was obvious. But I knew

enough about Sinclair to understand beauty wouldn't have been enough.

"Veda, this is Dempsey, our stepsister."

Veda offered me her hand and a small smile. "Nice to officially meet you. It's weird that we haven't already."

She dropped my hand and looked to Sinclair, who shrugged like I wasn't important enough to know.

He looked down at her, that same affectionate edge to his expression, and I wanted to grip his lapels and beg him to look at me that way.

I knew he never would, though.

"A pleasure to meet you, Veda. It's a lucky woman who can snag Sin."

Sinclair's eyes locked on mine, something passing between us for a split second. Then he took Veda's hand in his, pulling her away. "Let's go talk to your mother. Hopefully seeing us together will be enough to placate talks of proposals."

She beamed back at him like he was her knight. "See you soon, Dempsey."

She offered me a small wave, then they disappeared through the crowd together, Sinclair taking a small, pathetic piece of me with him.

CHAPTER 24

begrudgingly made my way through the grounds of Byron's excessive compound after being summoned by my mother.

She and Byron were at the small putting green around the back of the house, getting a golf lesson from some golfer who used to play pro. Why they bothered with golf, I had no idea. The sport was a good walk spoiled.

I rounded a section of rose bushes to a clearing, where the golf pro had set up mats and tees. Both Byron and my mother were hitting balls off the tees. Well, Byron was. My mother was hitting fresh air more than the ball.

Since when did she even like golf? I'd never seen her play it as long as I'd been alive. And what were they wearing? They were sporting matching tan plaid vest monstrosities. My mother had paired it with a white tennis skirt far too short for her age.

"You summoned me, Mom?" I said as I approached, careful not to get too close to her errant swings.

She glanced up at me, her face twisting with displeasure. "I didn't *summon* you, Dempsey. I wanted to talk to you."

And you sent a maid to tell me that.

"Well, here I am."

My gaze snagged on the golf pro giving Byron directions on his swing. He was so much younger than I'd have guessed. And hot, too. *Damn.*

He didn't have anything on Dacre, Presley, and Sinclair, but no sane girl would kick him out of bed.

"The annual cotillion ball is coming up at the country club," my mother said, drawing my attention back to her and away from my blatant ogling. "While you're much too old to debut, you'll be required to attend and need a dress for it. Would you prefer to shop for one yourself this time, since you were so outraged by my choice for the last one, or would you prefer to attend the tailor with me and have something made for you?"

Well, the honest answer was that I'd rather stick pins under my fingernails than spend a moment more than I had to with my mother, so that made the decision easy.

"I'll shop for something."

My mother lowered her club, propping a hand on her hip, the other leaning on the end of the club. "Nothing too revealing. I want it classy and tasteful, do you understand?"

I bit back my scoff, gaze dropping to her legs in her too-short skirt.

"Sure, Mom. Classy and tasteful." My tone dripped with sarcasm.

She went on about the importance of the event, but I tuned her out, eyes landing on the hot golf pro again. Only this time, he was looking back at me, his interest evident in the small smile that hooked the corner of his mouth.

"Dempsey? Are you listening to me?"

I startled. "Yes, Mom. Of course I am."

She glanced over her shoulder at the golf pro, then back at me.

"Alex, this is my daughter, Dempsey." My mom leaned down to place another ball on the tee.

Alex strolled over, a smile on his face and his hands in his pockets. He slid one out when he reached me, offering me his hand. "Nice to meet you, Dempsey."

His palm was warm against mine, but I didn't get the same spark over my skin that I did when one of my stepbrothers touched me.

I smiled back. "Likewise."

A throat cleared behind me, and Sinclair strolled by, so close I could feel the heat of his body.

"Byron..." He stopped beside his father, talking to him in a low voice about company stock prices and necessary trades.

"Do you play?" Alex asked, motioning to my mother's terrible swing.

I shook my head. "Never even picked up a club."

"You should give it a go. Maybe I could give you a lesson sometime."

My mother brightened. "That sounds wonderful. What a kind offer, Alex."

She turned back to her ball.

Swing and a miss.

Alex grimaced and I pressed my lips together to fight my laugh. Sinclair glanced my way, green eyes burning into me as he spoke with Byron.

What was his problem? He was acting like I was cheating on his brothers by even speaking to Alex, when Sinclair was the one with a girlfriend but spent half his time staring at me when we were in the same room together.

"I've always wanted to give it a try," I lied through my teeth to Alex.

He shifted closer, smiling. "I'd love to teach you."

A figure loomed over us, Sinclair suddenly standing a little too close.

Alex glanced at him, offering us both a tight smile and sliding his hands back into his pockets. "Nice meeting you, Dempsey. Hopefully see you around."

He made his way back over to Byron, offering him some advice to correct his swing.

I clenched my jaw, trying hard to stop myself from releasing the string of expletives I wanted to direct at my asshole stepbrother. Opting to ignore him instead, I turned on my heel and power walked my way through the grounds to the back patio. Sinclair caught up to me just as I was hauling the door open.

His fingers closed around my bicep, dragging me inside and crowding me against the wall.

"What the fuck, Sinclair?"

Hard eyes stared down at me. "Flirting with a golf pro is beneath you, Dempsey. You're an Aston now."

My expression twisted and I tried to ignore the way my blood rushed through my veins at his proximity. "What the hell does that mean?"

"We have standards. He doesn't make the cut."

"Are you kidding me? Presley fucked a waitress after the wedding. What the hell kind of standard is that?"

He shrugged and the sight of it infuriated me. I hated that he was always so composed when my insides were a jumbled mess every time he came near me.

"He's allowed." He shook his head slowly. "You're not."

I glared at him, irritation flooding me. "What the hell is your problem, you emotionless robot."

He blinked back at me. "Robot. That's a new one."

"Robots are devoid of all emotion. Reminds me of you."

His usual stoney expression didn't falter. Not even a flicker.

"I have emotions. I've just learned not to display them for everyone to see and use against me. I keep my weaknesses locked down because that's what it takes to be a fucking winner."

"Well kudos on winning at everything." I rolled my eyes and his expression hardened.

"Did you just roll your eyes at me?"

I stilled, my brow creasing at the sharpness of his tone. He shifted closer, his body flush with mine, my back pressing into the wall until my shoulder blades ached. The ache between my legs increased right along with it.

Why did I have to react this way to him? I wanted to hate him. I really did.

"Get off me," I snapped, trying to shove him back, but he was a brick wall.

"I would…" He leaned down so his mouth was only inches from mine. "…but you don't really want that."

A shiver rippled down my spine. He was right. *Damn it.* Having him pressed against me like this was exactly what I wanted.

"We can't do this," I said, my voice breathy and desperate, solely focused on his mouth.

His voice was low and husky. "And why is that?"

I tilted my face up to his, the smallest of spaces between our lips. Barely a breath. "Because you have a girlfriend."

His eyes flared, and he pulled back in an instant, the heat and pressure of his body leaving me in a rush. I pressed both palms to the wall behind me to stop my legs from giving out.

For fuck's sake, he was boiling hot, then stone cold.

He stared at me, the rapid way his chest rose and fell the only indication he felt anything at all.

A beat of silence passed between us.

Then another.

"Sinclair—" I started.

He shook his head, silence descending as we entered into the most sexually charged staring contest of my life.

I wanted him. And I wanted him to want me, too.

"Fuck it," he said suddenly, closing the space between us.

He gripped my jaw in both hands and crushed his mouth to mine.

Our tongues went to war, and if he hadn't been holding

onto me, I would have hit the floor with the way his kiss weakened me.

It was demanding and self-assured, just like he was. He controlled every second of it, and I was all too willing to let him.

Sinclair kissed like he was mad at the world. Or maybe just me.

When he pulled away, I let out a small whimper, my mouth chasing his.

His eyes locked with mine. "Stay the fuck away from the golf pro."

Then his hands fell from my face, and he turned and stalked away, leaving me cold at the loss of him.

I took a moment to catch my breath, letting him go. He was a total mindfuck.

I pushed off the wall and headed for the entrance hall so I could take the stairs to my room, lock myself in the bathroom, and take the coldest shower of my life.

I'd barely made it to the stairs when one of the maids stopped me to hand me a letter.

I tore it open, dreading the words on the page.

I'm done playing nice.

CHAPTER 25

rena slid in the seat next to me in the one class we had together today.

"Hey girl, I'm surprised to see you here."

I frowned in her direction. "What do you mean? I'm here every week."

"After what happened this morning with Dacre, I thought you'd be at home."

I stilled. "What do you mean?"

Her eyes widened. "Holy shit, you didn't hear? Dacre was jumped in the parking lot this morning. From what I hear, they did some damage. Which is hard to believe, because that dude is built."

I didn't wait to let her finish talking. I was up and out of my seat, making it to the aisle of the lecture hall and bolting up the stairs. I jogged the entire way to my Bentley in the secured lot, tossing my book bag on the passenger seat and flooring it out of the lot.

Why the hell hadn't any of them called me? Sent me a text? Or a damn Snap, for all I cared.

I stormed into the house, slamming the door behind me.

"Someone better tell me what the fuck is going on!" I shouted from the entrance hall.

It had ceilings higher than the heavens so my voice echoed through the house.

A few moments later, Presley appeared from the hallway to the left. His expression was drawn, which was completely at odds with his usual charming energy.

"He's in here, Sass."

He motioned down the hallway in the direction of the gym, following behind me.

A hiss of pain greeted me as I stepped into the room. Dacre was seated on one of the weight benches. He was shirtless, his ribs and torso covered in black and purple bruises.

Sinclair had pulled another bench up close, an extensive first aid kit open beside him. He was stitching a cut above Dacre's right eyebrow, a short cut on his left cheek was already taped, and his left eye was swollen shut.

I sucked in a startled breath at the sight of him. Arena was right, whoever had jumped him had really done some damage.

"You've got more money than sense, you think you might be able to pay a professional to do that instead?" The bite to my tone covered up the panic rolling through me at the sight of Dacre beaten and bloodied.

"We've been stitching each other up since we were kids. I know what I'm doing," Sinclair said flatly, his attention focused on his task.

Dacre glanced at me with his good eye. "I'm okay, Bambi."

I bit my lip. "Not from where I'm standing. What the hell happened?"

"He got jumped on his way to the art studio," Presley said from where he sat on the edge of the raised boxing ring, his arms folded over his chest. "Beat the living shit out of him and left him there."

My hands shook and I clenched them into fists.

"There were two, maybe three of them. They surprised me, otherwise I might have been able to hold my own."

I softened. He was a boxer. They'd clearly landed a couple of blows to his ego as well as his body when they got the jump on him.

"Did you manage to get the security footage from the lot?" Presley asked Sinclair.

He nodded once. "I've got a couple of my team working on it. It should be in my email any minute."

It was helpful having a tech CEO in the family.

I stared at Dacre, wanting to reach for him, but knowing it would likely only hurt him. "Why would someone do this?"

He shrugged, then winced at the pain it caused. "I don't fucking know. Money means enemies. It could have been any one of the jealous assholes we're forced to hang out with."

I bit the inside of my cheek, following along with every movement Sinclair made while stitching. Clocking every wince Dacre made when the needle pierced too deep or the stitch pulled too tight.

Fuck. It hurt me to see him hurt.

Sinclair finished the stitches, pulling back to check his work, then started packing up the supplies. His phone pinged with an email, and he pulled it from his pocket, tossing it to Presley.

"Check it. It'll be the footage."

I sidled over, sitting next to him as he pulled up the security video.

The camera was across the lot, but you could see Dacre getting something from the trunk of his car just as three guys approached him from behind. One gripped his shirt and yanked him out of the trunk. They tossed him to the ground out of shot behind some cars and the three of them converge on him, boots and fists swinging.

"Oh my god." My body shook at the violence of it all.

Presley went to comfort me, but I got to my feet. Striding for Dacre and taking a seat beside him. I slipped my hand in his, careful not to hurt him.

"I'm okay, I mean it. I've copped worse in the ring."

I nodded silently, knowing full well that wasn't true. There was a big difference between being hit by one person in a controlled setting for training and being wailed on by three when you're on the ground.

Dacre squeezed my hand. "I need a shower and a long ass nap."

I helped him to his feet, and he kissed my forehead before leaving.

"I want to know who the fuck did this," Presley said with more bite than I'd ever heard from him.

Sinclair's gaze landed on his brother. "I'm working on it."

I left them in the gym, determined to be there for Dacre when he was done in the shower, but one of the maids stopped me as soon as I stepped into the hall.

"Another letter for you, Miss Dempsey."

She thrust it in my hand, hurrying off in the direction of the kitchen.

I glanced at the closed door to the gym behind me, praying Presley and Sinclair hadn't heard her. Swallowing against the bile rising in my throat, I tore open the envelope, pulling the card out.

Hope your brother is still alive.

I sucked in a sharp breath, my hands shaking with a mix of rage and fear.

My father was escalating, and there was a chance he knew

about me and my stepbrothers. Or at the very least, me and Dacre. The video he'd sent me was questionable, but not damning.

But if my father knew the truth and had people tailing me, it meant we were all in trouble now.

CHAPTER 26

"Isn't this nice?" my mother said as I took my seat at the table. "A full family dinner."

She'd been hellbent on forcing us to eat together as a group since we'd arrived here, but it rarely happened. Either Sin was working late, or Presley was at football practice. Someone was always missing.

But tonight, we had a full table, and my mother was brimming with forced enthusiasm.

I was sandwiched at the table between Sinclair and Dacre, Presley lounging at the end on Dacre's other side like the prince of the Aston manor.

I frowned at the double serve of whiskey in his hand, his eyes already a little glassy. He just grinned back at me like none of it mattered. "Won't be long until we'll be having these dinners with an entire camera crew in the room to adequately show off what an excellent family man the future Governor is." Presley raised his glass in his father's direction, and I tensed, glancing at Byron for a reaction.

His hard gaze locked on Presley. "And you'll be drinking water when it does."

He turned his attention to my mother, who sat across from

me. The two of them eyed each other like they wanted to rip their clothes off and throw down on the dining table right in front of us. The sight of their lovesick stares made me want to throw up in my mouth a little bit.

It was great my mom was happy, but being married to Byron had become her entire personality, just like she'd been with my father. She became so obsessed with the men she was with that little else mattered. I barely existed to her anymore outside of being her prop at parties. It hurt. Being shoved to the side to make way for her new husband so she could worship at his feet was humiliating.

"So, how was everyone's day?" Byron asked, as the first course was placed in front of each of us. It was some kind of fish dish in a spicy Thai sauce and it had fast become one of my favorites from the house chef.

"Fine," Sinclair declared. "Fired a few people."

The smile that stretched across Byron's face was laced with pride.

"Atta boy, Sin," Presley offered from the other end of the table, his tone laced with sarcasm. "Way to make Daddy proud."

Sinclair shot him a flat look as his phone buzzed on the table and he stared down at it, reading it. Then he tapped a message and returned it to the table once more. My own phone buzzed, and I reached for it, staring at the notification from the group chat the four of us had going on.

SINCLAIR: No leads on the surveillance footage of Dacre's attack. All assailants managed to stay off the cameras.

I swallowed. My father's men were smart enough to stay out of range of CCTV cameras. They would have had the whole place sussed out long before they'd gone for Dacre.

"And what did you do today, Presley?" Byron eyed his current state with disdain, carrying on the table conversation. "Besides drink yourself into a stupor? Did you even make it to football practice?"

Presley's eyes landed lazily on his father. "As a matter of fact I did, but I got bored fifteen minutes in so I set my sights on exploring the inside of the head cheerleader's skirt under the bleachers instead."

Byron's expression hardened, and my gaze snapped to Pres.

He did what…? Surely after everything that had happened between us, he wouldn't.

His gaze connected with mine, the subtle shake of his head giving me all the reassurance I needed.

Presley liked to push the limits, test other people's boundaries as well as his own. I'd witnessed him and Byron face off more than once since I'd moved in. It was as though Presley pushed his father away just to see if he'd keep coming back.

"A very impressive endeavour, son," Byron's tone was clipped, making it clear he thought the opposite.

"Dacre, honey," my mother chimed in. "What did you get up to today?"

I didn't miss Byron's frown at Dacre's injuries, but he thankfully didn't ask. Maybe he was used to Dacre coming home battered and bruised from too many rounds in the ring at the gym.

My mother was clearly trying to keep the peace and stop Byron and his sons from tearing into each other across the table. Would it kill her to take an interest in her own daughter the same way? Maybe if she were an engaged parent my father wouldn't feel entitled to come for me the way he was. Instead, she was focused on doting on her new stepsons in front of her husband.

"Nothing to write home about. Took some classes, came

home and worked on a few canvases," Dacre said, eyes trained on my mother to avoid even a glance at Byron.

Byron set his cutlery down on his plate harder than was necessary.

"Again with the art, Dacre? When are you going to understand there's no future in it? I won't have it."

Dacre's jaw ticked from beside me and I wanted to reach for him, to take his face in my hands and smooth the tension away.

He was an incredible artist. And under that hard exterior, he had a soft, open heart. Every time Byron trashed his dream, it shattered him a little more. I'd seen it that day in the studio when he'd opened up to me. And I hated seeing it play out now.

"I don't know, *Dad*, maybe you could drill it into me a few more times and I might get it," Dacre cut back.

Unable to stop myself, I reached for him under the table, taking his hand in mine and giving his fingers a squeeze. His fingers closed around mine in a vice grip. He was working hard to keep himself in check. He rested our entwined hands against my bare thigh under the table, just below the hem of my dress, his fingers brushing my skin.

Byron shook his head in obvious frustration, staring down at his plate. My mother reached for him, brushing his arm as though he was the one needing comfort right now.

"It'll be okay, Byron, the boys will figure things out," she cooed like he was a small child who needed coaxing at bed time.

She lifted her head, smiling encouragingly at Dacre and Presley, and I've never wanted to throttle my own mother so badly.

Couldn't she see what they were going through? Didn't she understand what Byron's criticism was doing to them?

It made me wonder what their mother, Sinclair's biological mother, had been like. Had she been the mediator who tried to make Byron see things from their points of view? Or had she been like my mother, siding solely with her husband with weak attempts to keep the peace?

"Well, I had a great day," I declared to the table.

My mother's gaze snapped to mine, eyeing me with wary disinterest. "That's great, honey." She turned back to Byron. "Let's focus on our honeymoon, darling. We leave next week, and I know we're going to have the most amazing time once you have the space to unwind."

Byron smiled at her, and my mother's face lit up.

Dacre's hand released from mine, and I tried to ignore the way my stomach dropped at the loss. Then his fingers grazed the inside of my thigh, and surprise flooded me.

Was he really going to start something with me under the table when our parents were sitting across from us?

Not that they were paying a lick of attention. They were deep in conversation about their honeymoon, Sinclair throwing in the occasional comment.

Dacre's fingers trailed up the inside of my thigh, taking the hem of my dress with him and my eyebrows shot up my forehead. When I glanced his way, he was focused on his food, moving it around his plate with his free hand. He had an incredible poker face, because there was absolutely no way to tell his fingers were now grazing the bare skin between my legs.

His head snapped in my direction when he realized I wasn't wearing underwear beneath my dress. I hitched one shoulder in a subtle shrug and Dacre's jaw tightened.

His finger brushed along my seam, teasing me, and I gripped my spoon tightly to keep from squirming in my seat. He pulled back, palm sweeping over my thigh.

I glanced at him, brow pinched in confusion, when a hand slid in from my right, brushing over the bare skin between my legs and separating me. My gaze shot to Sinclair, who was bringing his spoon to his mouth with one hand, his fingers grazing my clit beneath the table with the other.

I sucked in a sharp breath, looking to Byron and my mother, but they were still deeply immersed in each other. Clearly it paid to piss off Byron when it meant you were completely ignored for the rest of the meal and could tease your stepsister to the edge of insanity.

Casting a glance in Presley's direction, his hooded and heated gaze was trained on my face, taking in every flinch and clench as Sinclair's fingers circled my clit, teasing me.

I opened my mouth to speak, but Dacre's hand tightened on my left thigh.

What was I going to say anyway? Stop? Don't? Our parents are right there?

But I didn't want to stop. And the fact they were torturing me like this, so illicitly, right under my mother's nose only heightened the sensations flooding me.

Dacre slid his hand higher, taking my dress with him, exposing me. He stared down at my lap, watching Sinclair's fingers work me over.

"Fuck," he muttered so quietly only I could hear.

Hearing the effect this was having on him only turned me on, and I let my legs fall open to give him a better view.

When Sinclair slid his middle finger inside me, his thumb playing with my clit, my fist banged on the table against my will, making the cutlery rattle. But it was either that or cry out in ecstasy and that wasn't an option.

"Dempsey, are you all right?" Byron asked with a concerned frown. "You're not choking on a fish bone are you? I'll have your meal returned to the chef immediately."

I shook my head, swallowing hard in an attempt to find my voice. The last thing I needed was to respond with a breathy moan right in front of my stepfather.

"No, I'm fine, thank you," I blurted quickly, just as Sinclair quickened his pace, working over my clit so fast I was practically panting. "It's just a little spicy."

Byron smiled back at me, and I thanked every God who'd ever existed for low hanging tablecloths, which meant Byron couldn't tell his son's fingers were deep inside me.

"Ah yes," Byron said, beaming with pride. "Our chef is the best in the state. He knows how to give things a good kick."

Presley's gaze was burning into my skin from my left, and I glanced at him, drawing Byron's attention over to his son.

"What's gotten into you, Presley?" Byron asked with a frown. "You haven't touched your food."

Presley reluctantly pulled his eyes from me to turn to his father, just as I gripped the edge of the table to stop myself from rocking against Sinclair's hand.

Sinclair leaned closer, reaching for the salt, pitching his voice low so only Dacre and I could hear him. "You going to come all over my fingers at dinner, Princess?"

Dacre huffed a laugh, his hand sliding in to take over rubbing my clit, Sinclair now solely focused on getting me to ride his fingers.

"Yes," I hissed, a little too loud.

"What's that, honey?" my mother asked, forcing me to tune back into the table conversation.

What the hell had they been talking about?

"Glad you agree with me, D," Presley offered, glancing down at my lap as though he could see through the table, then back at my face. "The football team could use some extra supporters on game day. I'll get you a jersey."

I nodded, biting my lip as an orgasm started to crest inside me.

Oh, fuck.

The combination of Dacre and Sinclair's fingers on and in me had it building so hard and fast I was going to scream my lungs out when I finally came.

I gripped my spoon, trying to bring it to my mouth, but my hand shook violently, and I dropped it back in the bowl.

"Dempsey, are you sure you're okay?" my mother asked again, and panic flared through me. I needed her eyes off me, there was no way I was going to come undone with my mother staring straight at me.

But Dacre and Sinclair didn't let up, pushing me closer and closer to the edge.

"Oh fuck," Presley swore suddenly, tipping the entirety of his whiskey glass across the white linen table cloth and over the edge of the table.

The amber liquid spread fast, and my mother snapped her focus to the potential stain. She sprung from her seat to direct the maid on how to clean it up. At the same time, Byron reached behind Presley to signal to his valet to get another glass for his son.

Sinclair thrust inside me hard, and Dacre pinched down on my clit. I covered my face with my cloth napkin, biting down on it and using it to stifle the small moan that tore from my lips as sensation flooded my body.

I tried to snap my legs shut, but Dacre's other hand gripped my thigh, holding them open as he stroked me through my explosive orgasm.

When I sat back in my chair, trying to control my panting breaths, only then did they remove their fingers. Sinclair looked my way, bringing his fingers to his mouth and sucking them clean in one long stroke.

"Oh my god," I whispered, tipping my head back against my chair, trying to work out how to breathe again.

Dacre leaned in, his eyes blazing with lust. "You're so fucking hot when you come apart for us, Bambi."

It was so fucking hot letting them tear me apart.

And I wanted to do it again.

CHAPTER 27

ater that night, I couldn't sleep, tossing around in my bed like a dying fish on land.

I was a sweaty mess just thinking about the way Sinclair and Dacre had pulled me undone, right there at the dinner table. Dacre possessed the most masterful fingers, I already knew that. With a killer mouth, too. But that was the first time Sinclair had touched me, other than our incredibly frustrating kiss near the golf green.

But it wasn't just frustration I was feeling this time, it was outright annoyance. Sinclair had a girlfriend. A long-term, committed, very serious girlfriend given the amount of time they spent together.

Which meant he had no right to be finger fucking me under his father's dining table.

My mind flashed with the way he'd sucked his fingers after making me come all over them, and I squeezed my eyes and my thighs shut at the memory.

Fuck.

Sleep wasn't going to happen.

I picked up my phone, glancing at the time. It was past midnight, I should be sleeping—I had a full day of classes tomorrow—but thanks to the brazen sex fiends that were my stepbrothers, sleep wasn't going to happen any time soon.

If I was going to lie awake, I may as well do it with chocolate. The chef had made the most incredible individual chocolate mousse cakes for dessert, which meant there would be leftovers in the fridge.

Padding down the stairs all the way to the kitchen, I pulled open the fridge to find several of the cakes sitting in their small glass bowls on the middle shelf. I grabbed a spoon and my late-night snack and made a beeline for the stairs, but the sound of metal hitting the hard polished stone floor of the garage stopped me still with fear.

Was someone trying to break into the garage? The staff had all finished for the night, and while some of them lived in the manor and could be called upon any time, there was no way any of them were out in the garage past midnight.

Fear flooded my veins as a thought flitted across my mind.

Had my father sent someone to try again?

I stood frozen with indecision, the dessert and spoon gripped tightly in my hands.

"Fuck," came a familiar voice and the clanging of tools again.

Marching to the garage door, I flung it open, following the sounds until I circled around an old Mercedes that Sinclair was fixing up.

He was wearing another of those black fitted long-sleeve shirts with a pair of loose-fitting jeans that hung low on his hips.

He must have heard me approach, because he stood tall, sweat glistening his forehead and his dark hair mussed in a way that was so damn hot I had to resist the urge to shove him against the wall and rub my body against his.

"Is there a reason you're staring at me like you want to devour me and not that cake in your hands?" he asked, his expression on lockdown like always.

The guy fingered me during a fish appetizer a few hours ago, and he still wanted to dish out the ice king routine?

"What are you doing out here?" I snapped back, discarding my snack on his tool trolley.

"Fixing my car. I can't sleep."

"Good, because we need to talk."

He tossed a wrench onto the tool trolley with clang, eyes narrowed in my direction. "Do we? What about, Princess?"

I stepped closer, annoyance flaring inside me at this casually dismissive tone. He knew what the hell I wanted to talk to him about, but he was going to make me spell it out anyway.

"How about how you played with me under the table while my mother and your father were mere feet away?"

The corner of his mouth twitched, but he wouldn't let a full smirk break free. "You didn't seem to have any complaints at the time."

His casual arrogance was infuriating.

"Of course I didn't have any complaints at the time, I was too busy coming down off an epic orgasm."

He leaned against the side of the hood, crossing his arms over his chest. "Then you're fucking welcome."

I marched over, closing the space between us until we were face to face. "Oh, you're so fucking smug about it? What would your girlfriend have to say about you burying your fingers inside another girl?"

His expression hardened in an instant, and he pushed to his feet, forcing me to move back, out of his way. "My girlfriend is none of your concern."

I scoffed. "Apparently she's none of yours either."

He rounded on me, backing me up until my spine collided with the tool bench against the wall. "What exactly is the problem here? You're jealous that I have a girlfriend? Or pissed off that it means you won't have the opportunity to come on my fingers again?"

I clenched my jaw so hard it hurt. His arrogance was fucking boundless.

But he might be a little right. Clearly tonight had been a lapse in judgment for him. Maybe he was like Presley and the thrill of public sex got him off. Maybe it was the illicitness of what we did that had him participating, not his desire to see me come apart for him.

The thought stabbed me deep down in my gut. Because while Sinclair and I might pretend to hate each other, we also wanted each other, too.

Or at least… I wanted *him*.

His hands landed on the bench on either side of me, his eyes bouncing around my face, assessing me in that way I couldn't stand "No need to answer, I already know what it is."

I lifted my chin, bringing our faces even closer. "You think you know me, but you don't."

The corner of his mouth curved again and the desire to grip the back of his neck and pull his mouth to mine reared hard and fast.

"I know you're holding back right now," he said, his voice low. He tilted his head to the side, eyes narrowing on my mouth like my lips had personally offended him. "I know you think about the kiss we shared in the hallway, and what it would be like to do it again."

I sucked in a slow breath, my lungs expanding, and my breasts brushing his chest. My nipples peaked at the contact, shining through my thin silk camisole like headlights in the dark.

He tilted his head to the other side, his gaze narrowing on my exposed throat. His mouth dropped to my ear, his breath skating over my skin and making me shiver. "I know after tonight, you're wondering what it would be like to have my mouth on you, not just my fingers."

I swallowed hard, not even bothering to try to hide it. I wanted him and he knew it.

But he wanted me, too.

I quirked a brow at him. "Are you talking about me right now? Or you?"

He stilled, pulling back to look at me with what seemed like a hint of pride. "Maybe both."

Silence passed between us, our loaded breaths the only sound.

My expression filled with challenge. "Then prove it."

It was all the invitation he needed. His hand slid into my hair, pulling me to him, and his mouth closed over mine, just like it had the day near the golf green. Only this time instead of just hunger, his kiss was edged with urgency.

He angled my head, his tongue sweeping into my mouth and owning me so completely. If he was that good when he was kissing my mouth, I could only imagine how hot it would be when his tongue was between my legs. No wonder his girl-friend clung to him whenever they were out together. I wouldn't want another girl to steal him when he kissed like that either.

The realization sobered me immediately, and I put both hands to his chest, shoving him off. "We need to stop."

His eyes narrowed for the briefest second. "Why?"

"Because you have a girlfriend, Sinclair."

He shifted closer, pressing his pelvis to mine. The hard length of him thrust between my legs, jamming me against the tool bench. "You don't care about her, so don't pretend you do."

When he gripped my face and stole the breath from my lungs with another punishing kiss, I didn't have it in me to protest anymore. My hands gripped his waist, just above his jeans, clawing at him and tugging him close.

He thrust his hips forward, his hard cock grazing my clit, and I let out a small moan.

Fuck, he was so good at this. Arena was right, Sinclair was just as dominant in the bedroom as he was in life. And it turned me the hell on.

He pulled back, staring at me with a heat in his eyes that set my body on fire.

He nodded at my top. "Take it off."

I hesitated.

"Don't act like you don't fucking want this, Dempsey."

From the giant bulge coming from behind his zipper, he wanted this too.

I reached for the hem of my camisole and tugged it over my head, dropping it to the floor. I gripped the edge of the tool bench, eyes trained on Sinclair as he drank me in, wearing nothing but my tiny black satin sleep shorts.

I wished he'd say something, anything, to prove I wasn't the only one desperate for this.

"Come here," he beckoned, barely moving.

I pushed off the workbench and closed the three paces between us. His hands glided over my hips and down to my ass. The feeling of his hands on me had me soaring on the inside. His touch was filled with purpose, like he was memorizing me for later.

He tugged at the backs of my thighs, taking my legs out from under me, and I gripped his shoulders, wrapping my legs around his waist. His mouth claimed mine once more, devouring me like he'd been starved his whole life until this very moment.

His confidence—his dominance—made me wetter than I think I'd ever been.

Carrying me in his arms, he stopped in front of his red Porsche, lowering me to the hood. "I know how much you like this car."

I shrugged, unable to tear my eyes away from him to even glance at the car. "It's okay."

His lips twitched in an almost smile. "You're a terrible fucking liar, Princess."

Had I had fantasies of me riding him in the front seat? Yes.

Did he need to know that? *Hell no.*

He reached for the hem of my sleep shorts, and my hands instantly pressed back into the hood behind me so I could lift my hips.

"Who knew you were such an obedient little thing?" Sinclair said as he dragged the shorts down my legs torturously slowly.

"I'm a lot of things," I said, letting my legs fall open. "When properly motivated."

He stared down at me, his jaw ticking like he was forcing himself to hold back.

Restrained.

It was the perfect word to describe him. In life and in this moment. Sinclair held back, held himself together, held himself to a different standard than others. He wanted to be the best, the smartest, the most calculating man in the room. But what would happen if he just let go?

The thought sent a shiver down my spine, and Sinclair reached for the button on his jeans, his eyes trained on me as he flicked it open.

I swallowed hard, his fingers sliding down the zipper. He let them fall to his feet, kicking them away, his thick, hard cock sitting proudly against his stomach.

Holy shit, how the hell was I supposed to fit that anywhere inside me?

And was that… *a piercing*?

Four straight silver bars with balls on each end pierced the underside of his cock. My core clenched at the thought of how that would feel inside me.

He stroked himself slowly, eyes trained on me. "Like what you see, Princess?"

"Aside from the fact that you're about to ruin my insides, yes."

He smirked, climbing over me until I was sprawled beneath him on the hood of his expensive red sports car. "Don't worry, I know you can take it."

Fuck, the dominating, self-assured way he spoke to me, even when he was about to fuck me senseless, flooded my body with heat. His talented mouth closed over my throat, my breasts, my nipples, soaking me between my thighs.

When he slid a finger inside, his brow quirked. "You're so fucking ready for me, Princess."

I nodded, squirming with desire. I was so ready to be filled by him.

Leaning slightly off me, he gripped the base of his cock, lining it up with my entrance. "Hold on tight, this might hurt at first."

I lifted my head in time to see his thick cock slam into me in one hard thrust. My head dropped back, hitting the hood of the car, and I didn't care one damn bit. Because Sinclair Aston was finally fucking me, and it was consuming every coherent thought in my head.

"Fuck, Princess, you're so damn tight."

His hands were splayed on the hood of the car on either side of me, but he shifted his weight, fingers closing around my throat. He held me down, pulling out and thrusting back in, making us groan in unison.

"Oh my god, Sinclair… more. I need more."

I could feel the piercing hitting all the right spots inside me, heightening every feeling and sensation. His grip tightened and he thrust in again, every nerve ending in my body lighting up like a fucking Christmas tree.

Sex with Sinclair was every bit as hot and all-consuming as I'd imagined it.

Several more thrusts, and I was teetering on the edge of

oblivion, ready to ride the waves of pleasure peaking inside me.

"You going to come on my cock just like you did on my fingers?" Sinclair coaxed, his muscles taut with tension as he slid into me.

He hit even deeper this time, and my body arched off the hood. "Yes, oh my God, yes."

"That's it, baby, let me hear it."

He dropped down, taking my nipple in his mouth and sucking hard.

The combined sensations of his tongue on my body, his fingers at my throat, and his cock driving into me pushed me over the edge. He thrust in harder and deeper, and I moaned his name on repeat.

His whole body tightened and he swore, pulling out of me just as my own orgasm ebbed, spilling over me, coating my stomach and painting me between my legs.

I stared down at him, this masterpiece of a man spilling his seed all over my skin. It turned me the hell on.

He pressed his fists to the hood either side of my head, both of us totally spent and satiated. "Fuck, that was so damn hot."

I nodded, too wrung out to speak.

Sinclair took my hands, tugging me upright so I was sitting on the edge of the hood.

He reached for a clean towel in the drawer of the tool trolley, using it to wipe me down.

"You don't have to do that," I said to him, when I tried to take over, but he swatted my hand away.

"I'm not the asshole you think I am, Dempsey."

I opened my mouth to protest, but it would be a lie.

It was so easy to label Sinclair an asshole and move on. But tonight, I'd seen a different side to him. He was definitely an asshole who had cheated on his girlfriend with his stepsister, but I'd also seen what it looked like when his carefully controlled restraint slipped.

And I wanted to see it again.

CHAPTER 28

The glass of champagne in my hand grew warm as I stared at Sinclair from behind my sunglasses. He was across the garden party my mother had forced me to attend, flirting it up with Veda.

He'd had me sprawled on the hood of his car three nights ago, fucked me senseless, and come all over my bare skin, knowing full well he was going to run back to her the next day. Anger flared inside me, but it was heavily outweighed by an annoying dose of hurt. And I didn't want Sinclair or his actions to have the power to hurt me.

Yet here I was, standing under a tree at the country club garden party, watching my stepbrother live his best life with some other girl at his side.

"Fuck," I muttered, turning away. I was a damn fool for letting myself get tangled up with these boys. It wasn't going to end well for any of us, but least of all me.

"You look like you could use this," Presley said, appearing at my side and handing me another chilled glass of champagne.

He looked so incredibly handsome in his fitted navy checked suit with the matching tie. The pants cut off at the ankles, showing off his dark tanned leather dress shoes. Sunglasses covered the usual mischief dancing in his eyes and his caramel-colored hair was mussed like he'd been running his hands through it.

"Thanks, I can," I said, downing the last of my warm glass and discarding it in favor of his.

"He'll never leave her, you know." Presley nodded in Sinclair's direction.

I shrugged, shaking my head slowly. "Not sure why you think I'd care."

Pres tilted his head at me. "I don't know, maybe the moans coming from the garage the other night."

He took a sip of his drink, fighting a smile at the surprise plastered on my face.

"You're loud when you're having a good time, Sass." He moved closer. As close as we could get away with, given we were very much in public. "And I fucking love it."

I shiver ran through my body at the memory of Presley and I in the shower together. And against his bedroom door.

If we didn't have to be at this damn garden party right now, I'd drag him home and beg him to do it again.

"Whatever. He made his choice. It has nothing to do with me." I tried to inject more confidence into my voice than I felt.

"How about we hit the bar and drown our sorrows?"

Presley offered me his arm and I took it.

"What do you have to feel sorry about?" I asked, shifting sideways as we moved around people to make our way towards the bar.

He grinned, dropping his voice. "Nothing. I'm just hoping if I get you drunk, you'll let me do a whole lot of kinky shit to you when we get home."

We stopped at the bar, ordering two vodka shots, along with two vodka sodas with lime for good measure.

"Why wait until we get home?"

———

Two hours later, Presley and I were totally plastered and giggling like school girls as we fumbled to undress each other inside what I think was some kind of gardener's shack on the grounds of the country club.

We'd wandered away from the party hoping to find a secluded spot in the garden to grind on each other without the watchful eyes of the society matrons, ready to pounce on any bit of gossip or scandal they could get on the Astons. Instead, we'd found this place, with its fogged windows, dirty floor, and the strong stench of fertilizer.

"This is crazy romantic, Presley." Sarcasm laced my tone as I drunkenly fumbled with the buttons of his white linen shirt, while he sucked on my neck and pawed at my ass like it held the secrets to all his problems. "No guy has ever wanted to get it on with me amongst rakes and brooms. Kinky."

He pulled back, grinning down at me. "Wait until I fire up that thing." He nodded to the ride-on mower at the other end of the small shed. "I'd have you moaning my name in about eight seconds with that vibrating under you."

I raised a brow. I didn't hate that idea one bit, but... "No time to find the keys. I want you now."

His eyes flared with heat, and he swatted my useless hands away from his buttons, grabbing both sides of his shirt and pulling it open. Buttons tinkled to the floor.

"Wow, someone's excited." My eyes snagged on his impressive torso, stealing my train of thought. "My god, your body is incredible."

I ran my fingers over his pecs and abs, and he leaned his head back against the shelves behind him, letting out a long sigh.

"You know, I could die happy with your hands on me."

I let out a small laugh. "Nobody's dying today, big guy."

His head snapped up, eyes popping open. "It does things for my ego when you call me that," he said with a sly smile.

"Glad I could help with that, given your ego is in such dire need of stroking."

His smile widened to light up his entire face. Goddamn it, he was beautiful.

They were all hot as fuck. But Presley… he was gorgeous in that boy-next-door kind of way. If the boy next door was a male model with abs you could cut diamonds on and a smile that left you breathless.

"I can think of more important things that need stroking. Now pull up your dress and take off your panties."

I snaked my hands around his neck and into his hair, our bodies flushing together. "I'm not wearing panties," I said, our mouths achingly close. "Why would I bother wearing them around any of you at this point?"

He groaned, his mouth crashing with mine. His tongue was fevered and sloppy compared to his usual finesse, thanks to the alcohol, but it was so damn hot. He didn't care about technique, he wanted me. Desperately. And knowing that only spurred me on.

I wrapped myself around him like a damn pretzel, our bodies fully entwined.

He slid a hand between us under my dress, playing with my clit.

"Fuck, you're so ready."

"I was ready the moment I laid eyes on you at this stupid party. There isn't a time I'm not ready to take you." I closed my mouth over his, kissing him with all the drunken desperate need I had for him in this moment, and he groaned against my mouth.

"Peach is my new favorite flavor." He licked at my lips, tasting my lip gloss.

With one hand wrapped around my waist, he used the

other to tug at his pants, managing to get the button and zipper undone and dropping them to his ankles.

"Climb aboard, Sass. I'm ready to hear you scream."

I clung to his shoulders, and he grasped both my hips, lifting me until my legs were wrapped around his waist, the tip of his hard cock lined up at my entrance.

He didn't hesitate, thrusting in. I tipped my head back on a cry, exposing my throat.

"That's it, baby. Let me hear you." His mouth closed over my throat, sucking and nipping at me, his hips thrusting in a lazy rhythm.

Sex with Presley was always an experience. But languid, drunken Presley was something else.

He deepened his thrusts, clamping his hands tighter at my waist to hold me down on his cock, hitting just the right spot inside me to make me see stars.

"Fuck, Presley," I panted, tilting my hips to welcome him with every thrust.

He leaned forward, biting down on my neck, and I cried out so loud the sound rang in my ears.

"Never forget who makes you moan the loudest, Sass."

Right now, I couldn't see anything or anyone but him and the way he was making my body vibrate with pleasure. Faster than ever, I was coming, my walls clenching around him inside me.

He groaned at the feel of it, spilling into me, then held me tight, his head dropping to my shoulder. We were quiet for a long moment, clinging to each other.

Presley put me back on my feet, gripping my chin and planting a sweet kiss on my mouth. "You're so fucking sexy, Sass."

I smiled up at him just as the door to the shed burst open, Sinclair striding in.

"What the fuck is wrong with you two? I could hear

Dempsey crying out from halfway across the grounds." His expression was pinched with anger.

"I fucked her like I meant it. Can't help it if she had a good time, that's the whole point."

Sinclair marched for his brother, getting in his face. "Do you want to get fucking caught? Do you want to get sent the fuck away and see this family ruined because you couldn't keep your dick in your pants in public?"

Presley sobered, but Sinclair wasn't done.

"You know how badly this will end if anyone finds out about her and any of us, Pres."

Presley sighed, long and low. "Alright, I get it. We weren't thinking."

Sinclair scoffed, taking a step back. "Because you're drunk again."

Presley went to protest, to defend himself, but I cut in. "And you think you're the moral fucking compass of this family?"

Sinclair rounded on me, his perfect, emotionless mask falling back into place. "What the fuck is that supposed to mean?"

I crossed my arms over my chest, drunken rage boiling inside me that I was struggling to tamp down. "I don't know, Sinclair. Maybe that you want to lecture him about fucking me in public, when you fucked me on the hood of your car three nights ago and you still seem to be with your cute little girlfriend."

Something flickered behind his eyes, then was gone. He slowly closed the space between us, leaning down so we were eye to eye. Or face to face, given his mouth was only inches from mine.

"You know, jealousy really suits you, Princess."

His gaze dropped to my mouth, lingering there and making my breath hitch.

Then he pulled back, standing tall. He opened his mouth

to speak, when the door opened again and a gardener strolled in, surprise slackening his expression.

I glanced at Presley, whose shirt was still torn open and his pants undone at his hips.

Well, shit.

"I have five hundred dollars in my pocket," Sinclair said in a commanding voice. "All of it is yours if you keep whatever you think you're seeing to yourself."

The man nodded wordlessly, and Sinclair pulled a wad of cash from his pocket, handing it over. The gardener didn't hesitate, taking it and backing out of the shed, closing the door behind him.

Sinclair pinched the bridge of his nose. "Fuck." He turned to face us. "Pull yourselves together and get your asses back to the party, *separately.*"

He stalked out, slamming the door behind him.

Pres and I glanced at each other, bursting into laughter.

"I love my brother, but fuck, he has a stick up his ass."

I grimaced, reaching for a packet of paper towels on a shelf to clean myself up. When I was done, he reached for me, tugging me against him. "I thought railing you the other night might have dislodged it, but no luck."

Screwing up my nose, I pushed up on my toes and kissed him hard. "I'll see you back there, big guy."

He grinned back at me as I slipped out of the shed, wandering across the grass as though I hadn't just let my smoking hot stepbrother nail me in a maintenance shed.

When I made it back to the party, I stopped by the bar for a glass of champagne, making my way through the crowd to Arena's side.

"And where have you been?" she asked with a knowing smile.

"Just out for a walk in the grounds."

"A walk? That's what you're going with?"

I was going to reply with something innocent, when

Presley reappeared, strolling into the party with his sunglasses covering his eyes and his shirt still open. He'd busted all the buttons, he had no way of closing it up again. Clearly he was happy to roll with it.

"Bitch, you have got to be kidding me," Arena snorted, unable to contain her laughter.

I swatted her on the arm. "I have no idea what you're saying right now."

"So you had nothing to do with the fact Presley's incredible body is out for all to see right now?"

I shook my head, taking a sip of my drink. "Nope. I don't know anything about it."

"Hmmm," Arena said in a tone that showed just how much she didn't believe me. "I wonder why broody brother number one keeps glaring at you like he doesn't know if he wants to murder you or make you moan."

My head snapped in Sinclair's direction, and sure enough, his hard gaze was trained on me, his jaw ticking. We both turned back to Presley, as Byron marched over, his expression livid.

"Oh shit, hold this for me." I thrust my glass at Arena and threaded through the crowd, reaching Presley and Byron at the same time Dacre did.

Byron's hard voice was pitched low, tearing into Presley.

"Woah, Byron, ease up." Dacre slipped between his father and his brother, putting space between them.

"Your brother is drunk *again*," Byron snapped. "And making foolish decisions *again*."

Presley laughed. "What foolish decision have I made this time?"

Byron's eyes narrowed on him. "It's clear from the tattered state of your clothes, you've been nailing some dumb slut."

Presley's expression hardened. "You don't know what you're talking about."

Sinclair appeared at his father's side. "Let's dial this

down, there's no reason to cause a scene. So, he had a few drinks? He's fine, Byron."

Presley stood tall despite being half dressed, his hands in his pockets, anger radiating off him at Byron's unknowing slight against me.

"Get out of here before you embarrass this family any further." Byron turned to me. "And you, young lady…"

I blanched in surprise at being on the receiving end of his outrage.

"Your mother told me you had far too many drinks today. So maybe you and I need to have another discussion about what it means to be part of this family and the standards you're expected to live up to."

He didn't wait for a response, stalking off back in the direction of his friends.

"You're really one of us now," Dacre said, shaking his head. "You've managed to piss off Byron Aston. Isn't it fun?"

Presley swiped a drink from a passing tray, downing it in one go. "It's a fucking blast."

"Alright, that's enough," Sinclair said, taking the glass from Presley and discarding it on a nearby table. "We're leaving before you can enrage Byron any more than you already have."

Presley sighed. "Whatever. These parties are mind-numbing anyway."

We all headed for the exit, Dacre slapping Presley on the shoulder as we walked.

"I think that might be the seventeen tequilas you downed, bro."

CHAPTER 29

'd just climbed into bed when my door opened, a dark figure stalking across the room.

"Sinclair, what are—?"

Before I could finish the question, he scooped me up and tossed me over his shoulder.

"What the hell are you doing?" I asked, gripping the back of his shirt.

His hand connected with my ass in a hard slap. "Be quiet or you'll wake the whole fucking house."

He carried me into his room, kicking the door shut behind us and tossing me on the bed. My heart was slamming against my sternum and heat was pooling between my legs at his dominance. I wasn't wearing much, just a sleep shirt, leaving my legs bare to him.

"Don't you think your girlfriend would have a problem with you man-handling me and tossing me on your bed?"

Sinclair started unbuttoning his shirt, staring down at me. "She's not my fucking girlfriend."

I pressed up to my elbows. "Excuse me? Did you two break up?"

"She was never my girlfriend."

I glared at him. "The two of you put on a pretty good show for two people who aren't dating."

"That's the point. It's a show."

My eyes landed on his ridiculously hot body as he removed his shirt at a torturously slow pace and all I could do was watch as he undressed. He tossed his shirt to the floor and my mouth slackened in awe.

His body was a work of art. Not just from the rippling muscles all over each inch of him, but the tattoos. He'd kept his shirt on last time we'd done this, keeping his body a secret from me.

"You've had that hidden away under there the whole time?" My eyes ran over the intricate designs running over his shoulder, pecs, and arms, stopping just before his wrists. The piercing had been surprising enough the first time he'd fucked me, and I was dying to feel it inside me again. But the tattoos were something else.

He smirked. "Did you think I was too serious to have tattoos?"

Actually, that was exactly what I'd believed. I'd always thought of Sinclair as the enigma. The brother who revealed nothing with his expressions or his words. But he was revealing it all now, showing me all the words and symbols that meant something to him, so much so that he'd inked them permanently on his skin.

These guys never failed to surprise me. Dacre, who looked like a bruiser but had the soul of a sensitive artist underneath it all. And Presley with his charm and bravado, who deep down was a damn golden retriever, desperate to be loved.

But Sinclair... *damn*. Sin had surprised me the most. Mr. Buttoned-up Suit with a secret ink stash.

"Why do you hide them?"

They were all strategically placed, nothing visible near his neck or wrists, which was how he'd been able to hide them from me and the rest of the world. He shifted slightly and I got a peek at more covering his back.

He stared down at me, stroking my cheek like a favored toy. "Because people don't take you seriously in my world when you're covered in art. They write you off as some kind of deadbeat stereotype. That's not who I am, so I'll look the part and play their game if it gets me ahead, but only to a point."

I reached for him, tracing the lines along his pecs and forearms. "You're full of surprises."

The corner of his mouth hitched. "Oh Princess, you don't even know the half of it." His gaze hardened as he stared down at where my sleep shirt had ridden up my thighs, exposing me. He flicked open his belt buckle, whipping the leather from his waist. "Now are you going to shut the fuck up or am I going to have to tie you up?"

I stilled, mouth hanging open at his words.

I'd be a goddamn liar if I said I hadn't dreamed about this moment. Seeing Sinclair shirtless, a leather belt in his hand, as he stared down at me expectantly, had me hotter than I'd ever been.

I lifted my chin, gaze locked on his. "You're going to have to tie me up."

That ghost of a smile twitched at his lips again, and it was my undoing. "My fucking pleasure."

Taking the bottom of my sleep shirt in his hands, he whipped it off over my head and tossed it to the floor. Then he gripped both my ankles and flipped me over so I was face-down on the mattress, pulling my hands behind my back and looping his belt around my wrists, pulling it tight.

Running a slow hand down my spine, he gripped my waist, tugging me back toward him so my ass was in the air, my cheek pressed to the bed.

He dropped one knee to the edge of the bed, leaning over me so his lips were a breath away from mine. "You've been driving me fucking crazy for months. Now that I've fucked you, you're in my damn blood. I'm taking it whenever I want."

My insides heated at his words, pooling between my legs. Everything about this was both unexpected and so fucking hot.

"Wearing the shit that you do," Sinclair said, smoothing a hand down my back again and over my exposed ass. "Running your mouth. Fucking my goddamn brothers."

His eyes were hard as they assessed me, just like they always were. Only this time there was something else there.

Hunger.

"It's my turn now, Princess."

Our gazes locked, and I nodded.

I wanted this. Had been waiting for this.

It was all the permission he needed, hand gliding over my ass to slide over my slick seam. "You're so fucking wet."

I'd never been tied up before, but everything about this was turning me on. His dominance, his need, being wanted by him. It was what I'd needed all along.

I had tried to resist the pull of his gravity, but it was no use; I was too damn attracted to him. He was an endless pool, and I was ready to drown.

He dipped a finger inside of me, and I sucked in a breath.

"Sinclair," I whispered, pleasure simmering through me. I wanted to arch my back at his touch, but I couldn't move, my hands too tight behind me. "Sin, please."

I needed *more*. So much more. Tying me up had been all the foreplay required, I was ready to go and wanted him buried deep inside me.

"Say it again." The command in his voice made my pulse race.

I forced my eyes open, his finger teasing over my clit and making me squirm beneath him. "Sin, please."

I couldn't care less that I was begging. I'd beg all night.

He'd barely touched me, and I was already addicted. One word was playing on repeat in my mind.

More. More. More. More.

"I want you. Inside me. Right now."

Without warning, his fingers thrust inside me, and I cried out at the intrusion, desire flooding my body for the second time. He worked my body over with his fingers, two inside me, his thumb working over my clit and making me cry out.

I was so close to coming when he suddenly pulled out and I cried out for a completely different reason.

"What the hell are you doing? Stop teasing me."

He laughed quietly and I wish I could have seen it. But he was still behind me, his hands caressing my hips and ass as he spoke. "You've teased me for months and now you think you can just demand what you want?"

"Yes," I ground out, trying to see over my shoulder at the bulge I knew was tenting his boxers right now. "Because you want it, too."

Dropping a knee to the edge of the bed on either side of me, he leaned over me, his warm body covering my exposed back. His eyes dropped to my mouth. "You're damn right I do."

He flipped me on my side, closing his mouth over mine.

It was a high I'd never experienced before. Not with Dacre or Presley. This was completely different. When his tongue slid into my mouth I moaned at the contact, desperate to touch him. To run my hands through his hair. To run my nails down his back.

I tried to move, but he stood tall, flipping me back over so my ass was in the air once more. "I'm the one who gets to touch. And taste. And feel."

He punctuated the words with a kiss between my legs, tongue swirling over my clit, driving me to the edge of madness.

"Sinclair, please!"

He let out a small laugh. "So fucking needy when you're not getting what you want."

His tongue circled me again, and my desperation reached new heights.

"Tell me what you want, Princess."

His fingers pushed inside me, everything on display from where he knelt behind me.

"I want you to fuck me."

He stilled. "But we're just getting started."

"I don't care. Do you know how many nights I've waited for this? How much I want you? Once wasn't enough. You're not the only one who's been desperate. I *need* you to fuck me, Sinclair. Now."

His fingers disappeared from my body, and I screamed into the bed in frustration. The sound of his zipper filled the room, then he was lined up at my entrance.

"I'm not going to be gentle."

I glanced at him over my shoulder. "I don't want you to be."

He ran a finger through my slick folds, brushing against my clit and making me jerk at the contact. "Fuck, you're glistening, Princess."

"Please, Sin," I begged, almost close to tears.

The desperation in my tone must have worked.

"You sure you can handle it?" he teased, gripping himself and rubbing the tip against my slick clit.

I bit my lip at the sensation rippling through me and nodded vigorously. "I can handle it. I want it so badly."

"Then I'll give it to you."

He pushed inside me with one hard thrust that sent me sliding up the bed, but he gripped my waist, tugging me back down on him. We both moaned together at the feel of him buried inside me. He pulled out, the piercing gliding along my inner walls, and I wanted to tear my fucking hair out. I'd never been edged like this, and it was making me so fucking desperate for his cock I'd do just about anything.

He thrust inside me again, all the way to the hilt, his pelvis slamming against my ass. My body jolted up the bed and I cried out at the pleasure that ripped through me. "Oh my god, Sinclair."

He pulled his hips back, sliding out, then thrusting back in. "Oh fuck, you're so fucking tight."

I clenched around him, and his fingers tightened at my waist, his grip possessive.

"I'm not going fucking slow," he ground out, thrusting in again.

And I moaned over and over as the pleasure built. "I don't want you to."

It was all the permission he needed, holding onto my hips and ramming into me over and over. He loosened one hand, gliding it up my spine. His fingers splayed across my scalp as he took my hair in his fist, tugging my head back.

"Are you going to scream my name when you come, Dempsey?"

He thrust in hard, the combination of him filling me and the pain in my scalp forcing a deep guttural moan out of me. "Yes!"

"You fucking better."

I knew he'd be dominant in the bedroom, but the reality of it was so goddamn consuming. He was possessing me, in every possible way. And all I wanted was more.

His hips worked overtime, slamming in and out of me roughly until I was on the edge of combustion.

"Sinclair, don't stop, I'm going to come…"

His grip tightened in my hair. "Oh, I'm not stopping. I won't stop until you're screaming my name."

Pleasure built inside me until I couldn't contain it any longer. He slammed into me again and I exploded, screaming his name just like he wanted.

"Fuck yes..." he grunted, punishing me, drawing every inch of pleasure from my body. "Fuck yes, say my fucking name."

"Sinclair," I whimpered. "Oh my god, Sinclair."

He let go of my hair, only to slide his fingers along my scalp to tighten his grip again, owning me entirely.

"You're so fucking hot like this, on all fours and tied up for me, like my own personal fuck toy."

I looked back at him, his face contorted in pleasure, the hard length of him still thrusting inside of me. The pleasure was building again, and I knew I could go a second time.

"I'll let you rail me like this any time you want, so long as you make me come that hard."

His jaw clenched and he thrust once... twice... three times so hard I moved up the bed, then he was pulsing inside of me, the sight, the feel, the sounds sending me over the edge a second time. We came together, moaning each other's names.

When he released my hair and my waist, I collapsed on the bed.

My wrists were chaffed from being bound by the belt, but I didn't care.

I was so thoroughly fucked.

Sinclair pulled out, reaching for the belt at my wrists and loosening it until it fell away. Then he flipped me over, climbing over me until his warm body was pressed against mine and he hovered over me.

"You're so fucking beautiful trussed up like that for me, Dempsey."

I smiled a deeply satiated smile. He reached for the blanket, pulling it up and over us, then wrapped me in his arms in a tender way I never would have expected from him.

I've never slept so well.

———

I woke up the next morning in Sinclair's bed.

Alone.

A part of me wasn't surprised, it tracked for someone like him. But that didn't stop the disappointment and rejection that reared inside me as I stared at the empty side of his bed.

Did that mean he regretted what we'd done last night? Where the hell did we stand now?

My rejection turned to anger as I threw my sleep shirt over my head. I marched into his bathroom, swiping his toothbrush and toothpaste from the vanity and using them both. Our mouths had been all over each other, if he had a problem with me using his toothbrush, he'd just have to get over it. He shouldn't have left me unattended in his room.

Hustling down the stairs, I stormed into the dining room.

"Woah, someone's on the fucking warpath this morning," Presley said from where he sat at the table with Dacre, Byron, and my mother, biting down on his grin. "Who's in the line of sight today?"

"Sinclair."

Dacre and Presley shared an amused look.

"Library," Dacre offered.

Ignoring our interaction, my mother frowned at me. "Dempsey, that outfit isn't appropriate breakfast attire. Please go upstairs and change, I can see your nipples through that shirt."

Byron frowned over the top of his tablet.

I pressed my hands to my hips. "You know what isn't appropriate breakfast conduct, Mother? Discussing someone else's nipples."

I didn't give her a chance to respond, turning on my heel and heading for the library. I burst through the doors, stopping short at finding Sinclair shirtless in nothing but grey sweatpants. He was man-spreading on one of the low leather couches, a book in one hand, a coffee cup in the other, and glasses I'd never even seen him wearing sitting on his face.

Fuck me, he was gorgeous. I was at risk of melting into a puddle on the library floor. He was a book nerd's dream man right now.

But I was still epically pissed at him.

"Sneaking out of your own bedroom and leaving me to wake up alone is a little low, don't you think?"

He glanced up. If I'd startled him it didn't show, but that was Sinclair—emotions chronically locked down.

"There was no sneaking, I walked out as usual."

I studied every inch of his face, trying desperately to read him. Clearly, he noticed my desperation and threw me a lifeline.

"I didn't want to wake you. You looked like you were finally having a decent sleep."

I pulled back, surprised. Not waking me was a kindness I wouldn't have expected from him. And what did he mean I'd been *finally* having a decent sleep? Did he know I got up most nights, worrying about the state of my life?

Whatever the reasons, a question filled my head…

Did Sinclair care about me?

He placed his coffee cup on the table to his right, the book following. Then he stared up at me and patted the couch beside him.

I hesitated for the briefest moment only, striding over and curling up at his side. His arm came around me in a move that was uncharacteristically sweet. All of his actions this morning were throwing me for a loop.

At least it answered one of the questions plaguing me when I woke alone in his bed. We weren't going back to exactly how it had been before last night, and I loved it.

"I didn't mean to leave you to wake up alone." He leaned in and pressed his warm lips to my forehead, and I nearly expired on the spot.

What on earth was happening right now?

Whatever it was, I was loving every second of affectionate

Sinclair. And it made it easier to ask something that had been playing on my mind.

I glanced up at him. "What you said last night, about you and Veda…"

He ran the hand that wasn't wrapped around me through his hair, sighing.

"You said she isn't your girlfriend. That she never was. How is that true?"

His eyes locked with mine, clearly assessing how much to tell me.

"Veda and I have an arrangement."

I frowned. "What kind of arrangement?"

If it was the friends-with-benefits kind, the raging green jealousy monster was going to make one hell of an appearance. I knew it wasn't fair; I'd slept with other people before I knew Sinclair, Presley, and Dacre. Hell, I'd let Trenton fuck me in the garden on my first night. But now that I'd had them, the thought of any of them being with anyone else had me instantly possessive in a way I'd never been before.

"The kind where we pretend to be together. For Veda's sake."

I sat up. "See, you're answering my questions, but things aren't getting any clearer."

He chuckled, toying with the sleeve of my t-shirt. Seemed this new Sinclair had to be touching me at all times, just like Presley. Dacre, too, really. I didn't hate it one bit.

"Veda's a friend. Three years ago, I learned something about her, and she asked me for help. I agreed and we've been pretending to be together ever since." He reached out to tuck my hair behind my ear, his touch whisper soft, and I wanted to melt into him.

"Why would you do that? You're hot as fuck, you could get any woman you want. Why would you pretend to be with her?"

A slow, satisfied smile spread across Sinclair's face. "You think I'm hot as fuck?"

I rolled my eyes. "You know you're disgustingly handsome."

He pounced on me in an instant, his strong body overpowering mine and forcing me back on the couch until I was pinned under him. His elbows rested on either side of my head, and he hovered over me. "Did you just roll your eyes at me again?"

I nodded wordlessly, fighting my smile at his low, commanding voice. He leaned down, mouth ready to close over mine, but I stilled him with two fingers to his lips.

"I want to do... *all that*..." I said, motioning to his mouth. "But I want to understand what I'm involved in."

Sinclair's expression turned serious. "If I explain it to you, I'm trusting you with information that isn't mine to share. Information I swore I never would."

I cupped his jaw with my hand. "I promise you I'll never repeat it."

He stared down at me, eyes locked on mine, then he nodded.

"Veda is gay."

My face lit with surprise.

"She has a girlfriend, also someone in our community. But if her parents ever found out, they'd cut her off and disown her." His expression filled with anger. "They're absolute fucking bigots, particularly her pathetic excuse for a father. They'd turn her out on the street if they found out her truth."

"So how did you find out?"

He stared at my mouth like it was a reward he couldn't wait to taste. "I walked in on her and her girlfriend at an event. She begged me not to say anything. When we talked about it later, she asked me to help her with her parents, pretend to be with her to stop them suspecting anything else."

I stared back at him. "And you agreed?"

He nodded as if it was a given. "She's my friend. I've known her since I was three. Veda has been there through everything with my parents, my brothers. She knows me just as well as Dacre and Pres do."

The jealousy tried to unfurl inside me, but I clamped it down. She'd been a support for him before I'd even known him.

"Does that mean... you and she... you've never..." I struggled to ask the question I desperately wanted an answer to.

Sinclair smirked. "Are you asking if I've ever had her pinned beneath me like this?"

I bit my lip, nodding sheepishly.

"Never." His head dipped, his mouth brushing over the sensitive skin at my throat, making me shiver.

He pulled back. "Are we done talking about this? Can I fuck you now?"

I grinned back at him. "Absolutely."

CHAPTER 30

"It all makes sense now," Trenton said, appearing at my back. He kept his voice low, so only I could hear.

We were at yet another social event to raise money for something, this one at Trent's own house, which I hated to begrudgingly admit was palatial. It was still smaller than the Aston's though. Only a damn Saudi Prince would have a compound bigger than the Astons.

But it wasn't just the fact that this gathering was at Trenton's house that made it borderline unbearable. It was that Sinclair, Dacre, and Presley were all in the room looking like walking sex dreams in their tuxedos, and I couldn't touch them. Couldn't so much as smile at them for too long in case someone noticed and suspected even for a second that there was anything going on between us.

It was slowly killing me. I was a heartbeat away from dragging whoever was closest to the bathroom and dropping to my knees.

Instead, I was stuck dealing with Trent and his insufferable ego. How many times did I have to cut this guy down and push him away before he stopped coming back for more?

Was the beating Dacre gave him on my behalf not enough for him?

I changed my mind. For my birthday I was going to ask Byron to pay for the scientific research into time travel, so I could go back in time and never even entertain the idea of hooking up with a weasel like Trent for even a second.

I stiffened at the feel of him behind me now, trapping me between him and the bar. "What makes sense now? You finally work out how to do basic math? I'm thrilled for you."

I turned, lifting my elbow to catch him in the stomach as I did, making him grunt in pain. He recovered quickly; the way his eyes tightened at the corners was the only indication that I was pissing him off.

His fake society smile remained as he glanced around us, lowering his voice and leaning in. "It finally makes sense why you're acting like such a frigid bitch around me."

I scowled at him, moving to walk away, but his fingers closed around my wrist. Fear instantly flooded me at the memory of those fingers wrapped around my throat, cutting off my air supply, and I jerked my hand away.

"Touch me again and I'll make you bleed."

A smile spread across his face and then he outright laughed. The sound sent a hot burst of anger raging inside me. Did he think I was joking?

"Well, look at that. Someone's certainly stepped into her role as an Aston. Didn't take long for that family arrogance to kick in." He shook his head in a move so condescending I wanted to slap him. "It doesn't suit you, Dempsey. You should try behaving like a lady."

I took a deep breath, sucking it in and blowing it out. I was a step away from crushing his toes beneath my very sharp heel. "And you should stop behaving like a desperate, panting dog, and take no for an answer when it's offered repeatedly."

His eyes hardened with anger in an instant. "No need to

get bitchy because you're sleeping with your stepbrother. Don't tell me Dacre isn't dicking you right?"

A full body chill washed over me, the blood draining from my face.

How the fuck does he know that?

"Oh, don't look like such a helpless fucking doe." Trenton glanced around the room again, the smarmy fucking smile still there. "It's not hard to work out. The meathead has been staring at you all night like you have a gold-plated pussy. He hasn't looked at anyone with that stupid puppy dog look on his face since Belinda."

I had no idea who Belinda was, but I wasn't about to let him know that.

"I don't know what the hell you're talking about, and clearly, neither do you."

Refusing to listen to him spin more of his smarmy bullshit, I turned on my heel and walked away from him, edging through the crowd. I stopped near the entrance of the hallway, downing half my drink and trying to catch my breath.

It didn't matter that I'd stayed away from my stepbrothers all night. Trenton had still worked it out, which was a fucking disaster.

Discarding my glass on the edge of a nearby art bust in a move my mother would kill me for, I ducked into the hallway towards the bathroom. Just as I approached, the door opened and Dacre stepped out.

His brow pinched, his face etched with concern as he scanned my face. "Hey, what's going on? Are you okay?"

I shook my head and Dacre instantly reached for me, backing us into the bathroom and locking the door behind him.

His hands caressed my arms and shoulders, soothing me. "What happened? Talk to me."

"Trenton," was all I got out.

His expression instantly shuttered. "What has that fuck-stick done now? Did he touch you again?"

Rage lit his eyes and he reached for the door handle in an instant, ready to storm out there and defend me. I clasped my hand over his, stilling him.

"No, I'm fine. He just..."

Dacre frowned. "He just what?"

I gazed up at him, biting the inside of my cheek. "He said he thinks you and I are fucking. He claims you haven't looked at anyone the way you've been looking at me all night since someone called Belinda."

Dacre's expression twisted. "What, has he been fucking staring at you all night? That's the only way he could know who's watching you. Fucking creep."

I nodded, leaning back against the bathroom counter and gripping the edge. I was a ball of stress right now at the idea that Trenton might out us. "Except he's right, we are..." I waved a hand back and forth between us, bringing a smirk to Dacre's face.

"Fucking?" he offered with a wry grin.

"Yes! What are we going to do?"

He moved in close, taking my face in his hands and tilting it so our gazes locked. "Nothing. It's petty gossip from a little bitch who's obsessed with you. Who's he going to tell?"

"A tabloid. A gossip site. Any kind of press."

He scoffed. "And say what? He suspects we're sleeping together? Unless he has a picture or video of us going at it, they're not going to give a shit."

A smile broke free at the ridiculous thought. "Wouldn't put it past Trent to be camped outside my bedroom window with a long lens camera."

Dacre dropped his hips against mine, my breath catching at his hardening cock between us. "I'd fucking kill him," he muttered low and menacing, then covered his mouth with mine in a slow and sensual kiss completely at odds with the harsh words he just uttered.

Of all three of them, Dacre was the one with the most contradictions. A gentle brute. A sweet yet vicious guard dog. He loved hard and rough, just like his outward demeanor, but he had a bigger heart than anyone I'd ever met.

And I couldn't get enough of him.

I broke the kiss when my heart rate started to pick up, pulsing between my legs. "We can't do this here. Trenton already suspects us, we can't get it on in his house and prove him right."

Dacre's heated gaze scanned my face, like he couldn't decide where to kiss me first. "I don't give a fuck about him. My girl is stressed, and I know getting her off is going to make it all better. So, get on the counter."

Indecision kept me rooted to the spot. Doing this here in Trenton's house when he already had questions about us was monumentally stupid. But all my solid decision-making went out the window when it came to Dacre. To any of them.

Tired of waiting for me, Dacre gripped my hips, lifting me off the ground and depositing me on the edge of the counter. He slowly dropped to his knees in front of me and his hands dipped beneath the hem of my dress, slowly trailing up my calves, then round to caress my thighs, taking the hem of my dress up with him.

"I'm dying to get my mouth on you, Bambi."

His words had heat pooling between my legs. He hitched my dress underneath me to keep it out of the way, his hooded gaze meeting mine. "No panties. What a good fucking girl."

I bit my lip, staring down at the reverent way he caressed my skin. He parted my knees, biting his bottom lip at the sight of me spread wide for him.

"So wet for me already." Then he ducked his head between my legs, the first flick of his tongue making me moan.

He pulled back, a satisfied smile spread across his face. "As much as I love the noises you make when I'm eating you out, you have to be quiet if you don't want to get caught."

Without waiting for a response, his mouth closed over my clit, sucking, licking, teasing me in an endless assault on my senses. I moaned his name over and over as quietly as I could. My fingers threaded through his hair, gripping it tight and I rocked my hips against his mouth. "Fuck, Dacre. You're so damn good at this."

He teased me with his tongue over and over until I was ready to combust.

"Let go, baby. Come all over my tongue and give us both what we want."

As soon as his mouth was back on me, he suctioned over my clit and my hips shot forward, an orgasm tearing through me.

"Oh my god, Dacre, yes!"

He lapped at me as I rode the wave and I fell back on both hands against the counter, totally satiated. Dacre climbed to his feet, swiping at his mouth. "Fuck you taste sweet, Bambi."

He reached for a towel, cleaning me up and tossing it in the trash. Then he righted my dress and offered me both his hands to help me off the counter.

"Now run along and play your perfect daughter role, and act like your stepbrother didn't just tongue fuck you in the bathroom like a good little whore." He patted me on the ass as we left the bathroom. His words rushed through me, making my pulse pound between my legs all over again.

Maybe after one more drink I'd convince him for round two.

Only this time, I'd make him fuck me in Trenton's bed.

CHAPTER 31

pushed harder, propelling my body faster through the water. Sinclair was gliding at my side, trying to reach the wall before me.

I managed to edge him out and touch just before him. I planted my feet on the bottom of the pool, panting with exertion. "When you said you wanted to work out with me, I thought you meant you'd actually be giving me a contest," I teased, eyes snagging on the drops of water clinging to his perfect pecs and shoulders.

God, I wanted him every minute of the day. Even now, wet and tired, I wanted to climb his body and cling to him, letting him thrust inside me until we were moaning each other's names.

His mouth hitched at the corner, and he shook his head. "Despite you trying to sass me with that fucking mouth of yours... I'll do anything with you, if it means being near you."

I stilled at his words, studying him. "Who knew Sinclair Aston was such a simp?"

He closed the space between us, my body instantly

heating when he crowded me against the side of the pool, caging me with a hand on either side of my head.

I wasn't about to push him away. Being trapped beneath his strong body was one of my favorite places to be.

He stared down at me, gaze filled with his usual intensity. "I keep my circle small and protect what's mine. If that makes me a simp, then I am."

I stared up at him, biting my lower lip, my heart pounding so hard against my sternum I was suddenly lightheaded.

"And yes," he said, gaze trained on my mouth. "You're part of that circle now. You're mine. And nobody fucks with what's mine."

A slow smile spread across my face. If you'd told me months ago that the stepbrother who I thought more likely to fight me than fuck me was calling me his, I would have dropped dead.

Sliding up the pool wall, I wrapped my arms around his neck and pressed my slick body to his, our mouths fusing. Wrapping an arm around my waist to hold me against him, he stood tall, and my legs closed around his waist.

"You still kiss like you're mad at me," I said, breaking away from him only to dive back in for more.

"I am mad." His lips landed on my throat, sucking on my skin and making me shiver. "Mad that we haven't been doing this since the day you got here."

His hand slipped between us, but I stilled him.

"I want you. All the time. But I want this to be more than just sex between us."

Those intense green eyes studied me. "It is more than sex between us."

I could feel it. Just like with Dacre and Presley, something had shifted between Sinclair and I the same way. Our connection was deeper than anything physical we could share between us. I cared about him, and I never wanted to be without him.

I prayed my mother and Byron never found out about us, because there was no way I was giving any of them up. I belonged to them. And they were mine.

But I wanted to know Sinclair. I needed to know what made him who he was and the *way* he was.

"Come to the hot tub with me?"

He nodded and I slid down his body, both us wading towards the steps. He climbed them, offering me his hand to help me out. Walking around to the other side of the pool, we moved behind the rock wall that held up the slide, stepping into the grotto cave beneath and slipping into the hot tub.

Hot water enveloped me, instantly warming my skin, and I groaned.

Sinclair levelled me with a flat stare. "Don't do that again or I'll have you naked up against the wall and then you'll never believe me when I say that I want you for more than how good you fuck."

I laughed. "I know you want me for more than that. But I feel like I barely know all three of you beyond what I've been told, or what little I've learned since I got here." I dropped down onto one of the bench seats under the water across from Sinclair. "And I want to know everything."

He leaned back, his head resting against the side of the tub, his dark hair falling into his eyes in a way that made him deeply irresistible. "Ask me what you want to know."

I stilled, studying him and weighing up whether I should ask what I wanted to.

"What was it like here before your mom left?"

Something flickered behind his eyes. "Way to ease into it, D."

"I'm sorry. We don't have to talk about it."

"I'll talk about it." His gaze dropped to the rippling water between us. "It was better when Mom was here. She cared about each of us, took the time to learn what we each needed from a mother." He glanced up at me. "Don't get me wrong, she could be self-obsessed and a raging bitch when she wanted to be, but she was a decent mom."

He ran a hand through his wet hair, lost in the memories.

"Presley was the most attached to her. Dacre was too, in his own way, but Presley has always been desperate to be loved. When she left… it broke him."

His face pinched with pain, and I pushed off the bench, gliding over to sit beside him and taking his hand under the water.

"Presley was young when my parents adopted him, but still old enough to remember his birth parents. Not fully, but enough to know he'd had a mom and he'd loved her. He latched on to Mom like a life raft, so when she and Byron split and she disappeared, even at sixteen, Presley lost it."

I shifted closer, desperate to hold him while he was lost in the memories. "Is that when he started drinking?"

He let out a humorless laugh. "Presley started drinking when he was thirteen. But when Mom left, he hit the bottle harder than ever, drugs too. What he's like now is nothing like he was then. He was coming home wasted every night. His football suffered and he would have been kicked off his high school team if Byron hadn't intervened and convinced them it was a bad move. But he sent Presley away because of it."

He stared down at his hands, swiping across the water.

"It was the first time since they'd been adopted that the three of us were apart. Dacre and I didn't know where he'd gone, Byron wouldn't tell us. We'd just lost our mother, and then our brother was taken away from us, too."

He looked at me, those intense green eyes haunted by feelings he'd buried.

"I'd handled it when Mom left, but when Presley was sent away, I shut down. I was freshman at Triple C, and I was supposed to be this model fucking son, but a part of me had been ripped out and sent away with him."

I cupped his cheek, pressing a kiss to his mouth. He kissed me back, his tongue sliding into my mouth, his kiss possessing.

There was nothing I could say to change the past or take the pain away. All I could do was be here for him. Offering him any small piece of comfort I could.

I pulled back, kissing him once more, my thumb stroking his cheek. "He's here now. And he's fine."

Sinclair let out another humorless laugh. "He's here, but is he any better?"

"He will be," I said firmly, voice filled with confidence. I didn't think I had the power to be some miracle balm that solved Presley's abandonment issues, but I'd be there for him. Make him feel so loved and included until there wasn't a doubt in his mind that he was safe.

A question gnawed at the back of my mind.

"What happened to Dacre when Presley was gone?"

Sin stared at the rippled water again, eyes unseeing. "Dacre was no better than me. He was suddenly thrown into high school politics without his ally. Pres was always the outgoing one, the life of the party who people flocked to. They still do. So, without him as an anchor, Dacre was aimless."

He blinked, shaking his head.

"He had friends, he didn't suddenly become an outcast overnight. But he disengaged."

He looked up at me, expression tortured.

"I could barely reach him, Dempsey, even at home. He locked himself away in his room, barely speaking. Just worked out, studied as much as he needed to get passing grades, and avoided life as much as possible. Byron couldn't stand it. He tried berating him, threatening to take things away from him, nothing worked. Dacre didn't care. He was so withdrawn, he was a shell."

My heart broke at the idea of Dacre barely living.

The three of them were bonded deeper than I'd ever real-ized. Even if they weren't connected by blood, they were more than brothers.

"Eventually I lost it. My family was torn apart and both my brothers were lost. I confronted Byron, told him to bring Presley back or I'd crush the fucking picture-perfect illusion of family he'd created for his precious image. It took two weeks of raging at him, but eventually Presley came back, more broken than before."

I pressed my lips together, willing away the tears that pricked the backs of my eyes.

"He didn't trust Byron anymore, none of us did. Screw up and you'd be sent away. All three of us were living in fear of being torn apart again. Presley had been betrayed by yet another adult who was supposed to care about him, which is why he does what he does now."

It made sense why Presley felt the way he did about Byron. And why his reactions to him were so volatile.

Sinclair's head dropped to his chest, and he scrubbed his hands through his hair. "I feel like I can't fucking breathe sometimes with the weight of it all. Because if I stop, if I take a fucking breath, it's all going to fall apart." He shook his head. "My brothers need me. Without me, Byron would be unchecked. He doesn't understand them or me. Doesn't understand how any of us think or what we've ever needed from him, even when we were kids. My brothers have always been there for me, and I've been there for them. It's why I work so hard, so I can protect them. If Byron ever decides to send Presley away, I'll be able to get him back. If Dacre wants to go to art school or open a damn gallery, and Byron cuts him off, I'll be able to cover it. My brothers have never let me down, and I'll never let them down." He looked up at me, a broken, battered boy staring back at me. "But the pressure of carrying this family, Dempsey… it's slowly fucking killing me."

I moved closer, climbing into his lap until I was straddling him. I took his face in my hands, his expression tortured.

"I just need them both to be okay. Because if they aren't, then I can't be okay."

Stroking his cheek, I stared down at him. "They will be okay. Presley has you, and Dacre. And he has me. And together we'll make him feel so loved, he'll wonder why he ever questioned where he belonged in this world."

Those green eyes had never been filled with more intensity than they were in this moment. "Where the fuck did you come from? And where the hell have you been?"

I offered him a small smile. "All that matters is that I'm here now and we're together. And we're going to stay together, no matter what Byron or my family or the world does to tear us apart."

His large palms smoothed over my waist and up my back, bringing me chest to chest with him.

"You're the best thing that's ever happened to us." He buried his face in my throat, murmuring over my skin. "You're exactly what I need to finally be able to fucking breathe."

I held him close, arms circled around his shoulders and held him against me.

We stayed that way for a long time, him wrapped in my arms, his lips caressing my skin. I'd made a promise to him out loud and I made one to myself now.

I'd never let anyone or anything come between us.

Because they needed me. And I needed them just as much.

CHAPTER 32

showed up at the library, as requested, the following night.

Presley instantly moved to meet me the moment I stepped into the room, taking my face in his hands and consuming my mouth with a deep, panty-melting kiss that made my heart stutter in my chest.

"Missed you, Sass."

I grinned back at him. "Missed you too, Superstar."

He slung an arm around my shoulders and walked me over to where Dacre was leaning against one of the shelves. Sinclair was sprawled in an armchair to his right, legs spread and hands splayed along the arms like he owned the place. As Byron's oldest heir, he technically, sort of, did own the place, but Sinclair owned any room he was in.

Dacre crossed his arms over his chest as Presley and I approached together. "Way to mark your territory, Pres."

"That was entirely the point," Sinclair said in his usually unreadable tone. Only this time I caught the flash of annoyance directed at his brother.

"I can't help it that I can't keep my hands off her." Presley tightened his arm around my neck, tugging me closer so he could kiss the top of my head.

"Try," Dacre offered.

Pres tilted his head like he was thinking about it. "You know, I don't really want to."

Dacre laughed, shaking his head. I slipped out from under Presley's arm, ignoring his sulking noise of protest, and moved to Dacre. Stopping in front of him, I stood between his legs, smoothing my hands up his hard pecs to wrap around his neck, then met his mouth in a searing kiss. The heat of his hands at my back and ass made my thighs clench, and I pulled away before we started something we couldn't finish right now.

"Get back here," Dacre growled, eyes lit with teasing.

"Not in front of the books," I said over my shoulder.

I stopped in front of Sinclair, staring down at him and waiting for some kind of permission to share an intimate moment with him. Dacre, Presley, and I had all had fun together. I knew where they stood about hooking up around each other. But Sinclair and I hadn't so much as kissed in front of his brothers. I had no idea what his boundaries were. Which was exactly why we were here to begin with—to lay out the rules when it came to this unique little situation we found ourselves in.

Sinclair's eyes locked with mine and he reached for my hand, pulling me closer. His other hand cupped the back of my thigh, bringing me onto his lap, my knees straddling his hips. Then he took my face in his hands and kissed me like the damn world was ending.

The kiss stole the strength from my body and the breath from my lungs.

A low whistle sounded behind us from Presley. "Fuck, that's hot."

I rolled my eyes at his voyeur tendencies, but didn't dare break the kiss. Not when it felt this good.

"Keep going, bro. I love the way her hips rock and she doesn't even realize it. It turns me on when she's doing it in my lap, but it's even hotter watching it."

Of course the brother with a fetish for public sex was getting off on watching me make out with his brother.

Sinclair's hands roamed my back, his broad fingers splayed across my shoulder blades and the middle of my spine, like he was waiting for me to pull away and he wasn't going to allow it. Presley moved closer until I could feel the heat of him at my back, strong hands landing on my shoulders. His fingers tightened over my skin, slowly massaging me while I kissed Sin.

"You're doing so good, Sass. Keep riding him just like that, baby."

Sinclair's hard length hit just the right spot between my legs, and I moaned into his mouth.

"Fuck," Dacre ground out from where he still sat a few feet away.

Presley's hands splayed over my collarbones, massaging my chest and the tops of my breasts. "Do you like that, Sass?"

I nodded, mouth still fused with Sinclair's, unable to break away even if I wanted to. Which I didn't. Nothing could tear me away from his hot mouth and practiced tongue. My hips rocked into him on their own accord, causing him to grunt into my mouth.

Presley's hands dipped lower, his fingers sliding into my bra and over my hardened nipples, sending sparks of delicious pleasure through me. He shifted closer, his jean-clad cock at the back of my head. He cupped my breasts and stroked my nipples, heightening my arousal. Having both Sinclair and Presley's hands on me was like a drug. I was a damn addict and needed more.

I opened my eyes, lips still fused with Sinclair's, and looked to Dacre, motioning for him to come to me. He pushed off the bookshelf, strolling over until he was at my side, his waistband at eye level.

Reluctantly I pulled away from Sinclair. Presley's hands were still buried in my shirt while I worked Dacre's cock free from his jeans. He stared down at me, expression full of heat, as I stroked his cock in my hand.

I turned back to Sinclair, making sure to keep a steady pace for Dacre. Sin's eyes were hooded, his cheeks flushed, and he reached for me again, mouth instantly claiming mine. His hips rocked in time with mine, both of us jolting every time the tip of his cock nudged my entrance through our clothes. Presley resumed his massage of my breasts, sending my senses into overdrive.

One brother in my mouth and between my legs. One driving me insane with the way he'd caged me in and was working me over. The last thrusting into my hand like he couldn't get enough.

It had never crossed my mind that things would play out this way between us all, but now that it had, there was no turning back. I wanted all of them. And if they were going to give themselves to me all at once, I was going to take it.

Sinclair's hands moved to my thighs, rising higher and taking my short skirt with him.

"You going to let me in, Dempsey?" he murmured against my mouth.

I nodded, and Dacre cursed under his breath. Presley's hands tightened over my breasts, giving them a hard squeeze. I didn't slow the pace of my hand, bringing Dacre along with me with all the sensation and arousal I felt when Sinclair reached between us to unzip his pants, freeing his steel cock. He didn't hesitate, shoving my panties aside and thrusting inside me.

I cried out, my grip tightening around Dacre. He pitched forward, hands white-knuckling the broad side of the armchair.

"Fuck, Dempsey, you've got my dick in a chokehold. I love it, baby. Show me how good Sin is making you feel."

I rocked my hips harder, Sinclair thrusting deeper, and I moaned each of their names.

"God, this is so fucking hot," Presley muttered from above me, shoving my top and bra down under my breasts.

Sin's gaze dropped to my chest, mesmerized by every sway and bounce of my breasts when he thrust inside me.

Presley moved around to the other side of the armchair, near Sinclair's shoulder.

"I need more, baby. You're going to take care of me too, right?" Presley unzipped his jeans, pulling his cock free and giving it a long tug.

Of course the big needy baby was asking me that. I loved how much he wanted me and there was no way in hell I wasn't going to take care of him.

I nodded, opening wide when he rubbed the tip of his cock over my lips. Swallowing him down, I ran my tongue along the underside of his hard length.

I was so full, so overwhelmed, my senses were in overdrive. Presley filled my mouth while Sinclair thrust deep inside me, and Dacre's pulsing length moved in my hand.

I'd never been more turned on or desperate to make all three of them come.

Dacre reached out, his rough hand squeezing and palming my exposed breast.

"That's a good girl," Sinclair said, his voice low and rough. He gripped my hips, staring down at his cock thrusting in and out of me. "You going to get us all off, Dempsey? Let us use this hot little body like a cum rag?"

His words were filthy, demeaning. But they only made me hotter and needier.

I nodded, taking Presley deeper, rocking my hips harder, and stroking Dacre faster.

Presley and Dacre tipped their heads back in unison,

groaning at the ceiling, and the sight and sound of it made me feel more powerful than I ever had. It was *me* making these big, angry men moan my name. They wanted me, and I wanted to please them any way I could.

A minute later, I was ready to combust. My insides were like liquid heat, Sinclair's punishing thrusts pushing me higher and higher.

I took Presley all the way to the back of my throat until I gagged and he swore, caressing my hair. "Such a good little slut, Dempsey. You know just how I like it."

My orgasm tore through me like a lightning bolt at his dirty words, and the overwhelming feeling of their hands on me. My pussy tightened around Sinclair and he gripped my waist, his cock pulsing inside me as he came along with me. Presley and Dacre were next, Pres shooting his load down my throat, while Dacre's hand closed over mine where it was wrapped around him, and he shot ropes of cum across my breasts.

I cried out as he painted my chest, all of my senses pinging with pleasure.

Being with all three of them was the hottest thing I'd ever experienced. And I wanted to spend the rest of my life doing it over and over again.

The room was still, our heavy breaths the only sound.

Presley slipped from my mouth, tucking himself back in his jeans with a grin and a loving stroke of my hair. Dacre leaned down and kissed the top of my head. "You're perfect."

I smiled up at him as he zipped up.

"I didn't think we'd end up having group sex when we came in here," I said lazily, feeling happier and more content than I could ever remember being.

"That wasn't the intention," Sinclair said distractedly. His eyes were locked on my breast, his thumb swiping through Dacre's cum and swirling it around my sensitive, aching nipple. The sight was so erotic, so hot, that I was instantly ready to go again.

My pussy clenched around him, still buried inside me, and his eyes shot to mine, darkening with heat.

I bit my lip, reluctantly climbing off him. "We have things we need to discuss. Like how all this is going to work." I motioned to the four of us. "Beyond the super hot way we just made it work, obviously."

He nodded holding my waist while I got to my feet on thoroughly fucked jelly legs.

Dacre appeared behind me, tissues in his hand. His body warmed my back while his arm came around me to clean his seed from my breasts. The gentle slide of his hand, the rough tissue, and the brush of his fingers over my nipples had me sighing, my eyes closing and head dropping back against his shoulder.

"If I dip my fingers under this hot skirt of yours, am I going to find you wet and ready for round two?"

I bit my lip and nodded, and he half-groaned, half-growled in my ear.

"Fuck porn," Presley said, dropping onto one of the couches and grinning in my direction. "Images of Dempsey are the only thing I'm beating off to anymore."

CHAPTER 33

“freaking love this song,” Arena said, trying to shake her ass in the passenger seat of my Bentley.

We were on our way to a party at some club downtown. I wasn't in the mood to drink too much tonight, so I'd decided to take my precious four-wheeled baby out for a spin. It was the first time I was going out with my stepbrothers now all of us had laid our cards on the table. I knew I had to keep my hands to myself, which was near impossible after I'd had a drink. Especially for me and Presley. Hence why I'd opted to be designated driver.

Arena was loving being my passenger princess, music playing way too loud, both of us hoarse from screaming along with the lyrics.

“And I'm *obsessed* with this car,” she said, running her hands along the creamy leather dash. “I am so glad you finally decided to take it out of the garage of dreams.”

“I am too.” I grinned at her, loving the feel of the engine beneath me. “And do you know the best part? We look damn good in it!”

Arena laughed, busting a move to the music. “We're going to have an epic time tonight.”

Just as she said it, my phone rang, killing the music and the vibe.

Gretel.

"Hi, Gretel."

"Hello, Miss Dempsey. I'm sorry to interrupt your night out, I wanted to let you know that another delivery has arrived for you. Twenty-five boxes this time."

"Twenty-five boxes?" Arena mouthed. "What did you order?"

I shrugged, shaking my head.

"Thanks, Gretel. Can you tell me what's in them?"

"Certainly." The line went quiet, a slight rustling in the background. "Peach lip gloss, Miss Dempsey."

My eyebrows crept up my forehead. My phantom package fiend had ordered me twenty-five cases of my favorite lip gloss?

"Ummm, okay… can you please store it for me?"

"Certainly can."

I thanked Gretel and hung up, the music instantly filling the car again.

"I know you love that lip gloss, but twenty-five boxes seems extreme," Arena said, eyeing me like I'd gone mad.

"I didn't order it. Someone keeps sending me boxes of stuff."

Arena pulled a face. "Like a really kind and considerate stalker?"

We both laughed.

"Exactly like that."

Twenty minutes later, after navigating downtown traffic we pulled into an outdoor parking lot a block from the club. I dropped the mirror, the lights illuminating my perfectly made-up face. Pulling my lip gloss (which I now had twenty-five cases of) from my purse, I swiped it across my lips, smacking them together and then folding the mirror away. Tossing the gloss back in my bag, I slid from the car in one graceful movement, eager to get inside and unwind with my best friend.

"God, I hope Trenton isn't in there. I've had my fill of entitled fuckers this week," I said to Arena across the top of the Bentley.

Arena went to respond, but her eyes snagged on something over my shoulder, widening with fear. "Dempsey!"

Rough hands gripped me from behind—one covering my mouth, the other wrapping around my arms, pinning them to my torso so I couldn't move. Panic flooded me and I thrashed against them, but they were too strong.

My desperate gaze landed on Arena as she bolted across the parking lot. I prayed she was headed for the boys and not just leaving me for dead or I'd kill her if I made it out of this.

I screamed into the hand covering my mouth, but the sound was muted and muffled, doing nothing to draw the attention of anyone on the street across the other side of the lot.

When I was lifted off my feet, my fight or flight response kicked in. I had no chance of running right now, but that didn't mean I was going to let this go down without a fight.

"It's you or we fuck up one of those pretty boy brothers of yours," a hard voice said in my ear.

No.

I didn't need to turn around to know it was Algor. My father was behind this.

While I didn't want Sinclair, Dacre, or Presley to be targets because of me, there was no way I could go back to my father either.

I thrashed with everything I had, trying to loosen the vice grip I was locked in, but it had no effect. Algor held me too tight, dragging me towards a black SUV with darkened windows at the end of the long row of cars.

Never let them take you to a second location.

The words I'd heard so many times in the true crime documentaries I binge-watched played over and over in my head, giving me an extra burst of energy.

Frantically kicking my legs, trying to swing my heels behind me, I connected with what I think were a set of balls. There was a groan from Algor and his arms loosened around me.

I fell to the ground, swearing at the instant pain in my knees, gravel embedded there. Ignoring the pain and my bleeding skin, I pushed up off the ground and bolted across the parking lot.

The sounds of thumping boots followed me a moment later, making my heart pound in my throat. I forced myself to pump my arms harder and move my feet faster. I was at a hell of a disadvantage wearing fucking heeled boots.

Just get to the street. Make it to the damn street.

I forced myself to put on another burst of speed, ignoring the pinching pain from my shoes or the blood running down my shins. I bolted past the boom gate at the entrance of the parking lot, rounding the side of the empty gate house and slamming straight into a hard body.

On the inside I whimpered at the thought that I had run straight into one of my father's men, my body recoiling.

But familiar hands gripped my upper arms, steadying me.

Sinclair's eyes were hard as stone as he stared down at me. "Where are they?"

His voice chilled me to the bone. I pointed behind me, my body starting to tremble from the adrenaline of trying to outrun my attacker.

Sinclair took off behind me into the parking lot, Dacre following him. Presley moved in front of me to take Sinclair's place and folded me into his arms.

My face pressed to his firm chest, and I let out a ragged breath.

"It's okay, you're safe now. Nobody can hurt you when you're with us."

I nodded against his chest, my body still shaking as the adrenaline ebbed away.

"Holy fuck, can we not just have one normal night around here?" Arena said, coming up to hug me from the other side.

I let go of Presley and flung my arms around her, her own tightening around me right back.

"Thank you for not leaving me for dead," I said, hands still shaking.

She let out a laugh. "I would never leave you for dead and you know it."

I pulled back, nodding. "Thank you for getting the guys. You saved my ass."

She gave me a sly smile. "It's such a hot ass, it was totally worth saving."

That pulled a smile out of me.

Sinclair and Dacre returned, their expressions murderous.

"How'd it go?" Presley asked over my head.

Dacre shook his head. "They're gone. Were already in their car."

Sinclair's body was vibrating with rage. "Peeled away like fucking snakes."

I reached for his hand, conscious of Arena's presence. "It's okay. I'm okay."

He glanced down at my bloodied knees. "I'd disagree."

I shrugged and Dacre held out his hand. "Keys?" Digging into my purse, I handed them over. "Let's get you home and cleaned up." His eyes were soft, masking his worry.

I loved the softer side of him, and I knew when we got home, he'd take care of me.

Presley went to wrap an arm around my waist to tuck me at his side, but I glanced at Arena, and he turned away.

Arena moved to my side instead, throwing an arm around my shoulders.

"Is there a reason someone keeps trying to chase you down?" Sinclair asked as we walked back to my Bentley, all of us somehow in silent agreement that the party was over for the night.

His gaze was probing, watching me like he suspected me of something.

I stiffened, shaking my head. "I have no idea."

Only I knew exactly the reason. My father was relentless, and he hated not getting his way. I was valuable to him, and he was ready to cash in.

I couldn't tell my stepbrothers that, though. I couldn't tell anyone that or they'd all be in danger. Although now that I'd escaped Algor, it seemed like they already were.

"Maybe it's because I have an uber rich stepdaddy now?" I offered as we reached my car.

Sinclair considered it. "It's a possibility. I'll look into it."

I wanted to beg him not to, given there was a chance he could uncover what I was really afraid of. But if I tried to warn him off, I'd only rile his suspicions even further.

"This isn't the first time someone has attacked you?" Arena asked, eyeing me with concern.

I shook my head.

"It's only, like, the third time," Presley said, opening the door to the backseat for me.

Arena thought about it for a second. "So, you're kind of like a cockroach at this point?"

I let out a short laugh.

Trust my best friend to lighten the mood and have me grinning when I'd just escaped an abduction.

"Yeah," I said, sliding into the backseat. "Something like that."

CHAPTER 34

slipped a diamond stud earring into my earlobe, securing the back, then reaching down to slide my feet into a pair of navy pointed stiletto heels.

In a surprise to no one, I was being dragged to another Cape Canyon social event by my mother. This one was a family affair, all of us required to attend in our finery. I'd given up trying to keep track of what charitable cause it was for this time. All of it was an excuse to party for the young people and a chance to schmooze each other with their wealth for the older crowd.

A knock sounded on my door, and I stilled, tipping my head back at the ceiling and sighing. It was going to be my mother popping in for her usual pre-event outfit perusal. If I didn't meet her standards, I'd be forced to change my dress or fix my face or select better shoes.

"Come in," I called, my voice flat.

The door opened and Dacre appeared, looking like he just stepped off the cover of a magazine in his tux. God, I wanted to strip him down and do very, *very* dirty things to him.

"You sound like you're headed to a funeral," he said with a smirk.

"I thought you were my mother."

He stepped into the room, followed by Sin and Pres.

"I'm insulted," Sin said, gaze running over me in that intense way of his. It made my cheeks heat.

Pres strolled over, pecking me on my heated cheek and giving me a look that said he knew exactly what had caused it.

"What have I done to be blessed by your collective hotness in my bedroom?" I asked, collecting the small purse from my desk and dropping my phone, lip gloss, and keys into it.

Dacre leaned a shoulder against the wall. "We have a gift for you."

Pres produced a discreet rectangle box from behind his back, handing it over.

"If it's the severed head of my enemy, I'll swoon."

Dacre chuckled. "So morbid, Bambi."

I grinned. "Let's be real, only Sinclair would be dark enough to gift me that."

He let out a laugh from where he'd settled on the end of the bed. "Just open it."

I flipped the lid on the box and found a small velvet drawstring bag inside. I glanced at each of them as I opened it and a hot pink sex toy fell into the palm of my hand.

"It's to go under your dress," Dacre said, hooded gaze heating.

"You want me to wear it tonight?"

All three of them gave me a nod and a thrill ran through me.

"This is the remote," Presley held up a small white control with matching hot pink buttons.

"There's a… wow," was all I could manage.

I strolled to the bathroom, shutting the door behind me. The toy was shaped like an almond the size of my palm, with a small rubber strap connected to each side so I could attach it to my panties and it wouldn't fall off. It had a small, ribbed suction hole that sat over my clit, with a vibrating dome at the other that sat right at my entrance.

Once it was in place inside my lavender lace underwear, I made my way back into the room.

"Can you see it?" I stood in front of my desk and did a twirl.

"No," Sinclair said from the bed, eyes trained on my ass.

The toy vibrated to life between my legs, and I sucked in a breath at the pleasure suddenly pulsing through me. I gripped the desk behind me, trying to ride the waves.

"Stop," I said, breathlessly.

Presley chuckled, hitting a button on the remote and halting the sensations in my core. I shot him a hard look.

"We had to make sure it works, Sass." His face was a picture of innocence.

And I thought this night was going to be boring. Not a chance now.

The ride to the event was filled with awkward silence. The four us were piled in the back of a limo with my mother and Byron. We'd been relegated to the far end, my mother and Byron taking the standard seats by the doors.

"How's business, Sinclair?" Byron asked, attention trained on his oldest son.

Sinclair replied, and the moment he did, the toy whirred to life. The vibrating between my legs made my knees snap together, and I squirmed in my seat.

"Dempsey, what on earth are you doing?" my mother sniped. "Stop the silly dance moves and sit like a lady."

The toy cut out and I stilled.

I ground my teeth. "Yes, Mother."

When I glanced at Dacre, Presley, and Sinclair in turn, each of them was fighting a smile.

Dacre had the remote at the house, but that didn't mean

he had it now. He easily could have palmed it off to Pres or Sin when we climbed in the car.

Five minutes later, thankfully without another vibration, we arrived at the event.

Rushing along the red carpet where the Aston names were called incessantly by photographers, the four of us headed for the bar.

"I never would have agreed to wear this thing if I knew you three were going to torture me with it."

Sinclair handed me a glass of chilled champagne. "That's entirely the point."

Dacre and Pres swapped amused smiles and the toy pulsed between my legs.

My hand shot out to grip Presley's arm. "Oh my god, stop it."

"She never says that when it's us getting her off," Pres said, keeping his amused voice low.

The toy died off and I stood tall.

"I hate this already."

Dacre raised a brow. "You won't be hating it when you're finally allowed to come."

The promise in his words had my thighs clenching.

Arena made her way through the crowd and my step-brothers excused themselves to give us some girl time.

"Try not to scream when it feels good," Sinclair said in my ear as he passed, the toy vibrating between my legs on a whole new level.

I let out a small cry of surprise and pleasure, and Sinclair smirked and walked away. The remote flashed in his hand as he slid it into his pocket and I wanted to call after him, but I knew better than to draw attention.

The vibrating died off, just as Arena reached me.

"My god, girl, you look insane!" Her gaze ran over my dress, then she peered at my face. "What's going on with you lately? You're glowing." Her eyes narrowed. "Are you getting laid and not regaling me with the dirty details like I do for you?"

I'm only boning my three disgustingly attractive stepbrothers every chance I get.

I laughed. "No, nothing like that."

"You better tell me the minute you get it on with anyone other than three-pump Trent." She took my hand, towing me through the crowd. "There's a crew from Triple C on the terrace."

The next hour passed in a blur of drinks, with me living on the edge wondering who had the remote to set off my panties any moment and if they would.

It went off when I was mid-conversation with a guy from one of my classes, making me lose my train of thought mid-sentence and squirming in my seat. When I'd looked around, Dacre inclined his head at me from where he stood across the terrace talking to a guy with a shaved head. There was a possessive gleam in Dacre's eye when he looked from me to the guy I'd been talking to.

It had happened again, right as I was accepting a fresh glass of champagne from a waiter. The surprise vibration made me flinch, and I spilled it all down the front of the waiter's uniform. That little gift had been from Presley.

Sinclair had waited until I was on the dance floor with one of Byron's work associates. The guy was younger, maybe a year older than Sin. But he wasn't my type at all, talking endlessly about how good he was at his job and how much money he made. None of that mattered to Sinclair though, he raised his glass in my direction and turned the toy up a level, the sensation causing my spine to stiffen and my knees to almost buckle.

I'd excused myself as soon as I'd regained control of my limbs.

I was walking back from the restroom after freshening my lip gloss when my mother called my name.

"Dempsey, sweetheart, come over and let me introduce you to some people," my mother called, holding an arm out with a tight smile that left no room for argument from me.

I moved to her side, the toy in my panties ominously still. I had no idea who had the remote now, though I knew beyond a doubt that they were waiting for the most inopportune time to torture me.

Eyeing the group, I inwardly cringed at the sight of Byron at my mother's side, Presley beside him. A man and woman I didn't know came next, then Sinclair on my left.

One glance at Presley biting down on his smile and his hand in his pocket and it was suddenly clear exactly who had the remote now.

I widened my eyes at him in warning. *Not here, not now.*

Not when my mother and Byron were standing between us with another couple.

"Darling, I was just telling Mr. and Mrs. Covington how much you're excelling on the Triple C swim team," my mother beamed at me with pride. Faux pride. She wasn't actually proud of me, only proud that I was living up to her expectations of me.

I dipped my head politely. "The credit goes to the excellent program Triple C provides and our fabulous coach."

Byron puffed his chest and raised his glass in my direction at the compliment. Triple C was his passion project and he loved to see it paying off.

"Do you have to train often, dear?" the woman across from me asked.

"Yes, we train tw—" I cried out at the sensation flooding between my legs, startling the group.

Presley took a sip from his glass to cover the devilish smile on his face.

I was going to kill him.

The toy buzzed again between my legs, harder this time, and I let out a small sound that was half cry, half moan.

"Goodness, are you okay?" the woman's husband asked, everyone peering at me with concern.

I forced out a smile, clenching every muscle in my body to fend off the waves of sensation rolling through me. "Yes, I'm —" The toy buzzed again, and I cried out, the vibration not letting up this time. "Cramps," I bit out, clutching my stomach to sell the lie.

My mother gripped my arm, right as Presley upped the speed on the vibrator, and I bent over, gripping my middle to hide the way my eyes were rolling back into my head.

I was so wet and moments away from coming.

Just as the thought crossed my mind, the vibrating stopped, and my muscles unclenched.

This was the worst gift I'd ever been given.

I stood tall, panting hard. "I'm so sorry..." I said to the four confused expressions I was met with. What else could I say? To them, I must have seemed crazy.

Presley was working harder than ever to cover his grin. Sinclair hadn't so much as flinched, just sipped from his glass like it was totally normal for his stepsister to double over dramatically in the middle of a fancy party.

"Take your sister somewhere to sit down, Sinclair," Byron ordered, brow pinched with concern.

"Stepsister," Sinclair corrected, discarding his glass on a high table behind him.

He took my arm, strong fingers brushing my skin, and motioned me towards a corridor nearby.

"I'm so sorry," I said again, just as Presley set the toy into high gear.

My knees gave out, and Sinclair caught me before they buckled completely. I glared daggers at Presley over my shoulder, but he only upped it again, and I had to turn around before my mother witnessed my eyes rolling shut at the waves of pleasure consuming me.

Silently, Sinclair guided me down a long hallway all the way to the end.

I bit my lip, trying to stifle my cries of pleasure the entire way. This thing was in overdrive, every one of my senses peaking to the point that I was in pain.

"I'm going to… I need to…" I ground out the words. Tears started to fall down my cheeks from the sheer torture. Pleasure and pain coursed through me as I fought the orgasm, my entire body trembling with the effort. "Get it off, oh my god, get it off or I'm going to scream so loud this whole place is going to be questioning my sanity." My breathing shuddered, my legs were weak.

Sinclair pushed open a door to our right, practically shoving me inside the bathroom and locking the door behind us, while I begged him to get it off me.

He dropped to his knees and shoved my dress up, the sound of my lavender lace panties ripping filling the small bathroom. He tossed them and the toy aside, sucking my clit in his mouth.

"Oh my god, I can't. It's too much, I can't take it," I moaned, wanting him to stop and desperately needing his mouth on me all at the same time.

He didn't utter a word, his tongue sliding over my clit. My legs fell wide open, my arms propping me up beside the basin. His lips closed over me and he sucked hard, sending me over the edge.

The orgasm that tore through me was like nothing I'd ever experienced before. Heat and pleasure flooded me harder and faster and bigger. Every inch of my body shutdown, my only focus on the pleasure roaring through me from Sinclair's mouth between my legs. The ripples from my orgasm lasted so long, my muscles ached.

When Sinclair finally lifted his head, he smacked a hand against my exposed clit, making me cry out. My hands, which had already turned to jelly, gave out, and I fell back, head hitting the mirror. I let out an exhausted emotional laugh that bordered on tears. I was so utterly and completely wrung out.

Sinclair got to his feet, pulling me up until I was sitting upright on the counter. He took my face in his hands, kissing me on the forehead, then letting my head drop against his chest while I caught my breath.

"Oh my god, that was the worst..." I said lazily. "...And also the best thing that I've experienced."

Sinclair huffed an uncharacteristic laugh.

While he'd no doubt relished the opportunity to make me come, he'd also done me a favor. The three of them had edged me so hard all night, it felt like I might explode. And I might have, if Sinclair hadn't diffused the bomb with his incredible tongue.

"I owe you," I said wearily, lifting my head to smile up at him.

"Happy for you to repay that debt any time. There's nothing that gets me harder than you on your knees with my cock in your mouth."

CHAPTER 35

The door to my bedroom burst open and hit the wall, making me jump out of my skin. I'd just stepped out of the bathroom, my hair wet around my shoulders, my body wrapped in a towel.

I'd come out to find a letter on my desk, left there by one of the maids.

Another letter. This one the most ominous yet.

Blew up a bank today.
Which means I'm coming for you, Darling.

I hid it behind my back, as Presley strolled into my room.

"Get your passport and pack your bags, Sass, we're going on a trip," Presley said.

I gripped the towel tighter around me with one hand. "Jesus, Pres, can't you knock?"

I tried to keep the tremble from my voice, fear from the letter still sparking over my nerves.

His gaze wandered over every inch of me, his face splitting in a deeply satisfied smile. "I've seen every inch of that gorgeous body. Know it all intimately." He winked at me. "And you're telling me I need to knock. In case you're, what? In here getting yourself off?"

My jaw ticked, and I resisted the urge to kick him out.

He flopped down on my bed, grinning back at me. "Because if you're in here flicking your bean without inviting me to either watch or lend a mouth for the occasion, then we have a serious problem."

I edged towards my desk, slipping the letter onto it behind my back, the towel almost slipping.

I scrambled to grab it before it fell too far, even as Presley's brow quirked in a way that said 'let it fall'.

"Why would I be in here getting myself off when the three of you are boning me several times a day?"

His grin turned to a smirk. "Yeah, we are. And I gotta say, my world has been infinitely better since you started riding my dick daily."

It wasn't daily, my vagina couldn't take it. But it was a lot. The three of us were having a lot of sex.

I moved to the bed, leaning over to press my mouth to his, the tremble of fear in my body slowly ebbing away.

His hands gripped my thighs, pulling my legs out from under me and rolling over so I was sprawled on top of him.

"Apology accepted," he murmured against my mouth, hands roaming to the bottom of my towel.

"Don't even think about it." I broke the kiss, smiling down at him. "You came in here for a reason. We're going on a trip?"

He nodded, fingers skimming the edge of the towel at my ass. "Mmmhmm," he said, distracted by his roaming fingers and what he could get away with before I stopped him. "We're going to Paris."

I pushed back off him a little so I could see him better, surprised by the destination. "We're going to Paris?"

"Would I lie to you, Sass?" He sat up, taking me with him and putting me on my feet. "There's some charity thing both Byron and Sin need to be at. So pack your bags and get your passport." He frowned. "You do have a passport, right?"

I walked to my dresser, pulling out some underwear to put on, while Presley strolled to the door. "Yes, I have a passport."

He stopped, leaning against the doorframe. "Don't bother putting those on." He pointed to my underwear. "Not unless you want them torn off later."

Shaking my head and fighting a grin, I chose a thin strap black slip dress and a denim jacket for the plane, skipping the underwear like Presley suggested.

Then I started packing.

———

Travelling with the Astons was like nothing I'd experienced before.

My mouth had been hanging open from the moment we'd stepped onboard the Aston private plane. I'd marvelled at the sleek grey panelling, the broad recliner chairs, the plush carpet, the full-length couches. Then Presley had taken my hand and shown me the full double bedroom and luxurious bathroom at the back, and my mind had been blown.

I'd thought the plane was Byron's but Sinclair had smirked, Dacre informing me that Sin had bought it his first year out of Triple C. When I said these guys were richer than God, I'd meant it.

As soon as we'd taken our seats, a stunning flight attendant, with long red hair and green eyes, dressed in the smallest mini skirt known to man, had served us drinks. I hated the way her gaze lingered on each of *my* guys. Had any of them slept with her? That jealous little monster inside me couldn't bear to know the answer.

Two hours into the flight, Dacre appeared next to me in the aisle, offering me his hand.

"Come with me."

There was a wicked gleam in his eye that had me rushing to unbuckle my seatbelt.

I let him lead me to the bedroom at the back of the plane, where he didn't bother to shut the door behind us, just sat down on the end of the bed, in full view of the plane aisle.

"Sit with me." He patted his muscular thigh and I didn't hesitate, turning and dropping my ass into his lap.

"Such a good, obedient girl, Dempsey," he murmured against my hair.

His hands came around me and he smoothed them up my thighs, dragging my dress along with them. Presley and Sinclair swivelled their chairs to watch us, their eyes trained on my legs and the path of Dacre's hands.

His lips pressed against my ear, his voice like a deep caress. "You going to put on a show for them, sweetheart?"

I nodded, heat already pooling between my legs at the promise of what was to come. I leaned against him so my back was flush with his chest and dropped my head to his shoulder.

Dacre reached for my knees, spreading my legs wide and exposing me to Sinclair and Presley.

"Fuck, you're glistening, Princess." Sinclair's hard cock was tenting his pants.

Across the aisle, Presley had already shoved his grey sweatpants aside and was stroking his thick cock with his hand.

"You look beautiful, Sass," he said, with hooded eyes, staring at the glistening heat between my legs.

Dacre's fingers brushed over my clit, pulling a sound from my lips.

"That's it, baby, moan nice and loud for me. Show them how much you love being fingered at forty thousand feet."

Dacre worked me over, pulling moan after moan out of me while Presley and Sinclair watched on. Sinclair was yet to touch his cock, his hands gripping the arms of his chair, eyes trained on Dacre's fingers between my legs.

The curtain at the other end of the aisle opened, the stunning flight attendant stepping into the cabin. Her eyes flickered with the briefest hint of surprise at the sight of me spread out and desperate.

I tried to slam my legs shut to cover myself, but Dacre held my knees wide with his own, a firm palm pressed against my stomach.

"Don't get shy on me, Bambi. Look at Presley, look how much he's fucking loving it. You know he gets off watching."

Presley's head was tipped back, his hand stroking his cock so fast he was surely about to explode.

Keeping my legs wide, I moaned loudly at the next swipe of Dacre's fingers.

The flight attendant strode down the aisle, keeping her eyes averted from what was clearly happening in the bedroom at the other end. She stopped between Sinclair and Presley.

"May I help either of you with that, sirs?" She glanced between them, motioning at their laps.

Oh, hell no.

I shot forward, but Dacre's strong hands kept me pinned to his lap.

Jealousy seared through me at the thought of her touching them. Touching what was mine. There was no way her perfect mouth or her dainty fucking hands were going anywhere near their cocks.

I opened my mouth to say as much, but Sinclair beat me to it.

"Not a chance. You're dismissed and don't come back in here unless one of us hits the call button."

She nodded, her eyes downcast as she made her way back behind the curtain.

The thought that maybe one, or all of them, had fucked her at some point took root in my mind again, a raging possessiveness flaring hot and fast in me.

It fled the moment Dacre pinched my clit between his thumb and forefinger, making me cry out and sending a full body shudder through me.

Sinclair pushed from his seat, striding into the bedroom. He stared down at me for a beat, heat searing in his gaze. Then he dropped to his knees in front of me, mouth closing over my clit.

I clung to Dacre's forearms, moaning like a bitch in heat.

"Fuck, Dempsey," Presley ground out from where he still sat in his seat, choking his cock with his hand.

Sinclair sucked and swirled all over me, getting me impossibly wetter.

"Oh my God, Sin!"

He groaned against my clit at the use of his nickname.

I tipped my head back against Dacre's shoulder, his hands coming up to slide the straps of my dress off my shoulders. He cupped my exposed breasts, thumbs flicking my hardened nipples.

"You like that, Bambi?" Dacre murmured against my ear. "Sinclair doesn't get on his knees for anyone."

I glanced down, infinitely more turned on at the sight of Sinclair's tongue all over me.

He smirked up at me, his lips closing over my clit and sucking hard, making me scream. I writhed in Dacre's lap, but he held me firmly against him as an orgasm tore through me and I exploded on Sinclair's tongue.

Dacre nipped at my earlobe, allowing me a few deep breaths to recover. "There's no way I'm not fucking you after that. Get on the bed."

I slipped my dress off, leaving me naked, and moved to

the bed. Presley got to his feet and joined us, stepping out of his sweatpants, his giant cock still in his hand.

Sinclair did the same, unzipping his pants and taking out his hard length, exposing the row of bars piercing the underside.

I kneeled on all fours on the bed. Dacre moved behind me, dragging the tip of his cock along my seam. "I'm going to take what I need from you, Bambi, and you're going to give it to me, like a good little whore."

His harsh words sent a thrill through me that made me shiver with the pleasure I knew was to come. He thrust inside me, and I moaned his name, both Presley and Sinclair moving closer to the side of the bed in front of me. They stood side by side, cocks in hand, making my mouth water.

I looked up at them from my position on the bed. "Come closer."

They obeyed, their shins brushing the edge of the bed. I opened my mouth, taking Presley down my throat. He groaned louder than I'd ever heard, his head tipped back to the ceiling. "Fuck, Sass. Your mouth is incredible."

He pumped into my mouth as Dacre pumped into me from behind, and pleasure began building inside me.

I loved being filled by them. *Craved* it.

Sinclair moved in close, his cock edging towards my mouth, smacking against my cheek while I sucked Presley off.

Pres pulled back, the head of his cock sliding from between my lips with a wet pop. Sinclair was in my mouth in a second, hitting the back of my throat. His piercing grazed along my tongue, the foreign feel of it turning me on.

"Goddamnit, Dempsey, you take us so well."

His whole body was rigid, his muscles taut as he worked to stop himself from coming.

Dacre's hold at my hips tightened, slamming me back against him, while Sinclair slammed himself down my throat.

I could barely breathe, and I loved every damn second.

CHAPTER 36

The hotel suite was just as impressive as the plane, with sweeping views of Paris. The Eiffel Tower glinted nearby, the entire view like a fairytale come true.

So far I hadn't lifted a finger on this trip. I'd been treated like a true passenger princess.

After our epic romp in the bedroom, Sinclair had carried me to the bathroom and run a steaming shower, the two of us going at it up against the bathroom wall as the water sprayed us.

Now, I gripped the edge of the wrought iron balcony railing, staring at the rooftops of Paris.

Did life get any better than this? Yes, the Aston family's wealth made for luxurious living, but even without it, things would be pretty damn great right now. With Sin and Dacre and Pres I was happy. Happier than I'd ever been. And I didn't want to give them up. Our connection was unconventional, but it was true and strong. I didn't care if we had to spend the rest of our lives keeping it a secret, I would do anything if it meant we got to spend it together.

Footsteps sounded behind me, Dacre coming to wrap his arms around me, his chin on my shoulder.

"Pretty impressive, huh?"

I smiled. "It's stunning."

"It's got nothing on you."

I turned in his arms, his eyes shining with sincerity. "You're a real softie, you know that?"

"Only when it comes to you."

His mouth descended on mine, and suddenly I was kissing my stepbrother, who I knew I was falling hard for, on a balcony in Paris.

Dacre's mouth moved over mine, his arms possessively wrapped around my waist. His kiss was sweet and tender and loving, just like him, and I realized if I died tomorrow, it would all have been worth it for us to wind up here.

I had to tell them about the threat against me. Had to tell them about my father. I'd been wrong to keep it from them for so long, even if I believed I was protecting them from it in some way.

But I hated the idea of tainting this magical moment with my sordid history. Besides, all of that felt like it was a world away.

I'd tell them on the plane ride home, I decided… if we could keep our hands off each other long enough.

Dacre broke the kiss, but didn't let me go, pressing his lips to my forehead as we surveyed the view.

"You need to go inside and get ready. Pres organized a glam team for you."

My eyes lit up. "A whole team?"

Dacre nodded once. "A whole team just for our favorite girl."

I went to pull away, to go inside and get ready, but Dacre's arms tightened around me.

"I have to tell you something first." His eyes were more

playful than you'd expect from someone uttering those words.

"Oh?"

"Those phantom deliveries you've been getting?"

My eyes narrowed on him, and I nodded.

"They're from us."

I paused. "You've been sending me granola and coconut shampoo and peach lip gloss?"

He groaned. "God, I love the smell of your shampoo. One sniff and I'm half hard."

I let out a small laugh. "Okay, weirdo."

His arms tightened around me. "We know you love those things, and we love making you happy, so we bought them for you."

I melted at his words and at the kindness of them supplying me with the things they knew I loved.

"Don't get too blissed out about it. Sinclair has ordered you about twenty sets of lavender lace underwear like the ones he apparently tore off you in the bathroom the day you wore the vibrator." He shook his head, trying not to laugh.

"How romantic… I think…"

He smiled down at me and I kissed him once more. "All part of taking care of our girl. Now, time for a party in Paris, I can't wait to see you in your dress."

He reluctantly let me go so I could get ready, a promise in his gaze.

———

Two hours later when I'd been primed and prepped and buffed and stuffed into my stunning gown, I descended in the elevator to meet my stepbrothers in the lobby.

Byron and my mother were staying at a different hotel. Apparently, Byron had his preferences in just about every city in the world, based on how well they served him. He and my mother would attend the event, then jet off tomorrow in Byron's plane for a belated honeymoon.

Au revoir, Mother.

The elevator doors opened, and I stepped out, my smile fading as I surveyed the lobby and adjacent bar area.

Dacre and Sinclair stood on the other side of the lobby looking damn near perfect in their tailored tuxedos that fit them like a second skin. But a deep, roiling sense of possession filled me at the sight of Veda on Sinclair's arm. He told me that he'd spoken to her, that they were calling things off between them, but that the process would take time given it was all for her parents.

Right now, she was pressed up on her tiptoes whispering in his ear. It didn't matter to me that their relationship was fake, or that Sinclair was only pretending to be with her to help a friend. Seeing it right in front of me now that he was mine caused my blood to catch fire. I wanted to march over there and rip her away from him, finger by manicured finger.

Then my eyes landed on Dacre beside him, deep in conversation with... his ex.

He'd pointed her out to me that day at Trenton's after we'd fucked in the bathroom.

Belinda looked incredible in a deep magenta dress that hugged her figure. Her black hair fell down her back like a midnight waterfall. Dacre's eyes were focused solely on her as he listened to whatever she was saying. The all-too-familiar cocktail of jealousy and possession reared its ugly head inside me and I turned away, looking for Presley. I knew if I found him, he'd scoop me into his arms with that giant grin of his and tell me I looked pretty, along with all the dirty things he wanted to do to me.

But when I scanned the bar, I spotted him there with two women. Presley had his back to the bar, elbows propped against it, the women surrounding him on either side. He smiled—not the same devious grin of his I loved so much and made my heart melt in an instant—but a smile nonetheless. He wasn't shooing them away like the annoying gnats I clearly thought they were.

One reached out to touch his arm, and my anger flared.

What the hell is going on here?

We'd laid the ground rules that day in the library. They belonged to me, and I belonged to them. No fucking around with anyone else. No flirting with anyone else. And no one could ever find out about us or it would ruin everything.

Yet here all three of them were, chatting to exes, indulging fake girlfriends, or letting other women flirt with them.

Hurt mixed with the anger and I bolted before any of them noticed me, heading for the front doors to the lobby to get some air. I pushed outside, sucking in several deep breaths to get a grip on my emotions.

Being with all three of them was overwhelming. Being possessive or jealous with one boyfriend was bad enough, but experiencing it three times over was all-consuming.

I hated being jealous, but when it came to them, I couldn't help it. It had come on fast, but Sinclair, Dacre, and Presley meant everything to me now, and I hated the idea of them looking at anyone else. Veda had clung to Sinclair like he belonged to her and not me. Those women at the bar touched Presley like he was theirs. And Trenton's words about Dacre and Belinda played on repeat in my mind.

My chest heaved and tears pricked the backs of my eyes. I moved down the path out of the lights and people coming in and out of the lobby.

I wouldn't let anyone see me cry.

The darkness swallowed me as the path narrowed through a small garden near the front of the hotel.

I was being stupid, I knew it. All I wanted was for one of them to find me, wrap me in their arms and tell me it was all in my head. I wasn't a damsel that needed rescuing though, and they weren't mind readers who instinctively knew what I wanted from them. If I needed them, then I had to tell them that. I knew they wouldn't hesitate to give it to me if I asked.

Chastising myself, I turned back up the path to tell them exactly that when a figure stepped in front of me. No, make that several figures.

My stomach dropped as I stared up into Algor's dark eyes. "Time to go, Dempsey."

I shook my head. "I'm not—"

But I couldn't get the words out. Algor's gloved hand closed over my mouth, the other wrapping around the back of my head. I sucked in a breath to scream and the overwhelming stench of chemicals filled my nose and lungs. My head spun and my limbs turned heavy.

My body slumped in Algor's arms, and he swung me off my feet, the world spinning around me as he carried me through the dark.

My head lolled against his chest as we moved, and I fought to keep a grip on consciousness. The sound of a trunk popping echoed in the darkness, and I was lowered into it.

It slammed shut, everything slipping away.

CHAPTER 37

I sat up with a start, sucking in a sharp breath that burned my lungs.

My eyes adjusted to the bright, burning construction light on a stand in the corner. It faced the army green colored wall, shining a strange glare that half-blinded me when I tried to survey that part of the room. I was seated on a low metal bed frame, a thin threadbare mattress beneath me.

Where the fuck am I? And how the fuck did I get here?

My heart rate kicked up several notches as the memories came back to me. Running out of the hotel, freaking out about Pres, and Sin, and Dacre. Turning back to make things right and running into… *Algor.*

I pushed off the bed to try to find a way out of here, but a chain clanked against the metal bed frame, stopping me.

What the hell…?

I stared down at the thick metal cuff on my right wrist. There was a solid lock on one side and a hinge on the other.

It was suddenly hard to breathe. Panic hit me like a tidal wave crashing against the shore.

I had to get out of here.

This was extreme, even for my father. Yes, I was valuable to him, but valuable enough to abduct me? Hold me hostage chained to a bed in a foreign country?

Clearly my father's business dealings had escalated since my mother and I had left. Or his mental state had deteriorated to the point he thought it was normal to abduct his own daughter and hold her captive.

I sucked in a breath and screamed. "Help!"

I screamed the word over and over until my mouth dried up and my throat ached, but I refused to give up. If my father was willing to do this to me, there was no telling what fate was waiting for me on the other side of it. If it was anything like the life he'd been trying to force on me before I'd left with my mother, I was in trouble.

So I screamed for what felt like an hour before I heard the sound of the door being unlocked on the other side of the room, behind where the light shone obscuring my view.

"Will you shut the fuck up?"

A man I didn't recognize stepped around the light, glaring down on me with the venom of a viper.

"No one can fucking hear you. No one is coming to save your ass. So shut the fuck up already."

I blinked up at him, smart enough to keep my mouth shut. It was a safe bet this goon worked for my father, and my father's men weren't known for their self-control.

"What? Nothing to say now that you have my attention?" the man barked, staring down at me.

I stared up at him. "I thought you wanted me to shut the fuck up?"

He huffed a humorless laugh, staring off at the wall like he was thinking.

I should have seen it coming. I'd mouthed off to him and no man who worked for my father would ever tolerate that.

He cracked me across the face with the back of his hand,

my head whipping to the left. Fire burned across my right cheek and my eyes smarted with tears I tried to hold back.

But it lit something inside me. A fire—an anger and a strength that burned deep inside me.

I lunged to my feet, gripping a section of the chain at my wrist in both hands and flinging it around his neck. We hit the ground in a mess of limbs, me on top of him. He struggled, but my grip held firm as I crossed the chain and pulled it tight, cutting off his air supply.

He clawed at my hands, but I didn't break. This might be the only shot I'd have to get the hell out of this place. When that didn't work, he got a hand under my chin and tried to push me backwards, but I still didn't loosen my hold on the chains at his throat.

The door burst open and Algor was in the room in a heartbeat, coming around behind me and wrapping his thick arm around my throat, squeezing tight until he choked my airway.

"Let him go, little firebird," Algor murmured in my ear. "You kill him, and I'll have to hurt you."

I didn't want to let go. I wanted to see the light snuff out in this guy's eyes and the thought should have scared me. All I could think was that, if our roles were reversed, he wouldn't have hesitated to kill me.

But my lungs seized from the lack of oxygen, and I reluctantly released the chain.

Algor adjusted his arm at my throat enough that I could suck in a desperate breath, but he didn't move away. He kept me in a headlock and pulled me off his friend, forcing me to my feet. He shoved me towards the bed, and I fell back onto it, then he leaned down and helped the other guy to his feet.

"You crazy bitch," the guy croaked, his voice hoarse and his throat already bruising.

"She was raised by the boss," Algor snarled, shoving him towards the door. "You think she was going to be a little weakling who'd sit in here and cry? I warned you to stay the hell away from her."

The man snarled in my direction as Algor herded him out. He slammed the door and turned to me.

"You've got one more night in here until we board a plane and you're back where your father wants you."

I sucked in a breath at his words. At the confirmation that I was going back to everything I'd been running from.

"But if you pull something like that again," Algor said, his voice dark and low. "I'll break your legs, are we clear?"

I nodded, too afraid to utter a word.

I knew Algor's reputation all too well. I'd seen what he was willing to do to someone who dared to cross my father.

There was nothing empty about his threat.

———

I'd been awake most of the night, having spent hours trying to slip my hand free from the cuff. When all I achieved was bruising the bones in the base of my hand and splitting my skin open, I'd moved on to trying to tug the damn chain out of the wall.

Eventually I'd fallen asleep on the floor, waking some time later with a start, my mind not being able to compute where I was.

When I'd remembered, I'd crawled up onto the threadbare metal cot and forced myself back to sleep. I'd need rest if I was going to survive my return to my father.

The next time I woke, it was to the sound of the door being unlocked. Algor stepped into the room. He moved for the bed, handing me an apple and some bottled water.

"Where is my friend?" I asked, accepting what he was offering.

His gaze was stern when it locked with mine. "Being kept far away from you in order to save your life."

I grunted, taking a bite of the apple. The sour sweetness burst across my tongue and my stomach growled with the anticipation of my swallow. I downed the apple in six bites, followed by half the water.

Algor discarded the remnants on the floor, then pulled thick black zip ties from his back pocket. "Hold your fists together."

I obeyed, knowing if I did there was a chance he'd remove the metal cuff. I had a better chance of escaping if I wasn't chained to the damn wall. And after my efforts last night, I knew there was no way I was getting out of it without the key.

Algor tightened the zip ties around my wrists like handcuffs, then pulled out a black hood. "This is going over your head. No reason for you to see where we are or where we're going."

He moved to put it over my head, and I pulled away. His eyes twitched at the corners.

"Don't make me hurt you, Dempsey. Because I will and you know it."

I swallowed, nodding, and when he moved to place the hood over my head again. I didn't pull away. Everything was instantly dark, the material of the hood not the slightest bit transparent. The harsh noise of a strip of duct tape being ripped from the roll filled the room, and Algor wrapped it around my throat several times, securing the hood like a collar.

Only then, when I was cuffed and blind, did Algor remove the metal cuff from my wrist.

He took me by the arm, hauling me to my feet, and my dress swished across the floor as we walked. The door gave the smallest creak as it opened, then we moved left down a hallway. We made several more turns before I felt the breeze kiss my skin, the bite of the cool air on my exposed arms.

Outside.

If only I knew what the hell I was up against.

Algor hadn't let go of me yet, but the moment he did, I had hoped to make a run for it. I could deal with my cuffed hands; my legs weren't restrained. But if I couldn't see where I was going or how many of my father's men were here, it was pointless to try.

Algor shuffled me along at his side, the sound of several car doors opening and closing filling the air. Then his hand pressed against the back of my head, guiding me downwards.

"Get in the car," he said, shoving me inside.

I fell across the backseat, sliding to the other side, my hands blindly searching for the door handle. Instead they were met with a hard body and soft clothing.

"She trying to feel me up?" came a low voice, almost amused.

Al gripped my arm, tugging me upright, then sliding into the seat beside me and slamming the car door. "Keep your hands to yourself or I won't make sure these men keep theirs away either."

It was a sobering warning. One I was all too willing to heed.

"Where are we going?" I said quietly, hoping they'd remove the blindfold.

"Back to your father."

I was in Paris; my father was entire oceans and continents away. How the hell did they plan on taking me to him?

Forty minutes later, my questions were answered when the car pulled to a stop, Al tugging me from the car behind him. The wind whipped at my hair, my dress sticking to my body and billowing out behind me. The unmistakable sound of a jet engine filled my ears, drowning out all other sounds.

"Get her on the plane fast, we need to take off *now*."

I didn't miss the urgency in the man's order. But why?

I was shoved towards a set of steps, my shoe colliding with the metal, but I reared back.

There was no way I was getting on that plane. I didn't care if they hit me, threatened me, or forcibly carried me. I wasn't getting on there without a fight.

"Walk," somebody grunted, shoving me roughly between the shoulder blades, but I pushed back against them, kicking out against the stairs.

"For fuck's sake," someone swore, two sets of strong hands closing around both of my arms and I was lifted off my feet.

I screamed and thrashed, trying to cause as much of a scene as I possibly could to draw attention. I had no idea who was around, if we were at some kind of airport or in the middle of a damn field somewhere. But once I got on that plane, this was over.

In the distance, the wail of sirens filled the air, and I hoped with every ounce of will in my body that those sirens were for me. I had no idea how long it would have taken for the guys to notice I was missing. Did their influence stretch to Paris? Sure, money talked, but did American money speak French?

The sounds grew closer and more cursing broke out amongst my father's men.

"Get her on the damn plane!" someone shouted, and I was hoisted off my feet once again.

I thrashed with renewed energy, my right arm slipping from their grip, and I hit the metal stairs face first. Pain shot through my nose, wrists, and knees, and I cursed out loud.

The sirens were so close now. So close that they had to be for me.

Had Dacre, Pres, and Sin really come for me?

The sirens grew so loud they were deafening, with what sounded like about eighteen police cars surrounding us.

Shouts rang out in French and the arms trying to lift me disappeared, the sound of feet shuffling nearby.

"Dempsey!" Dacre called from somewhere and my chest cracked at the sound.

A sob escaped me where I lay on the cold metal stairs. Shoes pounded across the pavement, and I ripped at the collar of duct tape at my throat, trying to pull the hood free.

I was scooped up into strong arms, held against a wide, solid chest. "I've got you, baby, you're safe now."

"Get this off me!" I sobbed, clawing at the hood, suddenly panicked at the unending darkness.

The sound of a switchblade flicked. "Hold still," came Sinclair's commanding voice.

He sliced through the tape, tugging the hood from over my head. Blinding light burned my retinas, and I forced them shut, holding up my still-cuffed hands to cover my eyes. I was slowly lowered to my feet, Dacre holding my head to his chest as he wrapped his arms around me and held me to him, my face buried against him. Adrenaline ebbed from my body, my limbs shaking with relief.

When my eyes no longer felt like they were going to catch fire when I opened them, I lifted my head, squinting.

"There she is," Presley said gently. Gentler than I'd ever heard him.

I offered him a tired smile, glancing at the chaos around us.

The guys had arrived with a serious convoy of police cars that surrounded the private plane. The French police had lined up my father's men, all of them on their knees on the tarmac, their hands behind their heads. Eight in total.

Al's hardened gaze followed me, a promise in his eyes that this wasn't over. But I was an Aston now—something that both he and my father had clearly underestimated.

"She needs to be seen by a medic," Dacre said, waving one over.

I shook my head. "I'm fine, honestly."

"You were just abducted in a foreign country," Sinclair snapped, like it was my fault. "Your wrist is all cut up and your nose is bleeding."

I glared back at him. "You think I don't know that?"

"What the hell happened?" he challenged, taking a step closer. His eyes were wild with worry.

Dacre's arms tightened around me protectively. "Back off, Sin. Give her a fucking second."

He walked me towards a small hangar where couches were arranged together haphazardly. I sat down in the center, Dacre taking a seat on one side of me, Presley at the other.

Sinclair paced in front of us. "Can you please put me out of my misery and tell me what the fuck happened?"

Pres leaned in close, pressing a kiss to my temple. "He's been going insane since the minute we realized you were gone."

I turned to Press, offering him a soft smile. He ducked his head, his lips meeting mine in a gentle kiss.

Sinclair was there in a heartbeat, on his knees in front of me, shoving Pres aside and taking my face in his hands. His lips were on mine a second later, his tongue invading my mouth in hard, commanding strokes that left me breathless. The kiss was overwhelming, like always, but I felt every tortured emotion behind it.

"Alright, Sin, give her a break," Dacre said, shoving his brother in the chest.

Sin's mouth disappeared from mine, and he fell back on heels, lips swollen and expression filled with anguish.

I looked to Dacre, cupping his cheek with my hand and guiding his mouth to mine. I didn't care who might be watching. I wanted to feel each of them. Know that they were there and they were real. They'd saved me from my father.

Dacre's lips were soft and sweet, like always, his presence like a balm to my soul.

When we broke apart, Presley took my hand. "You really need to tell us what the fuck happened, Sass."

"And why we've had half the Parisian police hunting for you."

I glanced at each of them. "You did that for me?"

"We'd set the entire fucking world on fire for you," Sinclair said, intensity burning through him.

I took a deep breath and closed my eyes.

"Those men work for my father," I said. "They were paid to take me back to him."

CHAPTER 38

I tucked my feet underneath me in the wide, luxurious plane seat.

Presley had put a pin in my explanation back in the hangar, insisting we went back to the hotel so I could shower, eat something and rest.

Now that we were forty-thousand feet in the air on our way home, the three of them stared at me expectantly.

Pres took my hand from where he sat in the chair beside me. "You need to tell us everything, Sass."

Sinclair and Dacre were seated facing us, their concern etched on both their faces.

Dacre leaned forward, elbows pressed to his knees. "You can trust us, you know that."

I scrubbed a hand over my face, breathing in the scent of Presley from his hoodie, which I was wearing. Presley's navy hoodie, Sinclair's grey sweats, and Dacre's black boxers. I'd wanted casual clothes for the flight home and each of them had offered me a piece of themselves. I didn't care that I was swimming in them, it brought me comfort when I needed it most.

"The men who took me work for my father. The attack

walking home that day, the one outside the club. It's been my father trying to get to me this whole time."

The three of them shared hard glances.

"He's been sending me letters. Threats, really."

Sinclair's eyes darkened. "Why didn't you tell us?"

"I was scared, Sin. I didn't know how to ask for help." I stared down at my hands. "I've been weighed down with this secret, this looming business deal of my father's, for as long as I can remember. Talking about it openly is new for me." I glanced at each of them. "Having people I can rely on is new for me."

Presley brushed a thumb over the back of my hand and Dacre reached out to give my knee a reassuring squeeze. Sinclair stared at me, his expression locked down. I wanted to reach for him, to crawl into his lap and beg him to tell me what he was thinking.

He'd been quieter than the others when we'd gone back to the hotel. And again on the way to the airport. I wanted him to open up to me. I'd pry him open with a rusty screwdriver if that's what it took.

"We know who your father is. He owns a chain of commercial businesses in Seattle," Dacre said, shifting in his seat.

My gaze shot to him. "How do you know that?"

Presley leaned closer, like he wanted to hold me but wasn't sure I'd let him. "We looked into you."

"Byron looked into your father before he proposed to your mother," Sinclair said. "He wanted to make sure your father wouldn't become a problem. I used my company to look into you the week before you arrived. The investigator returned a lot of information, mostly about your father and his businesses, same as Byron's."

I stared down at my hands in my lap. "Those businesses are just a front."

"For what?" Dacre asked.

"For his *other* ones."

I didn't need to spell it out for them.

"My father is involved with some seriously shady people. He does deals, makes promises, sometimes ones he can't keep, which leads him to make other deals to get himself out of them." I paused, biting the inside of my cheek. "I was one of those deals."

Dacre brushed a hand over my knee again. "Tell us what the hell is going on, Dempsey."

I sighed, blowing out a long breath. "Two years ago, my father made some deals, getting himself in deeper than he'd ever been with some seriously shady guys. He was looking down the barrel of more than one gun and he only had one thing to offer to buy his way out."

I bit the inside of my cheek, chancing a glance at each of them. None of them spoke, no one urging me to go on, letting me get there in my own time.

"The only way to get him out of his dodgy deals alive was to offer up his only daughter as collateral. He wanted to unite our family with one of the biggest crime families in Seattle, tie us to them in a permanent way."

Sinclair's hard voice cut through the silence. "With marriage?"

I nodded, tugging on the sleeves of Presley's hoodie so I could sink further into it. "The benefits for my father were endless. The family had the means to help him with his deals. His reputation would grow, which meant so would his reach in his underworld."

"But what did it mean for you?" Dacre asked, eyes narrowed on me.

I huffed a humorless laugh. "It meant I'd be married off to their only son. A man with the most vicious reputation that people feared him just by name." I glanced out the window, lost in my head. "He's apparently only twenty-three or four, but he's been feared in the Seattle crime world since he was fourteen."

Presley's thumb rubbed soothingly across the back of my hand once more. "What does that mean?"

I glanced at him. "That he beats the shit out of anyone who crosses him or gets in his way. He's known to kill off his enemies with ruthless efficiency. There was a story that did the rounds about a guy who tried to break into the family's compound to steal from them and he beheaded him right there on the marble tiles of the entryway without uttering a word. There are endless stories from women he's been with claiming he beat them during their time together because they didn't get him off how he wanted. He's violent for the sake of being violent, just because he can be."

Another glance passed between the three of them.

My voice trembled as I went on. "I begged my father not to force me into a marriage with him. He was guaranteeing me a life of pain and torture if he forced me to be with their son. But my father cared more about his standing in their world than he did about me being married to someone who was likely to beat me bloody if I burned his eggs in the morning."

Dacre's face pinched tight with anger. "You never met him face to face?"

I shook my head. "I've never laid eyes on him. My father made sure of it by barely letting me out of the house other than to go to school or swim meets. He tried to keep me as separate from his world as possible, tried to hide me away at home. He said it upped my stock. The more innocent and unobtainable I seemed, the higher price he could get for me. Like I was a piece of livestock he was selling at auction."

It was partly why I'd been so willing to hook up with Trenton or a random waiter at my mother's wedding. It was an act of pure defiance against my parents.

Silence hung over us, only the sounds of the plane engine as it sped across the ocean.

Dacre sat back in his chair, clearly lost in his own head as he stared out the window. Presley glanced between each of us, while Sinclair's hard stare remained locked on me.

"How did you get away from your father? You and Beatrice?" he asked eventually.

My lips twisted as I mulled over how much to tell him. "There was a shooting. I was out with some friends at the mall when someone had taken shots at us. They were clearly aiming for me, which meant I'd become a true pawn in my father's world. I went straight home to my mother, told her what happened, and begged her to save my life." I picked at the sleeve of Presley's hoodie. "She would have stayed with him. Would have died at his side if I hadn't begged with everything I had for her to get us out of there."

I shook my head at the memory. At just how much pleading it had taken to get her to put me first.

"She eventually relented. Packed our bags and stashed them in the back of the closet. We crept out in the middle of the night while my father slept."

Sinclair's brow pinched. "If you're so valuable, you didn't think he'd try to come after you?"

"Oh, he would have. Except my mother left him a note with a key to a safety deposit box at a bank downtown. Inside that box was everything she had on him. She was his spouse for more than a decade, she had everything she needed to bury him. She said if he came after us—came after me—she'd bury him."

None of it mattered now that he'd blown up the bank with the safety deposit box inside. That life insurance policy was long gone, and my mother had no idea.

Presley's brows rose, mildly impressed with my mother's moxie. And it had been impressive. Until she'd sold me out for a rich husband.

"It put him off for a while. For a few years actually. But then my mom met your dad and everything changed. It was like a switch flicked the moment my mother met Byron. She cared less about me and more about being Byron Aston's new wife. My father knew it, too. Knew my mother wouldn't risk her new life and social standing in order to save me again, so he grew bold." I ran a hand through my hair, shoving down the resentment I had for my mother the moment she sold me out for the payday of a lifetime. "Straight after the wedding, the letters started, telling me to come home or he was coming for me."

Dacre swore, shaking his head. "You should have told us."

"I didn't know you then. I didn't know I could trust you or that I'd come to feel the way I do about you. If the letters started tomorrow, I'd come to you without hesitation. But when they started, I was totally alone."

Silence descended again. This time unnerving.

"Before I came here, I had a plan," I said, staring out the window. "I was going to get some money together and go on the run. Start a life somewhere my father wouldn't be able to find me." I glanced up, taking in each of them. Each seemed riddled with worry. "Once I got here, I just wanted him to leave me alone. I never expected to fall for each of you the way I did. Never expected to ever feel this way about anyone, let alone all three of you. And then the idea of leaving started to eat away at me, even though I knew if I stayed, I was putting all of us at risk."

"Fuck the risk," Sinclair said. "I'll kill your father with my bare fucking hands if I have to."

Presley nodded. "There's no way in hell you're marrying that asshole, Sass."

Dacre got to his feet. He leaned down, hand sliding into my hair, and he pressed a kiss to my forehead.

"You're ours, Dempsey." His eyes blazed with anger. "And nobody is going to hurt what belongs to us."

CHAPTER 39

We stepped through the front door, and I resisted the urge to groan at the relief at being home.

"I want to have the world's longest shower then fall into bed. Like, I'm talking about Guiness World record levels of bathing, with all the expensive soaps and shampoos I can find."

Dacre walked up behind me, wrapping his arms around my waist, his lips at my ear. "I can think of so many more ways we could break records that don't involve showers."

I quirked a brow, glancing at him over my shoulder. "Oh yeah? I might like to see that."

Sharing everything I had on the plane had left me feeling lighter than I had in months. They hadn't judged me or shamed me for the decisions I'd made. Instead, they'd offered me support and pledged to be there for me, no matter what my father did.

After years of feeling alone, I finally had a place I belonged. And it was in the arms of my three stepbrothers.

"I want in on this record-breaking sex marathon," Presley said, standing in front of me. "That's what we're talking about, right? A sex fest?"

I rolled my eyes, fighting my smile. "Nuance really isn't your thing, is it, Pres?"

He reached for me, a hand snaking over my hip, moving in close until I was trapped in a Dacre and Presley sandwich. "You're my thing, that's all that matters."

I smoothed my hands over his hard pecs. "You're real smooth, Romeo."

He ducked his head, lips brushing my ear. "Let me show you how smooth I can be."

Staring up at him, I bit my lip and his eyes zeroed in on it.

"Hate to interrupt," Sinclair said from where he was leaning against the sideboard with his arms crossed. An envelope dangled from his fingertips and my stomach twisted at the sight of it.

He must have read the panic on my face. "It's a note from Byron telling us to take care of Dempsey while they're off on their honeymoon."

My gaze slid to each of my stepbrothers. "Does that mean we have this giant house all to ourselves for you to *take care of me* in?"

Dacre grinned against my cheek, lips brushing my skin in a tantalizingly quick kiss. "What do you want to do first?"

I didn't hesitate. "Skinny dipping."

Presley let out a full-bodied laugh and I swooned at the sound. I loved his laugh.

"That can be arranged," Dacre murmured against me. "Want help getting undressed?"

His hand trailed along the waistband of my borrowed sweatpants and his own borrowed boxers, fingers dipping beneath them.

I bit my bottom lip and nodded, Presley's gaze following the trail of Dacre's fingers. God, he was obsessed with watching me get off. Almost as obsessed with getting me off himself.

My gaze cut to Sinclair, who was frowning from his position across the room, but his eyes were locked on Dacre's fingers too.

Just as he slipped between my folds, his touch torturously close to being exactly where I wanted it, the doorbell chimed through the house, stilling each of us.

Dacre withdrew his hand, and my teeth clenched in frustration.

Stomping over to the heavy ornate front door, I hauled it open, staring at the guy on the other side.

He was a little older than me, maybe twenty-four at the most. Tall, with dark hair and tanned skin, his body packed with muscle that he wore like a warning. But it was his eyes that scared me. Dark brown pools that promised sinister things.

A shiver ran through me as his gaze raked over me from my feet back up to my face.

"Can we help you?" Dacre said, coming to stand at my back.

Presley and Sinclair flanked him behind us.

The guy smiled like a psycho, those brown eyes trained on me like he'd won a prize he didn't know he'd been playing for.

"I'm here for Dempsey."

Silence hung in the air.

No.

There was no way my father was coming for me again so soon. Unless he'd managed to pull some serious strings, Al and his other men were likely still in custody with the Parisian police.

Presley took a protective step in front of me, partially blocking me from view.

"If you work for her father, you can turn around and get the fuck out of here, because she's not going anywhere with you. I think we made that pretty fucking clear with his men currently sitting in an international jail cell."

The stranger glanced at Presley for half a second, his eyes instantly returning to me.

He assessed me with a hard intensity that surpassed Sinclair. "She'll be going with me."

Fear flooded my veins, along with a jolt of defiance. "What the hell makes you think I'd go anywhere with you?"

He smirked like he had a secret.

My heart rate ratcheted up several notches when he leaned towards me. I swallowed hard, waiting for his words and knowing I was going to hate every last one.

"You'll come with me." His gaze locked with mine. "Because you're my wife."

THANK YOU

Thank you for reading *Hearts of Fortune*.
I hope you loved reading about Dempsey, Sinclair, Presley,
and Dacre as much as I loved writing them for you.

Reviews mean everything to authors. Especially us indies!

If you enjoyed this story, I'd be so grateful if you would
please consider leaving a review on whatever platform you
get your books from.

ACKNOWLEDGMENTS

The first and most important thank you goes to you. For reading it.

There are more books in the world than you could ever hope to read in a lifetime, so I'm beyond grateful you chose to pick up one of mine.

Thank you to makeup artist extraordinaire, Dempsey, for lending me your amazing name! Meeting you at BABE '23 was a highlight of the weekend for me. You're a ray of sunshine in human form and an absolute talent with a makeup brush. And now you've got a book character named after you forever!

Thank you to my book babes—Steph, Ali and Emma. You read everything I write, prop me up whenever I'm feeling insecure, and make me laugh daily.

The biggest of thank yous to my early readers: Jess, Sam and Donna. You made this book the best it could be and I'm so thankful to you. A special shoutout to Sam for demanding a book with a Jacob's ladder. Sinclair is for you!

To Amy Maranville for being an editor and a friend. And to Quirah from Temptations Creations for the incredible cover. Thank you both!

To Ellie from Love Notes PR. You're a powerhouse in bookish PR, and it's a highlight every month to work with you and Nathan. Thank you for promoting my books so tirelessly. It's a joy to be able work with someone I consider a friend. I appreciate you.

To my husband, who has always supported my love of romance, never once telling me to keep my passion for spicy love stories a secret or have any shame over what I do. I'm so grateful for you.

ABOUT THE AUTHOR

E. Winn is a spicy romance author who dreams of getting pounded by Mr. Darcy at Pemberley or railed by Rhysand in the City of Starlight. Her favorite hobby is dreaming up fictional men that IRL men can never compete with.

WANT TO GET IN TOUCH?
   INSTAGRAM: @ewinnwritesromance
   TIKTOK: @ewinnwritesromance
   VISIT MY WEBSITE

MORE TO READ

E. Winn is a pen name from spicy romance author, Elouise Tynan.

If you like college basketball romance with playboys whipped for one girl, where each book follows a different player on the team, you might like these:

PIERSON U SERIES

WAITING TO SCORE

A spicy fake dating college sports romance

SHOOTING TO WIN

A spicy forced proximity, second chance college sports romance

DEFENDING THE PLAYER

A spicy reverse grumpy x sunshine and enemies to lovers college sports romance

www.ingramcontent.com/pod-product-compliance
Lightning Source LLC
Chambersburg PA
CBHW020335120726

47904CB00002B/421